CINDER THE FAE

FAIRELLE BOOK FIVE

REBEKAH R. GANIERE

Cinder the Fae © 2016 Rebekah R. Ganiere
ISBN: 978-1-63300-011-7
ISBN: 978-1-63300-012-4

Cover art by Rebekah R. Ganiere
www.vwzdesigns.com

DEDICATION

For those who read and those who love it.

NEWSLETTER

To claim your Two FREE Books and find out more about
Rebekah R. Ganiere and her other Upcoming Releases
You can Go Here:
www.RebekahGaniere.com/Newsletter

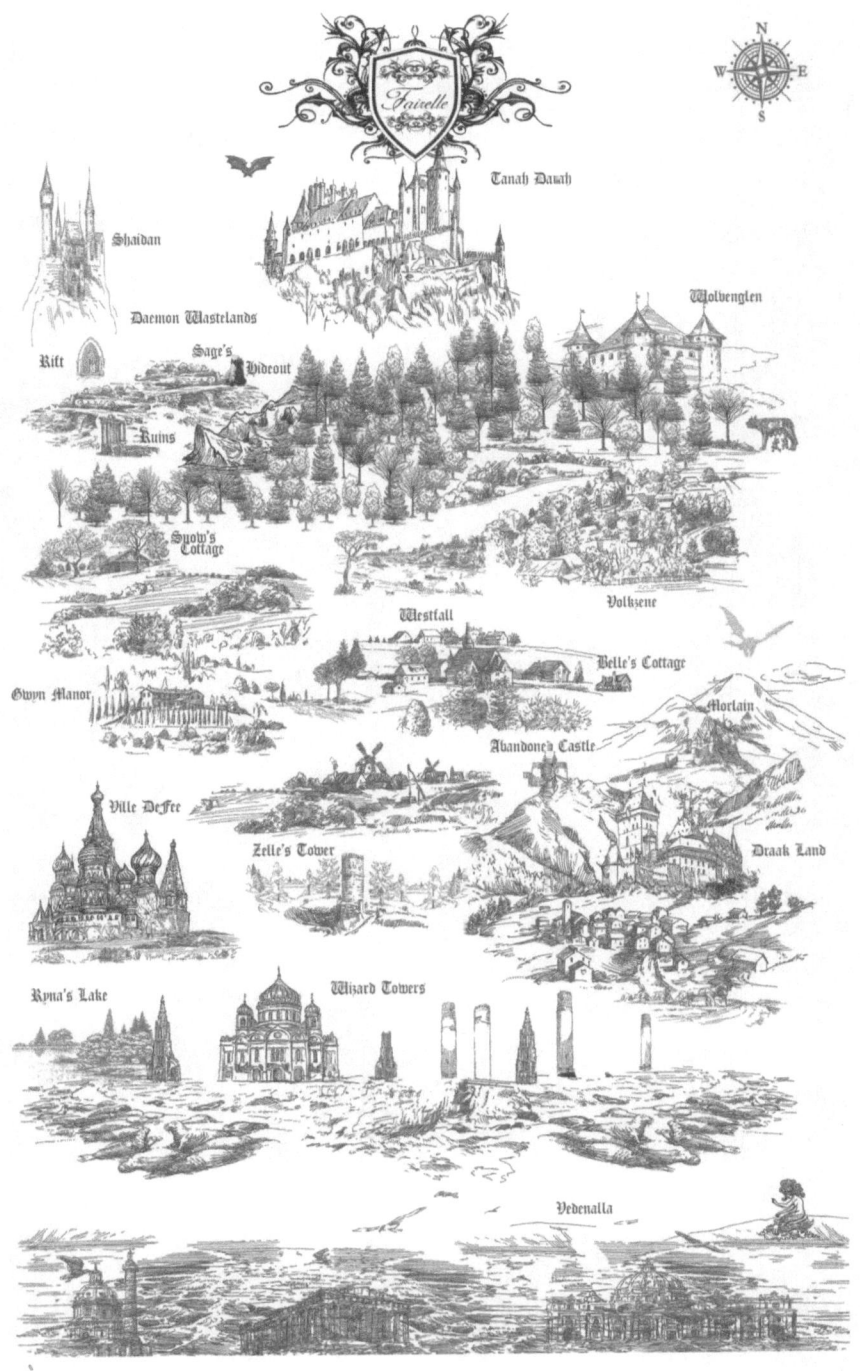

PROLOGUE

PEREUM, FAIRELLE YEAR 200

In the year 200, in the city of Pereum, the heart of Fairelle, King Isodor lay on his deathbed. With all of Fairelle united under his banner, his four sons vied for the crown. One by one the brothers called forth a djinn named Xereus from Shaidan, the daemon realm, to grant a single wish. But Xereus tricked the brothers, twisting their wishes.

The eldest wished to forever be bloodthirsty in battle, and was thus transformed into a Vampire. The second wished for the unending loyalty of his men, and was turned into a Werewolf. The third asked for the ability to manipulate the elements of Fairelle; he became physically weak but mighty in magick, a Fae. And the last asked to rule the sea. A Nereid.

When the king died, each brother took a piece of Fairelle for himself and waged war for control of the rest. Xereus, having been called forth so many times, tore a rift between his daemonic plane and Fairelle, allowing thousands of daemons to pour into Pereum.

Years upon years of bloody warring went by with all races fighting for control and eventually the daemons gained dominion of the heart of Fairelle. Realizing that all lands would soon fall into the daemons' control, the High Elders of the Fae and the Mages from the south, combined their magicks to seal the rift. The daemons were banished back to their own plane, but Pereum was wiped off the map in the process, leaving only charred waste behind forever known as The Daemon Wastelands.

Upon the day of the rift closing, a Mage soothsayer prophesied of the healing of Fairelle. Over the next thousand years the races continued to war against each other, waiting for the day when the ancient prophesies would begin.

Eight prophesies, a thousand years old, to unite the lands and heal Fairelle. The fourth is now upon us. Evil hides amongst the Fae.

CHAPTER ONE

VILLE DEFEE, FAIRELLE - LATE SUMMER, 1212 A.D. (AFTER DAEMONS)

The coins slid across the counter one by one, scraping the glass and shredding Cinder's nerves.

A pompous, buttercup yellow hat that she could only assume was the latest fashion in fae society, adorned the local fisherman's red hair. His bright fern colored tunic, embroidered in golden thread, cost more than her shop earned in a week. But for all his finery, he couldn't hide the excess of drink in his cheeks and excess food from his waistline.

She scooped the coins into the register and slammed the drawer, trying not to let her irritation show. She plastered on a smile, handed Silas his bag and thanked him for coming. Taking the man's money was easy. Having to stand his smell and manners was something else altogether.

His pale blue eyes scrutinized her.

"Was there anything else, Silas?" If she were to be leered at, it wouldn't be by a fisherman who smelled like a scuttle fish dipped in love potion perfume. She rubbed her nose at the nauseating mixture.

She tried to brighten her smile, but the flicker in his eyes told her he wasn't buying it.

He gave a crooked grin, revealing teeth so white and straight only magick could have done them. "That's Baron Silas to you, Cinder. You forget your place since your father's death."

Her eyes narrowed, and heat licked her cheeks up to the tips of her ears, deepening her anger. "My place stays where my father put it. His death did nothing to dilute my blood."

"How naïve you are, girl." Silas pulled himself up to his full six-foot height and scratched his jutted, cleft chin. "I might be able to secure you a place, however."

Cinder's skin crawled like spiders covered her, and she struggled to swallow the bile that scorched her throat. She might be considered a lowly shop girl by some, but she'd be damned if she'd let someone like Silas look down on her.

"I'm just fine where I am, thank you."

Silas leaned in and stroked Cinder's cheek with his long pudgy finger. "How long will you deny me? Do you think you can do better?"

Her thoughts traveled to Rome and her gut clenched. Though she'd loved him for years, he was the one fae she could never have. That didn't mean she'd stoop so low as to accept Silas though.

Suddenly Silas grabbed Cinder's face. "You are nothing more than a *Tingafae*. I'm a Baron. What makes you think you can deny me anything?"

Anger roared through her breast, and she shoved out

her hand. An icy blast of cerulean magick burst from her fingertips and hit him square in the chest. He flew a foot from the counter and hit a display table, knocking over a tower of tea canisters, and sending them spilling in every direction.

Silas flipped to his feet, hat askew, and advanced on her. "You little—" He stopped short as diamond white magick arced between Cinder's fingers.

"Get out," she warned. "My father may not have left me much, but he sure left me his temper. And the next time you lay a hand on me, Silas, you'll wish that jolt was all I'd done to you."

He stood, chest puffed out, cheeks as red as cinnamon candy. For a moment, she questioned whether she'd gone too far, but Silas would be too embarrassed to report what had happened.

The bell over the entrance rang, and someone stepped into the shop, but Cinder couldn't see around Silas' bulky form. Silas glanced sideways, toward the door, and relaxed his stance.

"Problem?" asked the newcomer.

"No." Cinder smiled at Rome and shoved her hand below the counter, flinging off the magick. "Silas stumbled."

Cinder waved her other hand, and the tea canisters righted themselves. She sucked in a breath, trying to stave off the fatigue that seeped into her muscles from the use of magick.

Rome strode toward the counter, his highly polished boots clunking on the wooden floor. His boyish smile and sparkling, azure eyes cheered her instantly; just as they had for the past sixty years.

He ran his fingers through his messy, chestnut hair and chuckled as Silas struggled to retrieve his purchases. The small vials had rolled in every direction.

"Tinctures for your foot fungus again, Silas?" Rome picked a piece of horehound candy from a dish and popped it into his mouth.

Silas gave up on the last vial which had rolled deep under a cabinet and stood. "It's from standing in sea water so much."

It was a lie. Silas had several human fishermen down south that brought him their catch every week. Though it was forbidden to have dealings with humans, no one saw the harm. Not the gate guards that looked the other way for a few coins, not the fae who loaded in the fish, and not the fae who paid for the fish.

Silas' eye caught Cinder's for a moment and then he looked at Rome. "Well, I must be going."

Rome waved toward the door. "Don't let us keep you."

Silas bristled and gave a tight smile as he bowed. "Your highness." He turned to leave.

"And to Lady Cinder?" Rome asked.

Silas' back straightened and his shoulders bunched. He turned around slowly. His gaze fell heavily upon Cinder, but then he smiled genuinely.

A shiver crawled up Cinder's spine.

"Lady Cinder, I hope you have a pleasant day." He inclined his head and then strode from the shop.

As the door slammed shut, Rome let out a bark of laughter. "What an ass."

"He certainly is." Cinder's eyes stayed glued on the door as she stilled her anger.

Rome looked at her, and his smile fell. "What happened?"

Cinder swallowed and met his gaze before looking away again. "Nothing."

She picked up the lid to the jar of horehound candy and replaced it, then grabbed a cloth and scrubbed at a spot on the glass counter.

Rome continued to look over her. He had ever been her loyal protector. Standing up for her with anyone who dared to put her down or treat her as a lesser. But she didn't need him getting in the middle of her battles. Not this time. She could handle herself.

He reached out and touched her face gently, placing his fingers just where Silas had before. Cinder swatted his hand away and rubbed her cheek. Rome's eyes narrowed.

"*Afa Kalinda Mae.* He touched you."

"No, he didn't." Cinder ground the cloth on the invisible spot. Out of the corner of her eye, she saw Rome bite his bottom lip and scan the shop floor. She knew that look. He was replaying what he'd seen.

"Rome–"

"I'm going to kill him." He rushed to the door, but Cinder was right behind him.

"*Dota.* Don't, Rome, please." She grabbed him by the arm.

His handsome face twisted into a mask of anger.

7

"He had no right to lay a hand on you. He should be punished."

"Please. If he reports me then I'll have to go to a hearing for using magick on him. You know what could happen to me. And if I lose my father's shop what will I have?" The begging coated her mouth like soapy water, making her stomach roil. But she knew this side of him. The royal side, the just side. His father's side. She took his hand and squeezed it like she had when they were kids and scared.

After a minute, his face softened, and he squeezed her hand in return. "You always have a place to go, Cinder. I'd never let anything happen to you."

His sincerity struck her hard in the heart.

She sat her fists on her hips and blew the hair from her eyes. "I know, but I can't rely on you to get me out of trouble. What kind of reputation would I have then?"

He laughed. "Since when do you care what other people think?"

"I don't, but it would be nice to marry someday, and who would want a woman with a tarnished reputation?"

"We've been friends forever. People know that."

"Yes, but what kind of female friend gets the Prince to help her out of trouble with the law?" She wiggled her eyebrows at him.

Rome's expression grew serious again. "You've never spoken of marriage before."

She shrugged though her insides squirmed. She'd not thought about marriage much, except to Rome. But Silas had been right. Due to her father's not claiming her as his heir before he died, she had little to no standing in the fae community at all. Men with higher bloodlines wouldn't want a woman like her.

"Well I can't spend forever waiting around for you to ask me, can I? Not that I'd say yes," she joked.

A sly smile grew across Rome's face. He brushed a hair behind her ear then ran his finger along the outside to the apex. "As if you would ever curb your independent side enough to be bound by the rules of being a princess."

The tone of his voice struck her as serious, and something else replaced the playful glint in his eye. Like he was prodding her, testing her. She swallowed hard at his nearness and the desire to kiss him burned deep inside like it had ever since he'd kissed her in the field of sungolds ages ago.

"I might." She leaned into him, taking in his wonderful, lemon balm scented cologne. "If the right prince came along."

His face held mock offense. "Oh?" He grabbed her around the waist and brought her hips into contact with his. His deep blue gaze sucked her in. "Am I not the right prince?"

His words held the same teasing tone he always used, but his eyes were fixed on her like nothing else existed at that moment. What was he playing at?

In the past months, something had changed with him. Ever since the night Flint Gwyn had come asking for help and Rome had carried her home, something had been different. Nothing she could put her finger on but his words seemed a bit more earnest at times and his actions more meaningful. All she could assume is that it had to do with his father's desire for Rome to finally settle down.

The most eligible male in the kingdom, Rome was prone to flirting, but she knew what his life held. Parties, dignitaries, delegations, festivals, royal everything. Always on his best behavior. Always smiling and judicious and... a royal wife. One with grace and poise; one that didn't break the law or combine her magick with a mage to help a human. And most importantly, that had pure blood. Blood was the most important. Always had been.

Which was why, no matter who her father had been, how close he'd been— or how close her step-uncle now was to the king, she would never be a princess.

So why did it feel like he was asking her if she was really interested in the job?

Her heart ached for him. Yes, Rome was judicious and a stickler for the law as the prince. But with her he was someone else altogether. He was funny and kind hearted. He always listened to her problems with her stepmother and offered logical advice. Something she herself wasn't prone to giving. He never saw her as a commoner, and he treated her with respect. They'd shared every hope, every dream, every new beginning with each other. He knew her inside and out. Her good, her bad and her ugly, and he was still there.

She stared at his lush, full lips and wondered if they would taste the same as they had the time he'd kissed her, when they had played seek and find as children. She'd pushed him away then, afraid that he was only toying with her like she'd heard he had with other girls. And as he'd never tried again, she could only assume he had been testing the limits of their friendship.

"What's going on here?" Came an angry voice from behind them.

Cinder stumbled as Rome let her go. Her stepmother came through the back curtain and walked to the counter. She took one look at Rome, and her anger melted away instantly.

"Why Prince Rome, I'm so sorry, I didn't recognize you. How are you this fine morning?" Cinder's stepmother glided toward them, a toothy smile, wide as the moon, planted on her face.

Cinder stepped aside, bumping into a table of herbs, as her stepmother shoved a burgundy silk cloak into her arms. Cinder bowed and moved to hang it up.

"Tell me, your highness, what can I get you today?"

Cinder peeked over her shoulder to see her stepmother link a slender arm in Rome's and pull him into the middle of the room. His eyes never left Cinder's, and her cheeks flushed with warmth as she walked to the back room. She bit back her shame of being treated so low in front of Rome and hung the cloak on a hook near the rear door. She listened to her stepmother chat at Rome as she lit a fire in the small stove and put on a kettle for tea.

Cinder knew the drill. Stay out of sight, pretend she didn't exist, unless someone needed something magickal made.

Cinder pulled up a stool and tended the fire, flicking sparks off her fingertips while listening to the light tinkle of laughter from her stepmother out front. Her heart sank, thinking of Rome and his offer to help her.

Her father had been an advisor to the king. But since her father's unexpected death, five years before, Cinder had been forced to be the breadwinner for her stepmother and half sister. Her father came from a respectable bloodline, and he'd taught her everything he knew about magick, as well as herbs. He'd left her stepmother the apothecary, but the woman knew nothing about running it. Fancy parties and charming men she could do, but providing for herself and her daughter was beneath her.

The curtain was thrown aside, and Cinder's head whipped up. Her stepmother's eyes narrowed on her, and Cinder's gaze traveled toward the shop floor. Had a customer arrived? She hadn't heard the bell ring.

"Prince Rome would like to speak to you about his grandmother."

"All right." Cinder swallowed hard and kept her eyes on the floor. She crossed to the curtain, biting her tongue to keep from saying what she really wanted to. Her stepmother grabbed her by the arm, digging long nails through her thin dress and into her skin. Cinder's gaze caught her stepmother's and for a second she could swear the woman's eyes flashed red.

"Remember your place, girl. You are nothing more than the product of a fling with a seductress. Only I and my daughter Olivia carry the name of Rondell."

Cinder dropped eyes again, and her ribcage squeezed her like one of her stepmother's magick corsets. How could she forget her place when she had so many people willing to remind of her of it? The slashes to her pride burned white hot.

"Yes, Stepmother."

The woman gave a guttural, wheezy hiss. "How many times do I have to tell you not to call me that? Are you dense?"

"No, Lady Sabine."

Sabine thrust a parchment with a list into Cinder's hand then brushed past her, grabbed her cloak and headed for the back door. "Bring those potions by the house when you break for lunch. I have some clients coming in that need them. And it's a complete mess back here. You are to straighten up before tomorrow."

"Yes, Lady Sabine."

Sabine's gaze raked over Cinder. "Tomorrow, see that you wear something nicer as well. I don't want anyone thinking that I can't afford to keep you well enough. And please, for the sake of the gods, put some shoes on those hideously enormous feet of yours."

Cinder crossed her bare feet and swallowed but said nothing as Sabine swung her cloak around her and stepped out the back door. She tried to keep her anger contained, but the blue tendrils of magick had already begun to swell within her, like a floating lantern.

It was Cinder and her magick that kept both the shop and her stepmother in style. Without her magick, Sabine would be forced to do the work herself. If anyone looked as if they couldn't afford nice clothing, it was Cinder herself.

For the first time, the desire to run away crossed Cinder's thoughts. It would be hard out in the world of Fairelle, and she would miss Rome all of her days, but perhaps the Gwyn brothers would help her. They'd ever been kind to her and more like family than her own. Her ribcage squeezed, Ville DeFee was her home. So why did she never feel like she belonged there?

Rome peeked through the curtain into the back room and glanced around. "Is it safe? Did she go?"

Cinder sighed. "She's gone." She walked to her flat shoes and picked them up, looking at them. "Do you think my feet are hideously enormous?"

Rome chuckled. "What?"

"Nothing." She slid them on.

Rome shook his head and stepped in. He folded his arms and leaned against the back wall.

"I don't know how you do it, Cinder, I really don't. I couldn't put up with a woman like that."

Anger pierced her, and the need to stand up for her stepmother crossed her thoughts. But she couldn't pretend. Not with Rome. He knew her too well. "She and Livy are all I have. Even if she doesn't want me," she finally said.

The bell rang, and several sets of footsteps entered.

"I need to go."

"Me too," he said. "But I'm going to bring my grandmother in tomorrow. She's got a cough that worries me. And I wanted to speak to you about something. Something important."

"You can tell me now."

He shook his head. "No. I want to do it when we have a bit of time."

She planted a forced smile on her face. "I'll be here."

Rome wrapped her in a hug and kissed the top of her head. "It'll get better. I promise."

Her cheek brushed against his chest, and the scent of him made her eyes close as she inhaled.

If only she knew who her mother had been. If only her father hadn't died before claiming her as his heir and giving her his name. If only she'd tried harder to win his affections. If only, if only, if only…

"Helloooooo?" Came a call from the front of the shop.

Cinder backed away. If only I were someone else.

He shot her his winning smile and pointed at her. "I'll see you tomorrow."

She nodded and ambled to the curtain.

"And Cinder?"

She glanced back.

"Your feet aren't hideously enormous. Only moderately enormous."

She flicked her fingers and a hand towel flew off the workbench in his direction. He ducked out the rear door, and the towel hit the glass window instead of his face.

He laughed as she glared at him. A smile snuck across her face, and she shook her head before going to the front of the store.

If only she'd let him kiss her again and again when they were young.

ROME WALKED INTO THE KITCHEN, ON THE FIRST FLOOR OF the castle and plucked at his tunic from the long walk from

Cinder's apothecary. From the apothecary he'd gone to tend to the duties his father had asked of him.

Rome scanned the plethora of food on the counter.

"Prince Rome. Is there something I can get you?" asked Bess the cook.

"A piece of pie if you have it, Bess. Thank you." His stomach growled loudly.

In the past months, his father had added more and more responsibilities to Rome's plate. Not that he minded, it was his duty, but Rome was no fool. He knew the real reason. His father wanted him to settle down. His thoughts went to Cinder and their encounter from that morning.

Rome sat at the round wooden table in the corner and undid the top buttons of his jerkin. Ever since Flint Gwyn had shown up, something had changed. Seeing her break the law, by combining her magick with Stil, and almost getting herself killed, made feelings he'd pushed aside for decades roar to the surface. A protectiveness that had him wanting more than just friendship. Just knowing that Silas had insulted and touched Cinder made Rome want to banish the fishmonger's entire family from Ville DeFee.

But in the past months there had been more than just the feelings, there had been the thoughts as well. Thoughts of life with her. And life without her. Of what he'd have done if she'd died that night. She was so willing to risk her life helping someone else. It was one of the things about her that he loved and hated most. She always followed her heart, no matter the cost to herself. Whereas he was bound by the law. Bound by his duty. Bound to his kingdom.

The fleeting moments he spent with her were the

happiest times of his life. Going to see her in her shop. Having her up to the castle for a walk. Eating with Stil and the three of them playing games. Things they'd done for decades. Things that were becoming harder to find the time to do with all the new responsibilities. And not seeing her on a daily basis had him even on edge about wanting her to be with him constantly.

Despite his father's fear that he'd never marry, Rome had thought about it quite frequently of late. The problem was... he had no idea how he was going to convince his father to let him court Cinder. And honestly, Rome wasn't sure he could court her. He didn't want to ruin their friendship and he was under no delusion that she would change who she was and conform to the life of a princess.

Bess set down a large piece of goldenberry pie. "Anything else I can get you, highness?"

Rome picked up his fork and his mouth watered. "No, thank you."

Bess nodded and headed back to the long table piled high with food. Rome glanced around to find the head cook making a list and going over it with several other servants. For the first time he noticed how many servants were about. Where only Bess and two others were usually in the kitchen, there were currently close to half a dozen people.

Outside the kitchen maids ran here and there, and the butlers barked out orders to the footmen. So much commotion for a weekday. He tried to remember if there was a special occasion he'd forgotten about, but nothing came to mind.

"Why is everyone so excitable today?" he called to Bess.

"For the feast of course."

"A feast?" He shoveled a bite of the crisp tart fruit into his mouth. There hadn't been a feast in the castle since his mother's death. "What's the celebration?"

Bess's eyebrows knit together. "You are."

"Me?" Rome wracked his brain again. What day was it? "It's not my birthday."

He shoveled several large forkfuls of pie into his mouth, and then poured himself a cup of ansleberb wine.

Bess wiped her hands on her apron and licked her lips. "You may want to speak with your father, your highness. I could be mistaken."

The nervousness that shrouded her left a gnawing feeling in Rome's stomach. Bess looked like a cornered cat as she waited to see if he would ask her anything else. All appetite gone, Rome set down his fork. If Bess was correct, and there were festivities planned in his honor, there could only be one person behind it— his father.

Pushing out his chair Rome stepped around the table. He gave her a reassuring smile and squeezed her arm.

"Thanks, Bess."

She nodded but wouldn't meet his eye.

He remembered his father's rushed appearance as he'd strode down the hall with Phinneaus that morning, asking Rome to go out and see to the guard. Had it been a ploy to get him out of the castle?

His mind went wild with ideas as he walked along the stone passage leading to the upper courtyard. The sunlight struck him with warmth as he crossed into the open space. A beautiful white stone fountain stood in the middle. Several swans swam as pink water sprayed in time to the sounds of a solo violin playing nearby. Maids bustled to and fro carrying fabric and decorations from one side of the castle to the other. Above, several of the court dressers used their magick to hang a crystal candelabra ten feet in the air.

Damn. Not good. He crossed to the entrance.

A maid with a large carpet bowed low, knocking into him and forcing him back out the door. "Excuse me, your highness."

He gave her a tense smile and waited for her to pass before continuing into the front hall. Everywhere he looked, servants prepared for the celebration. Vases were being polished. Paintings dusted. Flowers revitalized to the perfect state of bloom. Rome hadn't seen the castle that bustling in a long time. But for all the beautification, anxiety wound tight inside him, like a string ready to snap.

He walked past the ballroom and dining hall to the grand staircase and jogged up to the third floor. The noise died down, but there were still maids making beds, footmen stocking fireplaces and polishing every surface. There was definitely going to be a party. The guest rooms hadn't been that cleaned in close to a year, which meant his father was expecting company. Noble company.

He rounded the corner and continued up to the fourth floor, then to the fifth, where his father's rooms were. All the curtains had been opened, and the smaller, quieter area had a light, airy feeling to it. Something glittered in the large window to the left and he walked to it to see what it was. Down below in the courtyard glass tables were being set up in two long rows. Swathed in tablecloths, he watched as placemats were set out down the line. The castle was as abuzz with action as the city far below it.

He looked out over Ville DeFee. The brightly colored buildings, in hues of pinks, purples, and blues, were a stark contrast to the heavy golden gates and lush farmlands that surrounded the city. Beyond the farmlands were the dull brown woods that offered, even more, protection from the rest of Fairelle.

His gaze traveled to the part of the city where Cinder's shop stood and then beyond, to where her smaller home was smooshed between a hundred other tall, thin houses locked together on the sides. He had intended on going to see her that morning, but his father's need for him to help out had taken prescience. The door to his father's study stood ajar and voices floated out.

"This isn't right Alfred," said Rome's grandmother.

"And what would you have me do mother? He's no longer a child. It's time he stopped acting like one."

Rome's ears prickled and he stepped from the window and headed for the open door.

"Your Royal Highness, I too feel this is best. Not just for Prince Rome but also for all of Ville DeFee." Phinneaus, his father's advisor, spoke in his normal jovial manner.

His grandmother tsk'd. "This isn't the way. He needs to decide this on his own."

"I didn't get to decide, and things worked out quite well for me."

"That was different. You'd already known her."

"Your Royal Highness, with all due respect, he's been

given ample time, and he hasn't even shown the slightest interest in a girl," Phinneaus said.

"Shut up you sycophant. Ever since you became my son's advisor you've had nothing but one bad idea after the next."

"Mother—"

"I apologize, Queen Mother," said Phinneaus. "I meant no disrespect."

Rome raised a shaky hand and knocked on the door.

"Enter," called his father.

Rome straightened his shoulders and pushed his hair out of his eye.

"Ah, Rome!" His father clapped his hands and smiled. "I'm glad you've returned. I have some wonderful news."

"Do you?" Rome's gaze strayed to his grandmother. Her small, slender form leaned heavily on a brass cane. Her eyes held sadness, and she smiled at him weakly before coughing twice.

"We're having a feast." His father advanced. "And after the feast, a contest."

"Contest?" Rome's mouth went dry.

"To find you a bride." Phinneaus had been appointed after Cinder's father had died, even though he wasn't much older than Rome.

"Excuse me?" Rome looked from Phinneaus' friendly face to his father's gleeful eyes.

"It's time you grew up and married my boy. I'm not a spring fae anymore, and your grandmother has only fifty years or so left. We want to see you happy and wed with young ones of your own," said his father.

21

"Oh no." Rome's grandmother raised her hand. "You keep me out of this. I've already told you I'm against this whole thing. Besides, fifty years a still a long time for him to fall in love, marry and have faelens."

Rome caught his father's scowl.

"Enough is enough." The King donned his most royal voice and gripped Rome's shoulder. "You need to take responsibility. Stop gallivanting around with Stil and hanging out at Cinder's shop."

"What's wrong with Lady Cinder?" Rome crossed his arms.

Rome's grandmother's eyes glittered with interest.

"There is nothing wrong with Cinder. You know how fond of her I am. Her father was like a brother to me. And Phinneaus is her step-uncle. But it's time to put childish friendships behind you and look to your future."

"You need a wife of good breeding and with clean bloodlines," said Phinneaus. "And as fond as I am of Cinder, you know that with the death of her father, and him never claiming her, Cinder has no more pedigree than—"

"I wouldn't finish that sentence if I were you." Rome's fists clenched so tight his knuckles ached. He would be damned if he'd let anyone, especially the self-important Phinneaus speak against Cinder. Though she might not have the pedigree she carried more dignity and respect than the sniveling Phinneaus had in his left pinky finger.

Phinneaus held up his hands. "I mean Cinder no offense. Cinder is like family to me. I simply mean that she has no bloodlines to claim her."

Phinneaus' handsome face, with his long hair, so blond it

was almost white, pulled back into many braids, looked strikingly like his sister Lady Sabine. Only more feminine.

"I love Cinder," said his father. "But a princess needs to be of proper breeding. And as you refuse to pick a bride for yourself, we will hold a competition to find one for you."

How long had they been planning this? How had he not seen the signs? His father had hinted at the fact that he'd wanted Rome to marry, but this was so... obvious.

"Why can't you just let me pick in my own time? I'm sure if you will just-"

His father held up his hand. "It's too late. Announcements have already started to go out to the noble families."

Rome's gut squeezed. Married. His father wanted him to win a bride like a carnival prize. How could he think that would go well?

"A test, in three parts." Phinneaus shook his hands from his overly flamboyant, turquoise robes. "Three different houses of magick. To make sure the bloodline is pure and strong."

Rome's heart beat so wildly, he was sure it would give out. He didn't want any old female, especially not one that would entertain the idea of a contest, to get a husband.

"Three tests. So there could be three winners? Then what?" he asked.

"Well," his father shrugged. "We'll just have to figure it out if it comes down to that, but I doubt it will."

"I wouldn't be so sure," his grandmother muttered.

"And who's eligible to enter this contest?" asked Rome.

"All maidens who can trace pure bloodlines back at least

four generations." His father beamed, as proud as a rooster crowing.

Rome paced, staring at the creamy walls. How in the world had his life fallen into such a mess?

A contest to find him a wife. The person he was to sit with, to talk with, to sleep with and make love to. To have his children, raise them, and spend the rest of his life with. The idea was ludicrous. His grandmother was almost three hundred years old, and she had been married to his grandfather for over two hundred and sixty of them. That was a long time to be with someone you met at a contest.

"Rome, surely you must see that this is the best way," said Phinneaus. "I know this may feel a bit rash, but you'll get to choose from the best and most beautiful our kingdom has to offer."

"I don't want the best and most beautiful, I want to choose for myself."

As if he hadn't been exposed to enough preening, overeager supposedly noble females already. He didn't need a contest to have fae women throw themselves at him. Strong willed, stubborn, rule breaking, beautiful, gentle, kind. Those were the kind he liked. Or at least, one in particular.

Rome stopped. What if he could beat his father at his own game? He smiled despite himself. What if Cinder could produce four generations of pedigree- then she could enter. Or, he could get her a fake set. Even if she didn't want to, he could convince her to do it as a favor. Surely she'd want to help save him from marrying someone else. Hell, she'd broken the rules to help a human get a girl out of tower.

Entering his father's contest should be nothing to her. And there was no one like Cinder when it came to magick. She'd surely win. If she did he could prove to his father that pure bloodlines weren't everything, and that Cinder was good enough to become his wife. That she was indeed princess material.

But what if she said no? What if Cinder didn't want to help him? Or be a princess. The thought stuck him like a lightning rod to the chest. Worse yet... what if she didn't want to be his wife?

He had never told her how he felt about her. Though now that he looked back on it, his reasons seemed foolish. He'd been with women before, but none he'd fancied for more than a romp or two in bed. Funny how Cinder, who wasn't considered noble enough to become his bride, had more pride in herself to fall into a man's bed. Even his.

Memories of the one and only time he'd dared kiss her darted into his mind. They'd been young at the time. Playing seek and hide while on a picnic. He'd found her, but she'd run from him, and he chased her to the ground. They'd rolled in a patch of sungolds, and her laugh had infected him so that he'd wanted nothing more than to kiss her. So he had. But within a minute, she'd bucked him off and smacked him in the chest.

"You may be the prince but you have no right to me or my lips, Roman Geoffrey. The next time you feel so inclined to use me for kissing practice, you better ask permission first."

He'd been crushed that she'd think he'd been using her, but admired her even more for standing up for herself. Few girls then or women now would stand up to a prince and tell him no. But Cinder had never treated him like he was better than she was.

They'd been friends for decades. And he'd cared for her that entire time. But what if she'd never cared for him as anything more than a friend? His chest squeezed. Even so a friend would help him with the contest, wouldn't she?

He spent more time with Cinder and Stil than anyone else. But what about when he wasn't with her? Was she spending time with someone else? Certainly she would have mentioned suitors.

She had to care for him the way he did for her. She had to. Because if she didn't... His mind was made up. There was no more time for lollygagging. His father was putting on a contest to win him a wife and he needed to know if Cinder had feelings for him or not.

Rome strode from the room.

"Rome? Rome!" his father called.

"Let him go, your majesty," said Phinneaus.

Rome didn't stop. It was rash and unprecedented but he needed to know. Had to know. Right then, whether or not Cinder cared enough for him to enter the contest. Not the silly flirtations they had been bantering with, but if she truly cared.

He raced out the front door and down the winding steps to the village below. Though he'd already made the trek that morning, it didn't matter. He'd waited too long already — and now they were out of time.

. . .

ROME REACHED CINDER'S SHOP OUT OF BREATH. HE SLOWED at the side of the building practicing what he would say to her. He ran his fingers through his hair and buttoned his jerkin. He needed to look presentable or she wouldn't believe him when he asked her true feelings.

He waited for his heartbeat to stop thundering and though he'd caught his breath, his heart refused to calm. Finally he wiped his sweaty palms on his pants and sucked in a breath. It was now or never.

Rome rounded the building to the front door and tried the knob. It didn't turn. Stepping back he looked through the front window. A sign floated into view.

I've gone to see a sick customer on the far side of town. The shop will open again in the morning. My apologies for the inconvenience.

Rome sighed and looked around. He could go to her house and wait, but he had no inclination to be stuck with Lady Sabine all afternoon. He blew out a heavy breath. There was only one thing he could do- go home and wait until the morning when he brought his grandmother back to be looked at. All in all... it was going to be a very long day.

CHAPTER TWO

"**V**ery well," Rome strode through his father's door to find him, Phinneaus and his grandmother where he'd left them an hour previous. "I shall go along with your competition, on one condition."

"Which is?" His father's eyes narrowed.

"That if I find someone else to marry, before the competition ends, that I am allowed the opportunity to choose her instead."

Rome's father studied him for a moment. "No."

"But father—"

"You can't hold a competition under the guise of having you marry the winner only to have you choose someone else in the end. It would be bad form," said Phinneaus.

"Oh, give the boy a chance." His grandmother stood from the sofa and stretched. "You're forcing him into an impossible position. The least you can do is give him an opportunity to try and find someone for himself."

His father stroked his graying beard with one hand. "I'll compromise with you. After each of the competitions, you will get an opportunity to spend some time with the winner. In the event that you find she is completely incompatible, I will disqualify her, and we will continue. However, once a woman has been disqualified, you cannot bring her back and we will have to move forward with the ones that are left. If one maiden wins all three of the events however, then you must choose her."

Rome swallowed hard. His father wasn't going to let him off the hook, so there was only one thing left to do. Make sure Cinder entered the competition and won, at least one of the rounds.

"And what if no one wins?" Rome asked.

"I find that highly unlikely," replied Phinneaus. "We are after all the most powerful magical race in Fairelle."

"Then we are in agreement," said Rome.

Maybe if no one won, then he'd be able to choose Cinder after all.

ROME WALKED OUT OF HIS FATHER'S CHAMBER AND DOWN the hall to his room. When he threw open his door, the maids were making his bed and cleaning up his clothes jumped, then curtsied. He unbuttoned his jerkin and tossed it to the floor before plopping down onto his settee and propping his legs over the edge. He kicked off his boots just as a maid picked up his jerkin. She stepped back and then gathered up his boots as well. Rome leaned back and closed his eyes.

He'd been no more than ten, perhaps, when Cinder and her father came to the castle the first time. She had long blonde ringlets and bright, sapphire eyes, but her defiant spirit was what had caught his attention the most. That very first day she'd taught him how to scare the maids by magicking frogs into the linen closets. And how to multiply dust bunnies the moment they were about to be swept up.

If she was told not to use magick, she used it. If told she couldn't go down by the lake, she went. When dared to do anything, she did it. No matter the challenge, no matter the danger, Cinder did what Cinder wanted, and he loved her for it.

She'd spent more time inside the castle back then, than out. They'd attended dinners and balls and tournaments. Side by side laughing at the girls he danced with and then sneaking out with a bottle of wine to sit up on the highest balcony of the castle and looking over all of Fairelle. At one point he'd almost gotten up the nerve to ask her if she cared for him as more than just a friend, but then her stepmother had come into the picture, his mother had died, and everything had changed.

When her father came to the castle he'd brought only Lady Sabine and his new little daughter Olivia. Cinder no longer attended the dinners and his father no longer held balls or tournaments. Finally, after not having seen her for close to a month, Rome had snuck out to find her. It'd been the first time he'd experienced genuine anger.

She'd been on her knees, scrubbing the floors as punishment for something she'd done to upset her stepmother. Cinder had been more ashamed of him seeing her like that than she had been about scrubbing the floors. But seeing her treated so common had made him vow never to let her feel alone again.

After that, they'd snuck off together often down in the castle gardens, by the lake. Sometimes just the two of them browsed the marketplace or read in the great library or watched festivities. Sometimes with Stil. But always the two of them together.

Cinder and her magick fascinated him. She'd taught him how to bend his magick and use it in ways he'd never seen. She'd even shared her magick with him on occasion when he didn't have enough to do a trick or a spell. He'd watched her grow tired, after a day of helping people in her store, but one thing he'd never seen was her magick run out. He just knew if he could convince her to enter the contest she'd win.

A knock on his door interrupted his thoughts. Rome opened his eyes as a maid rushed to the door. She curtsied low to his grandmother as she entered. Rome hopped to his feet and took her arm, leading her to the settee.

She stared at him for a moment before patting him on the leg. "I'm sorry my boy."

Rubbing his face, Rome said, "I should have seen it coming."

"Your father really does want the best for you."

"But is he the best judge of what that might be?"

She shrugged. "He thinks he is."

"That doesn't make him right." Rome sighed.

"No." She shook her head. "No, it doesn't." His grandmother looked at the maids and waited until they left before speaking again. "Many things weigh on your father right now Rome. Rumors of things that are going on in Fairelle."

Rome's brows knit. "What kind of rumors?"

"That the prophecies have begun. That dragons are attacking in the south. Daemons have returned outside our walls."

A chill raced over Rome's skin. "But those are just rumors."

"Perhaps. Or perhaps not. We know that the werewolves have reunited with their mates. The vampire king and queen were overthrown, and the rightful heir has returned. Daemons were spotted coming out of the rift. There was a battle between them all, as well as the dragons, not too long ago, up in the Wastelands. It is only a matter of time before the other races reach our walls."

Rome's mind turned to Flint Gwyn, the human who'd asked Cinder to help with a spell, several months before. Was it possible he'd involved Cinder in something sinister?

"You know the prophecy I speak of don't you?" she asked.

"Of course," said Rome. "My mother taught it to me as a children's rhyme."

After the first, the second the third, the enemy will pull back.
They'll work in the dark, with the fae they'll hide and await
    their moment of attack.
Advantage they'll take, of the weak and the proud, and all
    goodness they will destroy.
Until the one girl, who answers to none, catches them in their
    ploy. "

"Then you know, that whomever this enemy is that has plagued Fairelle for the last thousand years, they're hiding within our walls. And if they aren't stopped, the prophecies could be broken, forever leaving Fairelle torn apart. Starting with our beloved city and your father in particular."

Rome nodded.

"So you understand why your father wants you to marry then."

Rome stared at his grandmother. "No. I'm afraid I don't."

"Because of the girl. The one from the prophecy. He believes that the girl you marry will be the girl that saves us all."

Rome shook his head. "He's putting all of that on one girl? A girl that he's choosing from a contest?"

"He believes that the contest will draw her out. By insuring that only those with pure bloodlines enter, he's narrowing the entrants greatly. From there, seeing who holds the greatest magickal skill, will be the next logical choice because let's be honest dear one, the magick in our family has been waning over the past generations. You aren't as strong as your father, and he isn't as strong as I am. But none of us come close to being as strong as my parents, or their parents before them. If we are to survive as royalty, and as a race, new blood is needed."

Rome nodded. "It's because we've become lazy with our abilities. Generations ago our ancestors closed the rift with the mages. Now we use our magicks to bring our clothes and butter our toast. Magick is meant to be exercised if we want to expand its influence."

His grandmother's smile widened. "And how is Lady Cinder these days?"

Rome lowered his gaze to his hands and laughed. "How did you know?"

His grandmother patted his knee again. "Dear one, what kind of fairy grandmother would I be if I didn't know your friends so well? Or their advice."

"I sound that much like her, do I?"

She laughed. "You do. But she's right you know. Ever since we stopped teaching magick to our children, they stopped knowing how to manipulate it properly." She coughed suddenly, and the wracking sound in her chest made Rome look up. She coughed again and again until Rome magicked over a glass of water for her. She sipped it until the coughing was under control.

"I want to take you to see her tomorrow," Rome said. "I want her to listen to that cough."

"Oh, pish tosh." His grandmother waved her hand at him. "It's nothing."

"Six weeks ago it was nothing. Now it's still here. I won't take no for an answer."

His grandmother looked him over and sipped her water a moment more. "I'll go. But before I do, you need to tell me how you plan on convincing Cinder to enter the contest."

Rome grinned and then blew out a heavy breath. He wished he knew.

CINDER WALKED TOWARD HER HOUSE, HER SPIRITS STILL depressed. The customer she'd gone to see was not doing well. There was little she could do for the old fae except offer some pain relief. She'd told the family that it shouldn't be long before her passing.

Seeing Rome had lifted her heart a bit, having to deliver potions to Lady Sabine, and doing it many hours later than anticipated was not something she wanted to do. The thing she loved most about being at the apothecary was being away from her stepmother.

She pushed open the front door to her house and stepped inside. She breathed deeply and could swear that, even after five years of absence, her father's scent still lingered. In his coat by the door. In his favorite chair by the fire. In his pillow and sheets that she washed weekly for her stepmother. It was as if his spirit still lingered, watching over them all.

Cinder closed the door and headed toward the kitchen with her crate of potion bottles.

"It was easy," said a man. "All I did was put the idea in his mind and give it a little push and the next thing I knew we were discussing party decorations and menus."

"We cannot take a chance," said her stepmother. "Olivia must prevail."

Cinder's brow furrowed, not understanding the conversation.

"She will, dear sister. Don't you worry. You just do your part, and I'll do mine, and together we will insure that your daughter comes to the position she deserves." *Phinneaus.*

Cinder shook her head. Poor Livy. Her mother was already trying to marry her off.

"Well…" The sly, crafty tone her stepmother had used a thousand times over with her father, crept into her voice. "Maybe if you let me borrow your-"

There was a sharp sound, like someone smacking wood. "I've given you enough of my magick, and I can't afford anymore. Use your own. Stop squandering it on youth and beauty."

She knew it! Cinder knew her stepmother had been using magick to glamour her appearance. No wonder she never had magick to do anything else.

"You're one to talk, Phinneaus. Look at you. You're almost prettier than I am." The silence stretched out for a moment. "Where is that damned Cinder? I need those potions."

Cinder opened the front door and then closed it loudly. She strode into the front room and stopped. "Lady Sabine?"

A chair scraped across the kitchen floor, and a set of light heels clicked on the wood and into the front room.

"There you are." She shook her shoulder length blonde hair. "You've kept me waiting almost three hours. Where were you?"

"I apologize. A customer detained me."

Her stepmother strode to Cinder and looked into the crate. "Is that everything I asked for?"

"Yes."

Lady Sabine glanced up at her. "And you're sure you made them correctly?"

Cinder bit the inside of her cheek.

"Of course, she made them correctly. Cinder is a master potion-maker." Phinneaus strode into the room, a broad smile on his face, his grass green eyes gentle and warm. "How are you, my dear?"

"I'm well, thank you, Uncle."

Phinneaus relieved her of the crate and set it on the small side table before taking her hands in his crisp thin ones.

"Phinneaus. Just Phinneaus to you. I'm not truly your uncle in anything more than spirit." His face was like a chiseled angel's. Large almond shaped eyes with long sweeping lashes. High cheekbones and full ruby lips. Though she'd never say so, Lady Sabine was right. He was prettier than she.

"Of course." She swallowed hard. Aside from Rome and Stil, Phinneaus was the kindest person in her life. "Can I make you something to eat before you go Phinneaus? Perhaps a cake or muffins? It will only take a moment."

Lady Sabine scoffed. "See how you preen over my brother but give me no more than pittance."

A little kindness goes a long way.

Phinneaus smiled. "Thank you, no. I must get back to the castle. There is much to prepare for." He leaned in and kissed her on the cheek. His light dusting of whiskers scratched her skin. "Don't let my sister sour your mood. You're more wonderful than you know."

Cinder's face heated as he planted the light kiss on her cheek. Over his shoulder, her stepmother's eyes narrowed, and her jaw clenched tight.

"If you have so much time on your hands, maybe you should make a cake for your sister and myself."

Cinder stepped away from Phinneaus and her fingers slipped from his. "I… I… should…" She cleared her throat. "I should get back to the shop. I don't want it closed for too long."

Phinneaus gave her a knowing smile.

"Don't be late tonight," her stepmother called. "I want dinner on the table on time for once."

Cinder held back a sigh of frustration and headed for the door. She wished she could spare a moment to look in on her sister Livy, but she'd wasted too much time as it was.

Swallowing hard she headed back to work.

CHAPTER THREE

D ax rolled his shoulders and stared at the large gate separating him from the possibility of getting answers to his past. He'd been hiding and waiting for three days, trying to get up the nerve to go in. He wasn't afraid of getting caught; he was afraid of what he'd find in there. The fear of not knowing wasn't as great as the fear of her telling him she couldn't help or even the fear of finding out the truth– who he was.

The sun hung low on the horizon, and the guards shaded their eyes as they ushered the last of the fae into the city before the gates closed for the night. Memories of the last time he'd tried sneak into the fae kingdom with Flint rushed back to him. All he needed to do was blend in and act natural. But he didn't suppose acting like a werebear would get him through the gate. So he had to act like a fae, not himself.

He grabbed his pack and slung it over his shoulders,

then fastened the cloak Cinder had given him around himself and raised the hood. He had no clue what kind of magick the cloak possessed, but the air around him shimmered and glowed with a faint iridescent light. He walked slowly, head down, from his vantage point just beyond the fields and headed for the gate.

His feet moved him forward but with every step, the heat of the cloak smothered him. He'd enjoyed the warm weather the past months, but not from under the weight of a woolen cloak.

The itch to turn and run started at the base of his spine and crawled upward, making his temples pound. He shook his head and clenched his jaw. He had to do this. If he ran now, he'd never get another chance.

"Good morrow," said a light female voice.

Dax raised his head long enough to see a young fae drop in alongside him.

Dax nodded but said nothing. His heart banged against his chest like an anvil hammer.

"Lovely day to be in the fields, don't you think? I just love the feeling of life growing around me; tending to the buds and making sure everything ripens to perfection."

She prattled on the longer they walked and as much as Dax wanted to shut her up, the cover of her incessant talking was sure to help him blend. They approached the gate; the girl said goodbye to him and turned to chat with the guards, offering them a piece of fruit from her basket. The guards barely even glanced Dax's direction. He blew out the heavy breath he didn't realize he'd sucked in.

Ducking behind the first shop he came to, he bent over, trying to calm his nerves. He had to keep it together.

As his heart and mind raced, he realized this was the first journey he'd taken alone in over five years– not since he'd been found in the woods of Wolvenglen running from vampires. His heart ached for the companionship of Flint and the Gwyn brothers, who had become like family to him. For Sage and Adrian, who had also become his brothers. He was happy they'd found their mates and their places in the world, but now he needed to do the same for himself.

He stood straight and squared his shoulders. Good, bad, or indifferent, he had to find out who he was, and Cinder was the only person that could possibly help him.

DAX STEPPED UP TO THE BACK DOOR OF CINDER'S SHOP AND peered through the glass window panes. No one stirred in the back room, so he slid down the side to the front and looked inside. A man and a young child stood at the counter, speaking to Cinder. She spoke to them with a warm, welcoming smile on her face. He waited while she handed the child a candy and hugged her, then the man and child headed for the exit. Dax dropped back into the shadows as the two stepped into the street and a "Closed" sign appeared on the front door.

He ran for the rear of the shop and stepped inside. After several tense moments, he headed for the curtain partition and peeked through. Cinder sat heavily behind the counter, on a wooden stool. Head in her hands, shoulders slumped, she looked impossibly tired. Guilt raced through him. He shouldn't bother her with his problems. But it'd been almost six years; he needed to know who he was.

"Excuse me, Lady Cinder?" He tried to keep his voice soft and gentle.

Her head whipped up and her glazed eyes connected with his, and then her brows knit together. She snapped her fingers, and the hood of his cloak dropped off.

"Dax!" She gave a weak smile and stood. "What are you doing here? Is there trouble?" She snapped her fingers again, and all the lights in the store extinguished as she headed for the curtain. Dax backed out of her way.

Stepping into the back room, the extent of her fatigue etched on all of her features.

"Are you all right?" He reached out to steady her. "You look like you're ready to collapse."

She squeezed his arm, and he pulled up a chair for her. "Thank you. To tell you the truth, I am quite tired. Using so much magick takes a lot out of me."

"Doesn't anyone help you? Your stepmother?"

"No." She chuckled. "Lady Sabine would never use her magick to help others."

Was she in charge of providing all the magick in the shop? "How can you do this, day after day? Using yourself up to pay for your entire family?"

She shrugged. "What else am I to do? I have no formal education. No title, no lands, nothing."

It wasn't right that a woman of Cinder's caliber be treated as a common serving wench. "But you're a lady. You have your father's name."

"Only in certain circles. Lady Sabine has seen to it that

everyone knows I was not a legitimate daughter. My mother was… of ill repute, let's say."

It wasn't possible. Though Dax had nothing against whores, he doubted very highly that Cinder herself could be the daughter of one.

"I didn't realize the fae even had such a thing," he mused.

She stared at him for a moment. "I'm sure you didn't come all this way just to talk about me. You came because Flint told you of my offer."

"He did."

"How are Flint and his woman in the tower?"

"Married. Happy. He was blinded trying to save her, but he's made it work."

Her brows drew together, and a rueful smile crossed her lips. "How very adaptable of him. And how very uncharacteristic."

Dax chuckled. "True. The process was painful, but I believe he's better for it."

"Well, good for him. And as for you my werebear friend…" She yawned. "You are shrouded in magick. It wafts off you as if you're made of it."

His heart sank a bit. Was she going back on her offer? "So you can't help me?"

"I didn't say that." She waved her hand at him. "But not tonight I'm afraid. I need to rest and replenish my magick so I can try to figure out what someone did to you. Do you have somewhere to stay?" She shook her head. "What am I asking? Of course, you don't."

She walked across the backroom to a smaller, separate room.

"Come on." She waved him over and flicked her fingers at a candelabra in the corner, lighting it. She picked it up and Dax followed her into the smaller room filled with crates and barrels of supplies. He squeezed through the narrow gaps to a dark corner.

"Sorry it's so tight in here. I haven't had the energy to tidy up and organize all the supplies with everything I've had going on."

She handed him the candelabra and pressed both of her palms to a section of the wall. The wall shook, and there was a creaking noise, before it popped open.

"Wow. A secret passage."

"Not exactly." She pulled open the panel and took the candelabra from him before walking into the dark beyond. "This used to be my playroom when I was a child. My father worked, and I occupied myself in here. It hasn't been used for decades but there's a bed, and you can have these candles for light. There are some books if you get bored, and there's food out in the storeroom. Take whatever you need."

"I can pay you."

She held up her hand. "Insulting me is a good way to get kicked out on your rear Dax."

He inclined his head. "I apologize. But I refuse to take so much from you for free. I can work."

She handed him the candelabra once more. "We'll talk about it tomorrow. Tonight I need to get home and make supper for my stepmother and sister before they have my head. I'll spell the door, so no one sees it but you'll need to stay out of sight."

"I appreciate everything you've done for me. I won't do anything to get you in trouble."

"I haven't done anything yet, and I can handle myself. You, on the other hand, will not get any closer to finding out who you are if you're in the Ville DeFee dungeon."

"Again, I thank you for your kindness."

Cinder nodded. "I really must go." She turned but then stopped, and with a twist of her wrist, all of the cobwebs and dust in the room disappeared; every surface gleamed. Even the fresh scent of flowers lingered in the air.

"Goodnight Dax. I'm sorry I'm unable to do more."

"You've already done more than most would."

She gave him a weak smile and walked out, shutting the door behind herself.

Dax looked around the room. An antique yet simple bed waited in the corner, and a beautiful rug covered the floor in blues and greens. Murals in cheery children's stories adorned the walls, and the ceiling looked like the night sky. A white bookcase held dozens of books and toys scattered the floor. It looked as if Cinder had just walked out the day before and everything stood awaiting her return.

He walked to the small nightstand and sat the candelabra on it. He removed his cloak and bag and set them on the end of the bed before sitting. The absolute quiet of the room stood in stark contrast to the variety of sounds he was used to in the woods. Between Wolvenglen, the hideout in the Wastelands, and traveling with Flint, the silence wasn't something he was used to. The urge to yell, just to hear the sound of his own voice, ballooned inside him.

He blew out a deep breath and settled into the fact that he was in a secret room in a land he wasn't supposed to be in. If he got caught, it wouldn't just be his hide, it would be Cinder's as well. Even though she'd said she didn't care, he did.

His gaze traveled to the door. Nervous energy wound inside him so tight, he hopped up, making the bed creak. He stretched his muscles and jogged in place for several minutes. It would be hours before he slept. His stomach grumbled, and he sighed. He hated eating her food on top of getting a place to sleep. An idea popped into his mind, and he smiled.

If he wasn't going to sleep, he might as well be helpful.

CHAPTER FOUR

C inder awoke the next morning to squeals of delight from down the hall. She sat up and yawned as the front door closed. Glancing around her small room for her father's old pocket watch she located it on her nightstand and flipped it open. It was barely past six.

A booming knock on her door had her on her feet.

"Get up you lazy girl. I'm starving."

"Yes st– Lady Sabine." Cinder stripped out of her dressing gown and walked to the washbasin in the corner. She waved her fingers over the water pitcher, and then poured the cool liquid into the basin. Another booming knock had her scrubbing herself raw, quick as light, and stepping into her chemise and light blue dress. She brushed her hair into a low ponytail, and then walked out of her room.

She hurried down the narrow hallway, past portrait

after portrait of her stepmother and half sister, to the end, where a single portrait of her father hung. His long black hair was pulled back into a low ponytail, and his deep green jerkin and breeches were the height of fashion thirty years prior.

She caressed the face she both adored and hated. "Good morning, Papa."

"Cinder!" her stepmother screeched.

Cinder walked down the stairs, the wood creaking with every step. She turned the corner and headed through the pink dining room, where her stepmother and half sister waited. Icy daggers stabbed at her from her stepmother's gaze. Gods above forbid Lady Sabine should bother to heat a piece of bread or boil water for some tea.

"Good morrow, Cinder." Her half sister smiled, lighting up her sweet, yet plain face.

"Good morrow, Livy."

Lady Sabine hissed. "You know I hate it when you call her that."

"It's all right mother. I like it."

"Your name is Olivia. Your father named you that after his mother. Your name is not Livy." Lady Sabine's gaze scoured her daughter's face, and Olivia dropped her gaze to the table. "Oh don't be so common Olivia. Hold your head high, shoulders straight. Remember who you are and what you represent."

Olivia lifted her head and straightened her spine, but the sparkle had left her round, doe eyes. "Yes, mother."

Lady Sabine's gaze traveled to Cinder. "What are you gawking at? Fix us something to eat. But go easy on the fat today. Olivia needs to watch every morsel she puts in her mouth now."

Cinder looked to Olivia, perplexed, then headed to the kitchen. She flicked her fingers at the stove, and it burst into a roaring fire. The pull on her magick was more than it should have been and she yawned. She needed more sleep.

She set a teakettle and two pieces of bread on top to warm. She walked into the small larder and cut three pieces of ham, shoved one in her mouth, and brought out the other two with a vine of bearberries and two beautiful pink apples. She cut and arranged everything on two plates and poured the tea into cups when it whistled. Then she walked everything out and set it down. Lady Sabine immediately snatched the bread from Olivia's plate and handed it to Cinder.

"No bread. Just the fruit and meat from now on."

Cinder held the bread in her palm and looked to Olivia, whose face seemed to sag with longing as she eyed it.

"Are you ill?" Cinder asked. "I can tend to you if you need."

"No," said her stepmother. "Olivia isn't sick; she received an invite to the ball."

Cinder stared at her stepmother, who cut her piece of ham into tiny slices before putting a piece between her teeth.

"A ball?" The lump in Cinder's throat threatened to choke her.

"Yes," Olivia gushed. "They're giving a tournament and ball for Prince Rome."

Cinder's stomach plummeted to her toes. "It... it isn't

his birthday." Her mouth dried and she could barely get the words out.

"No," said her stepmother. "He's looking for a bride. There is to be a contest and the winner will marry the prince."

Cinder's head spun, and she focused hard on the wooden table to keep from falling over. Was Rome having a contest to find a wife? Why hadn't he told her? Her chin quivered, and she sucked in a deep breath.

"Well," she finally said. "That's wonderful. May I see the invitation?"

Her stepmother laughed. "Why would you need to see it? You're not eligible."

"I'm not?" She hadn't meant to sound so hurt.

"Of course not. Only girls who are able to prove their heritage, going back four generations, are allowed to participate. And we have no idea where your mother came from. Even if we did, I'm sure your blood wouldn't be pure enough."

Cinder crushed the piece of bread in her hand as anger flared inside her. "My father was a Lord. I am Lady Cinder of Ville DeFee. I should be allowed to go."

Her stepmother's eye twitched, and Cinder was sure she would lash out. Instead, she set her fork down on her plate and took Cinder's hand in her own.

Lady Sabine had only ever touched her once before. The feel sent chills racing over Cinder's body.

"Of course, you are Cinder. Your father was a great man and a great friend to the king. You are right. You should be able to participate. I'll appeal to the king myself on your behalf. I'm going to visit Phinneausssssss today for tea. I'll make sure to mention it to him so he'll get me an audience with the king." Lady Sabine smiled at Cinder, the way one would a sickly dog that could not be saved.

The drawling *s* that her stepmother sometimes used made Cinder's skin crawl. An odd speech impediment Cinder had learned at a young age it only appeared when Lady Sabine was angry or nervous.

Cinder's stomach soured, and she pulled her hand away. "You're too kind."

Lady Sabine beamed up at her. "In the meantime, I'd like for you to close the apothecary for the day so that you can reserve your energy to help Olivia."

"Close the shop?"

"Yes. You do want to help your sister don't you?"

Cinder looked to Olivia. Her half sister was only twenty years younger than Cinder. And despite her mother trying to keep them apart, they'd always had a close bond.

"Of course," Cinder replied.

"Splendid. Then today I want you to stay home and together we'll help Olivia prepare for tomorrow's celebration." Lady Sabine picked up her fork and placed another bite of ham into her mouth.

Cinder's mind reeled. She needed to check on Dax at the very least. "I… I must go in this morning. Prince Rome is bringing his grandmother the Queen Mother by for some herbs and healing. I'll close up as soon as they leave. That will give you time to speak to the king about me."

Lady Sabine stopped chewing and took a sip of her tea before turning her smile up at Cinder. "Of course. Of course. Olivia and I will go as soon as I finish breakfast. She's going to take a walk with the prince after he escorts his grandmother."

"I am?" Olivia asked.

"Yes, my sweet." Lady Sabine gave Olivia a rare, motherly smile.

Cinder nodded to Lady Sabine even though every muscle in her body wanted to slap the lie right off her stepmother's pretty face.

CINDER PUSHED OPEN THE DOOR TO HER SHOP, AND ANGER knotted her stomach. In the past hour, she'd done everything without thinking. She'd moved through her morning doing her chores and preparing for the day with only one thing on her mind. Rome was getting married.

She set a basket of food on the back counter and removed her cloak. She shook it off and hung it on the hook by the door.

"Good morning."

She jumped and spun around to find Dax standing in the doorway to the back room. His large frame took up the entire entrance.

He gave her a tight smile. "Sorry. I didn't mean to frighten you."

She crossed to him and held out her basket. "I brought you some food."

"You didn't have to do that."

Dax was nice to look at, for a human. His large, bulky form was so different from Rome's lean, clean lines. But the masculinity, he exuded was completely primal. In his arms, a woman would be completely protected. For the first time in her life, she wondered what it would be like to live outside the walls of Ville DeFee. If Rome married another, was there a point in staying? He wouldn't come around to see her and then what would she have, besides her sister?

"I wanted to show you something," he said, breaking the silence.

She shook her head, realizing she'd been staring, and followed him into the storage room. "Holy blessed fae mother. Did you do all this yourself?"

He gave a genuine smile that lit up his hazel eyes, and he ran his fingers through his shaggy blond hair. "I did."

The entire storage room had been cleaned and organized. Crates had been stacked alphabetically. Goods lined the shelves. Barrels had been opened and left for her to sift through. The entire job must have taken hours.

"Thank you, Dax." She threw her arms around his neck and hugged him tight. He stiffened, then relaxed and hugged her back.

"You do me more kindness than organizing a thousand store rooms."

"Come," she said. "Let me make you some tea and we can talk. I'm only expecting one customer today and then I am to close the shop and head home."

"Is there a problem?"

"No." She shook her head. "The Prince is having a contest and a ball, and I am to go home and help my sister prepare for it."

His eyebrows drew together. "The prince?"

Cinder's gut clenched. She'd spent the entire walk to the shop crying over Rome, realizing everything she'd hoped for with with him was just a dream. A wish she should have known would never be fulfilled. She'd wasted so much time hoping their friendship would become more. It was time to accept what everyone had told her for years. She wasn't good enough to be a princess.

"But... why aren't you competing? I don't understand." Dax sat at the small workbench and opened the basket.

She set a kettle on the small stove and lit the coals inside. "Competitors have to prove their bloodlines for four generations. I have no way of proving mine."

"That doesn't seem right. Your father was a Lord."

She laughed. "Tell that to the king. His is nothing if not about his bloodlines. My father died without leaving a writ of lineage. Therefore, I am nothing and stepmother gets everything. When she passes on, my father's name and possessions will go to my half sister."

Dax crossed his arms over his chest and shook his head. "But I thought..."

"Thought what?"

"I thought you and Prince Rome were... friendly. Flint told me about him."

"Rome and I have been friends for sixty years."

Dax snorted. "Sixty? And he still hasn't asked you to marry him? The man must be either blind or stupid."

"I can assure you I am neither." Rome stepped through the curtain, a look of anger crossing his handsome features. "Who are you and what are you doing here?"

"Hold a minute," said Cinder. "This is my shop, and I'll have whomever I like here. This is Dax. He's a friend."

Rome's angry gaze turned on her. "You sure seem to have a lot of friends lately."

Cinder's anger peaked, and she had to swallow hard to keep from lashing out.

"Is that a problem? Seems *friends* are all I have anymore."

Rome's eyes narrowed. "And what is that supposed to mean?"

"Why don't you tell me."

"I think I'll eat in the other room." Dax picked up the basket and headed for the storage room.

"That sounds like a grand idea," replied Rome.

"*Nona.* No." Cinder snapped her fingers and Dax sat back in his seat with a thump. "You were here first. There's no reason you should have to leave. You were invited."

"So was I," retorted Rome. "I was told I could bring my grandmother."

Why was Rome acting so overbearing? Yes, technically Dax wasn't supposed to be in Ville DeFee without permission, but it barely warranted Rome acting like a total pigheaded dungbeast. If anyone had a right to be angry, it was her. He'd not even told her about the contest.

"Fine. Then let us go out and see to your grandmother." Cinder waved him toward the front of the store.

Rome clenched his fists tight, and magick sparked off his knuckles. Cinder reached out and spun him toward the curtain.

"Let's go before you do something I won't be able to

fix." She pushed against Rome's back, shoving him toward the partition. "Don't make me spell you Roman Geoffrey."

Rome relaxed and walked through the curtain to the front of the store.

Cinder turned to Dax. "I apologize for him, and for shoving you into your seat."

Dax raised a hand and nodded. "I've been through worse."

Cinder's chest tightened. "Yes, you have. Which is why it makes what I did that much more terrible. I promise not to do that again."

His eyes took on a sincerity that melted her heart. "Thank you. I'm gonna head into the secret room."

Cinder nodded. "That's probably best."

She waited until Dax disappeared and then took a deep, centering breath and heading to the store front.

Rome stood behind his grandmother; his face masked like she'd never seen. She'd only witnessed Rome's anger a couple of times, and it usually involved his father. The fact that he currently directed his anger at her struck an eerie chord inside. It didn't matter though. He'd made the choice to marry, without even talking to her. Therefore, what concern was it of his whom she allowed in her shop? Other than the fact that it was against the law. The law didn't seem to be his motive, however.

"Good morning, your majesty." Cinder curtsied to the royal mother.

Rome's grandmother chuckled. "Oh pish tosh child, none of that. You're the one who's helping me, remember? There's no need for such formality."

Cinder's gaze met the old woman's. Rome certainly didn't get his courtly airs from her. Slender and petite, his grandmother was a beautiful woman, even in her advanced age. Her silvery hair hung in ringlets down to her waist and her skin still held the pink flush of youthfulness. Jade green eyes sparkled with mischief as she looked Cinder up and down.

"You look just like your mother," she said.

Cinder's heart thundered. "Ex- excuse me?"

"Your mother. You look just like her. Same beautiful blue eyes. Light peachy skin and hair the color of corn silk. Same as your grandmother too I would guess."

Cinder looked between Rome and his grandmother. Her mouth opened and closed several times, and then she cleared her throat and wiped her slick palms on her dress.

"I... I'm sorry your majesty I didn't realize you knew my mother. My father never spoke of her. Do you... I mean... Could you... tell me her name?" She felt so foolish asking. But of all the things she'd ever wanted to know, that was the one she wanted most. A name. Such a simple thing. Letters strung together to make a sound. Yet above all, it was what she'd wished her father had given before he'd died.

Rome's grandmother stared at Cinder for a moment, and then sadness came over her face. "I'm so sorry my dear but for the life of me, I cannot remember."

Cinder's hopes fell so fast, she had to steady herself on the counter to keep from falling over. Questions wracked her mind. So many things she wanted to know about her mother. Things her father had never spoken of and that her stepmother had forbidden her to ask.

Rome's grandmother coughed several times. The coughing hardened and within an instant they'd caused his grandmother to keep from breathing. Cinder rounded the counter, pushing her problems from her mind and magicked over a small sucking drop.

"Give her this." She shoved it at Rome and then magicked over a goblet of water. She poured a vial of tincture into it and held it out to Rome's grandmother.

She sipped from the cup and then took a deep breath. "Thank you," she said in a croaky cracked voice.

"That doesn't sound right." Cinder shook her head and approached Rome's grandmother. He stepped back and she refused to meet his eye, for fear she'd lose control of her angry tongue; the last thing she wanted was to look common in front of his grandmother. "May I touch your chest, your majesty?"

"Please, call me Elise." She laid her soft hand on Cinder's arm. "And yes, you may."

Cinder's arm grew warm as blue wisps of white magick flowed through her. The feel of power that washed through her making her hair stand on end. She'd never been on the receiving end of shared magick before. Cinder stared into the woman's eyes as warmth and calmness flowed into her. Meeting another fae with as great a magick as she possessed was a rare treat.

Cinder placed her palms, one atop the other, over Elise's heart and told her to take a deep breath. A sticky rattle emanated from within.

"Morphos mold," said Cinder. "You have morphos mold in the castle."

"*Goth Rospa*. Preposterous," said Rome. "Every room in the castle is spotless."

Cinder's gaze slid to him. His indignation was enough for her to give him a tongue-lashing.

"I assure you, your highness, it is morphos mold. Predominantly found in wet, underground chambers. Particularly in catacombs. If you do not think I am correct in my assessment, you are certainly welcome to seek the advice of another healer." She kept her voice as calm as possible, but she was sure her body language and expression told another story. Her face was one place she'd never been able to hide what she felt.

"There is no need," said Elise. "She's right, Rome. And you would do well to trust Lady Cinder's judgment on things in the future."

Rome's brows knit together and he looked at his grandmother. "But there is no mold in the castle."

"There is. In your grandfather's tomb. I've been visiting it almost daily for the last six months. I've been missing him more frequently of late."

Rome's eyes softened, and he hugged his grandmother. "It's not your time yet," he whispered.

His grandmother chuckled. "Child I'm not going anywhere." She patted him lightly on the back, then pointed her finger at him. "I believe you owe someone an apology."

"Me? But... I..." His gaze connected with Cinder's conflicted.

"*Geat Morpent*. Roman. You apologize."

Cinder held back a snicker. Rome looked like a little boy, caught with a stolen pie in his hands.

He swallowed and inclined his head to Cinder. "*Aktae*. I apologize for my rudeness."

Cinder nodded. "Accepted. Now if you'll give me a minute, I'll fetch the ingredients needed to help clear up that cough. And the catacombs need scrubbing. Otherwise you'll be back here in a month."

Elise smiled at Cinder. "I would like to visit you again, my dear, but not for a cough. For tea perhaps?"

Cinder curtsied. "I would enjoy that very much. Thank you." If she was still in Ville DeFee.

Elise turned to Rome. "You get my herbs please and any instructions. I'll meet you in the marketplace. I'd like to pick up some flowers."

"Of course." Rome kissed his grandmother on the cheek, and she waved goodbye to Cinder before heading out the door.

Rome's gaze stayed locked on Cinder, and as soon as the door closed, the air between them heated and snapped with intensity.

Cinder moved to the shelves and pulled down various bottles and canisters. "I'll mix this up for her, but she'll have to drink it three times a day until the cough is gone. Then she'll need to drink the tea I prepare for the next thirty days, at which time—"

"Cinder we need to talk."

"…She will come back and see me and I can make sure she is completely clear." Cinder took her load of herbs and tinctures to the counter and Rome grabbed her arm.

"We need to talk about the werebear in your back room," Rome said.

"Do we? I don't see a reason to. He's none of your concern just as your business is obviously none of my concern." She pulled away and set the items on the glass counter. Then pulled out her mixing bowl, mortar, and pestle.

"What do you mean by that?"

She stared at him, was he really that stupid. "How long have we known each other, your highness?"

"*Mendas rathspa,* stop calling me that." He rubbed his face with his hands. "We've been friends for sixty years Cinder."

"So, one would think that after decades of friendship they could tell a person when they planned to marry."

Emotions raced over his features. Confusion, recognition and finally guilt. "You heard."

She poured the herbs into the pestle and pounded them until her wrist burned with fatigue.

"It's fine. You did not see fit to let me know you were planning a competition for a wife. Maybe because you knew I'd tell you how demeaning something like that was. Or possibly because you were afraid I'd say how stupid it is to try and find a spouse by a few simple tasks. Or maybe—"

"It wasn't my idea. It's my father's and I didn't find out until yesterday."

She slammed the mortar on the counter so hard it cracked the glass. "You're going along with it though aren't you?"

His expression held sadness. "I tried to talk him out of it but you know how he gets. Please. I want you to be there."

Cinder planted her fists on her hips and blew the hair

from her eyes. "You want me to be there? Why? To watch a bunch of self-indulgent *quondi* try to win their way into the royal family? I'd rather roll in dragon dung and walk through the city naked."

"Cinder I need you." He reached for her hand.

She pulled away and snapped her fingers at the herbs. They mixed themselves and then flew into a container. She waved, and the liquids mixed and dripped into an open amber bottle. She placed the stopper in the bottle and thrust both the bottle and the container of herbs at him before flicking her hand over the glass, fixing the crack.

"You don't need me anymore Rome. Our days of childish friendship are at an end. You are moving on with your life, and I need to as well. I wish you the best of luck with your upcoming nuptials."

She didn't wait for a response. Instead, she rushed from the store into the backroom and then out to the alleyway. Her chest burned, and her heart pounded so thunderously, she feared her body would burst into flames and break apart.

She shoved her fist into her mouth to keep from screaming. Tears stung her eyes and coursed down her cheeks. How had she let this happen? All these years she'd pined away for him, waiting for him to show interest. They'd occasionally flirted before, but there'd never been anything more. She knew everything there was to know about him. She knew the first time he'd kissed a girl. The first time he'd broken the law. She'd been the one to drag him home the first time he'd gotten drunk on ansleberb wine. She knew what he liked, what he didn't like. The way he took his tea.

The kinds of cookies he preferred and the face he made when he had a good hand at cards. She even knew about the two women he'd slept with. The maid that had been his first and the lady-in-waiting that had been his second.

He'd been testing out the waters of manhood, she'd told herself. He wanted to know what it felt like to lay with a woman. It was common.

But she'd been wrong. She was only his friend, nothing more.

And now, she would keep all of those things to herself and lock them away with the tender feelings she had carried for him. She could no longer hope. No longer wait. No longer wish her prince would come.

CHAPTER FIVE

Cinder waited until the front door of her shop
closed before stepping back inside the storeroom.
With nothing but emptiness in her heart, she
walked to the front, put her herbs and tinctures away and
locked the door. She had no time to dwell on the pain. She
needed to get home and help Livy.

Dax stepped from the storeroom as she threw her cloak
about her shoulders.

"You need to go?" he asked.

"I'm afraid I do."

He nodded. A solemn expression sat on his face.

"I can spare a few minutes, though." She removed her
cloak and hung it back up. "This might take a few tries," she
said. "The magick surrounding you is potent and foreign
to me."

"I can be patient. I've waited this long."

"Have a seat." She pointed to the stool.

He sat on it, making the wood creak beneath his bulky frame.

Cinder studied him.

"The air around you shimmers. Like… a red blanket is always on you. But it's darkest and strongest near your head."

"Red?"

"Yes. The magick is red. I've not encountered it before. Does that mean something to you?"

"I don't know. We've been finding red stones amongst our enemies lately."

"What kind of enemies?" She'd heard rumors of wars happening outside the borders of Ville DeFee, but she couldn't be sure of their authenticity.

"When I was with the wolves we thought it was the vampires. But it wasn't. There was a woman among them, leading them, twisting them. She wasn't a vampire; she was something else. A daemon. And then with Flint— the man who had taken his wife Zelle prisoner and blinded him; he was controlling the dragons with a red stone. And there was a woman…" His gaze drifted off as if lost in a memory.

"Did you recognize any of them?"

"I… can't remember. The woman I think possibly."

"Well, if this is daemon magick it's ancient and very powerful. It will take some time for me to break if I can at all. My best hope right now is to weaken it enough to see past it and help you find the answers you seek."

"Anything you can tell me would be greatly appreciated."

"All right then." Cinder rolled up her sleeves. "Let's see

what I can do to start with." She stepped between Dax's thighs. "We need to touch. The closer the contact the better the connection. I'm going to put my hands on either side of your head, and I want you to put your hands on my waist."

Dax swallowed hard and nodded. His large hands almost wrapped completely around Cinder's waist. The sensation sent a chill up her spine. Rome's hand only spanned half as much.

She shook the thoughts of Rome from her head and wiggled her fingers, preparing for contact. She placed her palms on either side of Dax's face and looked into his eyes. Concentrating, she tried to see beyond the red haze. The magick shivered and shook around him. She blew out a breath and focused her energy. But the harder she concentrated the tighter his grip became on her waist. The redness around him deepened and then she saw it. A small thinning in the fabric of the magick. Like an over washed piece of cloth that had begun to fray at the seams. She probed the watery, reddish pink area and an electric shock zipped through her painfully. Dax's body shook with strain, and finally, he cried out.

"Stop." His breathing came in hard, short bursts.

Cinder dropped her hands to his shoulders. His body trembled, and she closed her eyes, resting her forehead on his. "*Aktae.* I'm sorry. I'm sorry."

She sucked in a deep breath trying to calm the whooshing sound between her ears. Her magick swirled and pulsed inside her as if drawn to the magick that shrouded Dax's mind.

"It's all right," he said. "It just hurt like hell."

She straightened and pushed the hair back from his eyes. "I won't give up until you tell me to."

He nodded. "Thank you, but I think maybe I should lie down."

"Do you want something for the pain?"

"No. Thank you. I think some rest will do." He stood and shuffled shakily to the smaller room. "I don't mean to overstep," he said. "But I'm sorry for what you're going through with Rome. I couldn't help but overhear your conversation."

Cinder's cheeks flushed with heat. "Thank you," she said. "Unfortunately, it's time for us both to put our childhood friendship aside and move on."

"Is it? I just mean that you seem to care about each other a lot, and it's not often friendships like that come along."

"You think I should support him like a good friend?" She tried to keep the edge out of her voice.

"I do. But only you can decide in which capacity."

"Meaning?"

He leaned on the doorframe. "You have magick like I've never seen. You can do just about anything. Decide for yourself what you want. Go as a friend and sit by his side. Or—"

"Or?"

"Or win him in the contest. That is... if you want him."

Cinder stared at Dax. She couldn't enter the contest. She wasn't allowed. If anyone found out, who knew what would happen to her. She could be arrested or exiled or...

Or she could win. She could fight for him and prove she was worthy no matter who her mother was. Show the king that purity of blood wasn't necessarily the best way to find the strongest magick. After all, Rome's magick wasn't near as powerful as hers.

"Your stepmother is coming." Dax pointed to the back door and then ducked out of sight.

The door opened, and Lady Sabine stepped in. "Where have you been? Olivia has been waiting for you."

"The prince and his grandmother just left."

"Liar. Prince Rome and Olivia finished their walk not twenty minutes ago."

Twenty minutes. Cinder looked at the clock. It'd been over an hour since Rome had left. How was that possible? How long had she been searching Dax's mind?

Lady Sabine's eyes narrowed. "You don't want to help Olivia do you?"

"Of course, I do. I'd do anything for Olivia."

"Then prove it," she snapped. "Get back to the house and prepare her to win."

Cinder threw her cloak over her shoulders.

Sabine grabbed Cinder by the wrist, her eyes alight with anger.

"If Olivia loses because of you, so help me, girl, you'll wish you'd never been born."

Cinder yanked her away. "Your threats don't scare me. Unlike you, I have nothing left to lose."

"I wouldn't be so sure about that."

Cinder strode from the store and down the alleyway.

Her shoes clicked on the colored pavement so hard that she could hear nothing but the sounds of her heartbeat and the tapping of her feet. She was tired of being everyone's drawing room rug. Rome, Sabine, even her father. She would do what they asked of her, but after this, she was done. It was time for her to move on and make her own destiny in life.

ROME'S BLUR OF EMOTIONS HAD HIM SPINNING LIKE A child's toy. He'd replayed the scene with Cinder in his mind so many times he couldn't see straight. The hurt she felt over not being told didn't begin to compare with the betrayal he felt at her response. She hadn't even given him the opportunity to explain his side; to tell her how he really felt, or how much he wanted her to enter— not to sit at his side and cheer on his father's charade.

She'd run from her shop so quickly he'd not even been given time to think of what to do. He'd waited for several minutes, hoping she might return and when she hadn't he'd closed the shop and left for home. He'd hardly walked through the door when for some bizarre reason, he'd been forced by Phinneaus to walk with Olivia around the garden. Not wanting to be unkind to Cinder's younger sister he'd agreed, unable to even take the herbs to his grandmother. And though Olivia was always a sweet girl, he'd had little patience for her nervous chatter. Even she had been uncomfortable about the situation they'd been thrown into.

By the time he walked his grandmother back to her room mid-morning, he was all but shaking with anger.

"Cinder said you should take this one three times a day for a week, and you should make a tea with this one every day for a month. I'll get a maid to bring you some hot water." He turned to leave.

"Roman." The sound of his full name on his grand-mother's lips was enough to stop him in his place. "Sit with me a moment would you? I can ring for the water."

He looked back at her, and she flicked her wrist, causing the bell on the wall to ring. He licked his lips and sat on the light buttercup couch next to her. The beautiful tangerines and lemons of her room had always enchanted him as a child.

She smiled at him softly, then raised an eyebrow. "What will you do now?"

"I don't follow."

"Don't play coy with me boy, I know you almost as well as your friends Cinder and Stil. You know exactly what I mean. Cinder found out about your father's contest, and it's obvious it upset her greatly. It was not my place to interfere but… what are you going to do about it?"

He smoothed out a wrinkle in his breeches without meeting his grandmother's eye. "She's made her decision to move on and told me she wishes me the best. It's obvious she has no intention of entering the contest. What more can I do?"

"There are a million things you could do, the question is, are you going to?"

Rome jumped to his feet. "*Tothmock Beastae*. What should

I do? She's stubborn as a dragon and wild as a centaur. She's angry as a daemon at me and stormed out when I tried to explain. What am I to do with a fae like that? Father is right, there would be no taming or making a princess out of her."

"What indeed?" His grandmother raised an eyebrow. "Do you love her the way she is?"

"Do I... What? Do I love her?" He'd never admitted his feeling to anyone. Not even Stil. His shoulders slumped, and he shook his head. What was the use denying it to his grandmother? Anything he said, she would see right through as she always had. "Gods help me, I do."

"Then you accept her as she is and tell her. Tell your father. Call off this stupid charade of a contest and marry the girl. Today. You've had fifty years with her. It's time to make it official."

"But she isn't princess material. And her bloodlines–"

"Says who?" His grandmother's voice took on a rough edge, and her eyes narrowed.

"Grandmother, she continually breaks the law. She won't pander to the courtiers. She'll do what she wants when she wants with no regard to status."

"That's what makes her so unique. It's time we broke up the way things are done around here. All this stuffy pomp and circumstance is the very reason our bloodlines and our magicks are drying out. We've killed the fae spirit. The ones that break the laws and do what they want. The ones that learn and teach and grow organically, not through archaic lessons from a book. Cinder has never been formally educated, yet look at the power she holds." His grandmother's eyes grew melancholy. "Power like that was lost to us over a generation ago."

Something about the look on his grandmother's face struck Rome with great sorrow.

"There's something you aren't telling me," he said. "Something about the magick. About Cinder."

She shook her head. "The past is in the past. What you need to be thinking about is the future. And I tell you now. That girl is our future."

"And what about her mother? You said you knew her."

His grandmother's eyebrows drew together. "Did I? I don't recall."

A maid entered, carrying a tray of hot water and cups.

"Set it on the table," said his grandmother.

Was his grandmother joking with him or just hiding something? He couldn't be sure.

"I should go," said Rome. "I'm supposed to meet someone." He walked over and kissed her on the cheek, and she hugged him tight.

"Think about what I've said. And then go back to that girl, apologize, and beg her to marry you."

Rome nodded and strode from the room. He should do as his grandmother said. Go to Cinder. Ask her to marry him. Tell his father that he'd made a decision and wed her that very day. A thrill of pleasure raced through him. Him and Cinder. Cinder as his wife. Together. No more waiting, hoping she would change. Being able to hold her in his arms and kiss her soft sweet lips forever. Yes! He'd do it. He'd go to her, beg her forgiveness and ask for her to marry him.

Rome jogged down the hallway, smiling the whole way. There was just one thing he needed to get first.

ROME HEADED FOR THE ROYAL TREASURY. HE DESCENDED lower and lower into the bowels of the castle until he reached the guarded room. He nodded to the guard and passed his hand over the door. The enormous lock clicked and the heavy door swung open.

Rome entered the cavern, struck by the smell of metal and dirt. He scanned the plethora of wealth his family had amassed. Centuries of jewels, gems and precious metals. The room held wall-to-wall treasures, but none of them held his interest. He was looking for one particular item.

Heading straight for the jewel vault he scanned the trays of gems as he aimed for a small wooden chest. Pulling a small key off the shelf above he opened the box. Inside sat a lone, large, blue diamond, the color of Cinder's eyes. He'd picked out the stone for her over two decades prior while surveying the vault with his father. It had called to him, and he'd locked it in the box to insure no one used it for anything. He held the stone in his hand, hardly being able to wait to see it on her hand.

Next he headed for the rings. He dismissed gold band after gold band until finally his eyes rested upon a brilliant silver and gold band entwined with leaves. It was perfect. He smiled. All he needed was some help putting them together. And he knew just the man to do it.

.   .   .

"It's about damn time," Stil chuckled. "I have to be honest, I never thought you'd do it."

Rome's eyebrows drew together. "So you knew?"

"Knew? Of course I knew." Stil flipped through the pages of his spellbook. "I was getting ready to pull this out and find a commitment spell to place on the two of you."

"Then you think I'm doing the right thing?"

Stil looked up at Rome and shook his head. "What does it matter what I think, or what anyone else thinks for that matter? It's your life. Live it as you please and with whom you please." He turned the page and scanned it. "Would it make a difference if I told you I think you're making a mistake?"

Would it? "No," Roman answered without hesitation.

"That's the correct response. But with that said, yes, I think you and Cinder were made for each other."

Rome smiled. Just hearing the words from his best friend reassured him again; he was doing the right thing.

"Ah. Here we are." Stil rolled up his sleeves. "Step back and let's get this wedding ring fashioned for you."

The sun hung low in the sky as Rome walked through the closing marketplace. He gripped the ring in his pocket, feeling the smoothness of the band with his fingertips. His heart pounded so loudly, he feared Cinder would hear him coming from all the way across the city. He was really going to do this.

The lights in the sky flickered on for the evening and shops closed their brightly colored windows and doors. He stopped at the flower shop where his grandmother had bought flowers earlier that day. A beautiful bouquet of vibrant purple, pink and blue flowers hung waiting. He snatched them up and handed money to the florist.

"For the winner of tomorrow's competition?" the shop-keeper asked.

Rome smiled. "Something like that."

"Good fortune to you and your house."

Rome nodded. "Thank you. And to you."

He hurried down the street with a lighter step and hope in his soul. He smiled at every person he passed. Their well wishes for his upcoming nuptials only added to his excitement. By the time he reached Cinder's sungold colored front door, he was surprised his feet were still on the ground. He placed the flowers in a pot by the entrance so he could surprise her, and then he knocked.

Footsteps hurried around the room and then Lady Sabine cracked open the door and peered out.

"Why, Prince Rome. How wonderful to see you." She opened the door wider and gave a deep curtsy, her ample breasts almost spilling out of the top of her dress. "What can I do for you?"

"I had hoped that Lady Cinder might be around." He tried to keep his nervousness from creeping into his voice.

Lady Sabine's smile fell a fraction but then whipped back into place. "I'm so sorry your highness but Lady Cinder has already retired to bed for the night."

"So early?"

"I'm afraid she outdid herself today with her magick. But, we're all so excited for the contest and ball."

"Yes..." He'd rarely seen Cinder deplete her magick to the point of fatigue. Sour thoughts gnawed at him. Could she be ill?

Rome wracked his brain, trying to find a reason to get Cinder out of bed without raising suspicions. "I just... needed to speak with her for a moment. Earlier today when she saw my grandmother I forgot to ask how much of the tincture I was supposed to administer."

"I see. Well, let me look in on her and see if she's awake. Why don't you come in? Olivia had a wonderful walk with you in the garden."

"Yes... I, uh, I enjoy spending time with little Olivia."

Lady Sabine's eyes twinkled. "She isn't quite so little anymore. She will be entering the contest tomorrow."

"Really? But she's so young." Olivia hadn't mentioned it on their walk. Or had she? Cinder had occupied his thoughts so he barely even recalled their time together.

"She's close to thirty," Lady Sabine replied.

Barely a teen.

"Olivia," Lady Sabine called.

Cinder's younger sister entered from the dining room in an overly elaborate ball gown. Lady Sabine put her arm around the girl's shoulders.

"Olivia, Prince Rome is here."

Olivia stepped forward and gave him a kind smile. "Hello, your highness."

"Why don't you entertain him while I see if Cinder is awake."

Olivia rubbed her hands together. "Oh... of course."

Lady Sabine disappeared. The wooden staircase creaked with each step.

"How are you this evening?" Olivia asked.

Rome's gaze fell on the girl again. "Fine thank you. And yourself?"

She fluffed her bright petal pink gown. "Aside from feeling like mother's pin cushion, I'm well."

They both chuckled. Olivia's resemblance to Lord Rondell was unmistakable. Her round face, wide set eyes, and masculine jawline were purely her father's. For a human her features would probably pass as average but for a fae she came off somewhat plain. Her best qualities, that he'd seen, were her soft brown eyes and kind spirit.

"So you're preparing for tomorrow?" he finally asked.

"Yes. Cinder has been lending me her magick all day to boost me up." She threw her hand over her mouth and her head whipped in the direction of the stairs. "Oh. I'm sure I wasn't supposed to tell anyone that." Her eyes filled with tears. "Please. Please don't tell on me. Mother would be frightfully angry."

So that's why Cinder was so exhausted. Sharing magick with someone else was not only draining, but it could also be deadly if done wrong. Anger surged through him. It had been Lady Sabine's idea, no doubt.

Rome patted Olivia on the shoulder and smiled. "Don't cry Livy. It'll be our little secret."

She nodded and wiped her eyes. "Thank you, your highness. That is most kind of you. I enjoyed talking to you today on our walk. You are an excellent listener."

Rome cleared his throat. "Uh… yes. It was a beautiful day for a walk."

The stairs creaked, and Lady Sabine descended once more. "I am so sorry your highness, but she is completely asleep. I tried to wake her but to no avail. I will be sure to have her write down the dosage in the morning and will happily to bring it to the festivities tomorrow for you."

"If you could only wake her for a moment. Or possibly I could go up and see her—"

"Your highness I could never allow such impropriety in my home. What would her dear father think of me if I was to let a man, even one of royal blood, up to his daughter's bedroom unattended? I'm sorry but on her father's very soul I could not do it." Lady Sabine's face donned a mask of sincerity that even he was tempted to believe.

Rome licked his lips, unsure of what to do. Lady Sabine stood like a blockade in front of the stairs, and he wasn't sure if he pressed the issue that Cinder would even come down to see him. Not after what had happened.

"Of course. You're right. I'll just have to await her reply tomorrow."

Olivia reached around him and opened the door. "I look forward to seeing you tomorrow, your highness."

He gave her a tight smile. "And you as well Livy."

"Olivia," Lady Sabine corrected. "Her name is Olivia, Highness."

He bowed. "Of course. My mistake."

Rome stepped out the door and Olivia closed it behind him. He stood in the street glanced up at the bedroom windows, trying to figure out his next move. He had no idea which of the three was Cinder's. If he tossed something and hit the wrong one, or if Lady Sabine found out he had... He couldn't risk getting Cinder in trouble, or having her any angrier with him.

After several minutes, he turned and shuffled back toward the castle. The competition would begin in less than twelve hours. There was no way out of it now.

CHAPTER SIX

The sun's rays had already peeked over the horizon when Cinder's heavy eyelids opened. She peered around her room, fatigue blurring her vision. She glanced at her father's pocket watch and leaped from bed.

Damn. She'd overslept!

Racing around her room, she threw on clothes and shoved her shoes on her feet. Her hand shook as she lifted a glass of water and gulped it down. She'd not been this fatigued since helping Flint. Lady Sabine had drained her down to her toes the day before. Having her magick Livy a dress and shoes and accessories, then having her make dinner and clean the house before sharing what little she had left with her younger sister. Cinder didn't begrudge helping Livy, but she knew, in the end, it would do no good. Livy had no more magick than Silas, the fisherman.

For hours, the night before, she'd lain in bed, fatigue crashing in on her like waves of the sea, and she'd come to realize, no matter what happened, she couldn't let them force Rome into a marriage born of a contest. Mad as she was, she still loved him, and he deserved better. And she was possibly the only person who could help him in the end. She wouldn't just leave him to the machinations of his father. But more than that, she couldn't allow the king to go on treating those, who couldn't prove generations of magickal bloodlines like they were less than those that could. How was it that their very status in the city, came down to a simple piece of parchment carrying names of their ancestors? It wasn't right.

She tiptoed down the stairs and grabbed a piece of bread from the kitchen before ducking out the front door.

Cinder raced down the streets, between buildings that were just beginning to open their doors. She had a lot to get done and less than an hour in which to do it. She dashed down the alleyway, separating her shop from a tailor, and hit the back door with a bump. She sucked in air, trying to catch her breath while unlocking the door.

Inside she didn't even bother to take off her cloak. She strode to the storage room and looked through the shelves of supplies for a piece of parchment. Then she located all the colored ink she could find and took it all to the back counter.

Laying out the supplies she then pulled out the copy she'd made of Olivia's parchment. Olivia's right of birth order followed her father and mother's lines back eight generations.

Cinder studied the coat of arms for each one and then opened the jars of ink. She waved her hand over the black ink and then over the parchment, replicating all of the lines and branches necessary to produce four generations. Then she waved her fingers over the purple and green ink and replicated her father's coat of arms in the right corner of the paper. She held one hand over Olivia's parchment and one over her own and the names from her father's side appeared, scrolled beautifully, on her own page.

She blew out a breath. "That was the easy part."

"It's early." Dax appeared from the back, rubbing his face. "What are you workin' on?"

She concentrated on the parchment. "Sorry. I didn't mean to wake you."

"Is there anything I can help with?" He sat on the wooden stool.

Cinder looked him over. He'd been wearing the same clothes for the last two days. He looked like he could use a shave and a bath.

"As soon as my stepmother and sister leave the house I'll take you over so you can wash and we'll find you some of my father's old clothes to wear. They may be a bit small on you but I'll fix that."

"I don't want you to get in trouble."

"It's no trouble," she said. "Besides, they'll be at the celebration with most of the city."

He looked at her parchment. "What are you doing?"

"Trying to recreate a birth order document for myself."

"What for?"

"I'm entering the contest."

Dax smiled and got to his feet. His large hand fell on her shoulder. "Good for you. How can I help?"

"I need to think of some names. Four generations worth. And a crest. One that isn't too recognizable but that no one will think looks suspicious as well."

"How much time do you have?"

"According to the invitation my sister got? Less than forty-five minutes."

"Then we better get to it."

FOR THE NEXT THIRTY MINUTES, CINDER AND DAX WORKED on the parchment. Using customer names as reference they came up with four generations of valid fae names that looked plausible on paper. She searched through some old books her father had stored in her playroom and found half a dozen reasonable looking crests.

"Thank you, Dax." She hugged him tight. "You've been more helpful to me than I have been for you I'm afraid. Though I did think of something."

"Really?" He crossed his arms over his bulky chest.

"Yes. I have an aunt named–"

Dax stood suddenly and sniffed the air. "Sabine's around the corner."

"You can smell her that far?"

He nodded once and headed for the secret room. Cinder turned and waved her hands at the ink. The jars resealed themselves and then floated into the storeroom. She rolled up the parchments just as Sabine entered.

"There you are," she said. "I've been looking for you. You left this morning without cooking breakfast or helping Olivia get ready or anything."

"I'm sorry." Cinder turned to face her. "I wanted to get here early in case anyone needed me before I go to the competition."

Sabine laughed. "Go? You can't go. The competition is for those with pure bloodlines and the ball is for royals, courtiers and competitors only."

Cinder's stomach clenched. She'd almost ruined everything before she'd even begun. But she had to find an excuse to not be in the store.

"You spoke to the king yesterday didn't you? You asked him if I could compete." She'd completely forgotten about her stepmother's offer until that moment.

A flash of guilt crossed Sabine's face. "Of course I asssssked but unfortunately he said only those with pure lines I'm afraid. If he made an exception for you he'd have to make one for every girl." The lies dripped off Sabine's tongue like honey.

Anger swirled inside Cinder so hot it burned her flesh. "Why lie? You didn't ask him and we both know it. Are you afraid I might actually beat Olivia?" Something within her had been awakened over the last days. Something that she suspected had been growing inside her for decades, but now, with no prospect of having Rome for herself, she had no fear of what her stepmother might do.

Sabine walked forward and cupped Cinder's cheek. The iciness of Lady Sabine's touch shot straight through Cinder.

"My dear girl. You have me all wrong. You see, I don't care whether you enter or not because Olivia will win. I'll see to that." She ran her hands down Cinder's arm. Her mock apathy all but disappeared when her hand landed on the parchment in Cinder's hand. "What is that?"

Cinder pushed the parchment behind her back. "Nothing."

Sabine snapped her fingers and the parchment flew from Cinder's hand to her own. A red gemstone locket at Sabine's throat shone bright with a red churning light. Cinder's heart thumped like a rabbit's.

Sabine opened the parchment and her eyes narrowed on Cinder. "What are you doing with this?"

"I made a copy for Olivia. In case the first one was misplaced."

Sabine's eyes narrowed. "Now who's the liar?"

Sabine waved her hand and the second rolled parchment flew from the table to land at Sabine's feet. Cinder made a grab for it but Sabine was too quick. She snatched it up and opened it. Her mouth fell open.

"Where did you get this?"

Cinder's fists clenched tight as her magick swirled around inside her, ready to attack. "Give it back."

"It's a lie. This isn't who your mother was. You forged this." Sabine snapped her fingers. "*Enflamé.*" The parchment burst into flames and fell to the floor.

"No!" Cinder stomped on the fire, her hopes of entering the contest beaten out with every extinguished flame.

Sabine stepped close to Cinder, their bodies almost touching. "You listen to me girl. You are nothing. You came from nothing and you will always be nothing. You will never enter that contest. Olivia is the one who deserves to be on that throne, not you. You better stay here and tend to this shop or else—"

"Or else what?" Dax stepped from the storeroom.

Sabine's eyes flew wide, and she let out a small shriek. "What are you doing here?"

His gaze traveled to Cinder. "I'm sorry Lady Cinder, but I just couldn't stay quiet any longer."

Cinder nodded. "It's all right Dax." What did it matter now anyway? With no hope of getting in to the contest and nothing to go home to, Cinder might as well just pack her bags and walk out the gates alongside Dax that very minute.

"You... you can't be here." Sabine backed up as if seeing a ghost.

"I told him he could stay."

"No." Sabine shook her head. "I forbid it."

The look of absolute terror on Sabine's face told Cinder her hunch about where the spell on Dax had come from, could very well be true.

"Don't you have a contest or something you should be at?" Dax folded his arms over his chest.

A knock on the front door of the shop pulled everyone's attention.

Sabine tried to regain some of her commanding presence and sucked in a deep breath, straightening her cloak.

"I command you to leave immediately," she said to Dax. "And I forbid you to help him. If you do, you're on your own. I'll not shelter you under my roof any longer. Nor will I employ you. I mean it. He leaves today, or don't bother coming back to my house." Sabine sped out the door and out of sight.

They stared at the backdoor for a moment before another knock on the front door broke the silence.

"Perhaps I should go," Dax said.

"No." Cinder's shoulders slumped. She was bound to help Dax and she wouldn't go back on her word, even if it meant leaving Ville DeFee. One thing her father had impressed upon her most, was the need to keep one's word. "Don't leave yet," she said. "At least, not until I can gather my things and go with you."

She headed for the curtain.

"Go with me?"

She sighed. "If I can't enter the contest, there's nothing more I can do to help Rome and I can't stay in that woman's house one more day. I fear if I do, one of us may not make it out alive." The statement hung in the air but Cinder couldn't deny the truth of it. Something was not right with Lady Sabine and the necklace she wore gave off an odious vibe. The viciousness of her remarks of late left no room to doubt her intentions. Lady Sabine would have Livy on the throne and she'd do whatever it took to get her there.

A louder knock sounded, and Cinder walked out to the shop floor. Rome's grandmother stood on her doorstep.

Cinder pushed at her hair and hurried to open the door, smoothing her dress as she went.

"Your majesty, I'm so sorry to have kept you waiting."

"Elise."

"Yes, of course. Won't you come in?" Heat flushed Cinder's cheeks. What was Rome's grandmother doing there? "Shouldn't you be at the contest? Is something wrong? Are you worse?"

Elise waved her hand. "No. No. I've not come here for your help. I've come here to help you."

"Me? What do you want to do for me?" Cinder followed the woman to a seat at the counter and waited. Maybe Elise was there to offer more information about her mother.

The older woman's eyes twinkled with mischief as she looked Cinder up and down.

Cinder crossed her feet, trying to hide them under her dress, and fought the urge to fidget.

"I want to lend you my magick," Elise finally said.

Her magick? "Your magick?"

Her eyes crinkled in the corners, the same way that Rome's did. "Yes. I want you to enter the competition."

Cinder tried to form words. Was it a trick? A Trap? "But... I'm a nobody."

"Don't sell yourself short, my dear. Even a nobody can be a somebody in disguise."

What was going on? It didn't make any sense. "I don't understand."

Elise reached out and patted Cinder's hand. "And you don't have to. *Yet.* All you have to know is that I want you to enter the competition, and I want you to win."

Cinder dropped all attempts at social acceptability and plopped onto a stool next to Elise. "But... Even if I did enter and win, it wouldn't be valid. I have no royal blood. I could be imprisoned or worse."

Elise chuckled. "I'd never let you be imprisoned or banished, you should know that up front. I believe in you."

"But why me?"

"Because you remind me of someone I think I used to know." Elise's sharp eyes softened. "Consider it a gift from a… fairy grandmother."

"I've never heard of a fairy grandmother."

"Well, you have now. So let's get to work." Elise smacked the counter. "We don't have much time. You'll need a few things to compete. First you need a birth order parchment."

"I don't have one."

"Yes, you do. Right here." Elise pulled a parchment from her purse and handed it to Cinder.

She unrolled it; on one side were her father's names and on the other a crest made of purples and pinks in the shape of a unicorn. The names flowed and merged so beautifully. Done by a masterful hand.

"Now, you need a disguise."

"Disguise?"

"Well, we can't have you go as yourself. Lady Sabine would have you disqualified first thing. So what should we go with? Hmmm… pretty, but not overdone. Dark hair I think. Skin just a slight shade darker."

"Can you give me smaller feet?" Embarrassment heated Cinder's cheeks. It was a stupid thing to ask for.

Elise chuckled. "I don't think anyone will recognize you by your feet my dear."

Cinder nodded.

"All right. I have a good picture in my head so stand still. This might sting a bit." Elise's tongue stuck out of the corner of her mouth as she whipped her hands back and forth, swirling them in and out and over each other. Finally, after a minute, she threw them toward Cinder and a great ball of light hit her square in the chest.

It burned its way through her skin, deepening her flesh tone and turning her hair to coal. Her face burned as her nose and jaw changed and morphed into someone not herself. It took only a minute but when it had finished, Cinder felt like she'd run around Ville DeFee for the last hour.

She lifted her hands and touched her face before rushing to a shelf, that held a mirror, and looking at herself. The effect was nothing short of startling. Her face was the same, but not the same. Her nose appeared slightly shorter, with a rounder appearance and her now green eyes were wider apart. Her skin held the glow of having worked in the fruit fields all day and her hair bore a striking resemblance to her father's. All in all she was pretty, but not herself. Even her clothes had changed. Her new, pale lavender dress was comely, and understated. Well made yet not overly done.

"Now," said Elise. "The effect will only last until midnight I'm afraid. After that, it will wear off. So be sure to be gone from the ball before then."

Cinder turned from her reflection. "The ball?" She had not a thing to wear.

"Don't worry about that. Every competitor will have a room of her own. I'll find out which one is yours, and I'll have a gown sent down to you."

"I… I can't thank you enough," she said.

"You can thank me plenty by winning the contest." Elise grasped Cinder's hands in hers. Once more Cinder was flooded with the sweet warmth of Elise's magick as it flowed into her veins. It healed her own frayed magickal threads and bound them back together.

"I think that should get you through. Not enough to be considered cheating. Just sufficient to make you whole."

Cinder nodded. "Thank you."

Elise stood from her stool and headed for the door. She stopped with her hand on the knob. "It's none of my business but I thought you should know. Rome wanted no part of this contest. As soon as he found out, he wanted to tell you himself. Unfortunately, it seems someone informed you before he could. He cares for you a great deal Cinder and though he may not vocalize it, he wanted you to enter the contest the moment his father told him."

"He did?" Cinder's heart cracked a fraction, knowing how angry she'd been with him the day before.

"Very much. So much that I'd dare to say he wants you to win." Elise's eyes sparkled again.

Cinder's hands twisted together. "He's never said anything. Not in all these years."

"Men speak more with their actions than their words my dear. Any mere woman can be wooed with words. It's the wise woman who can see the intention behind them." Elise opened the front door, and the sounds of a crowd flooded in. "You better hurry."

Cinder nodded. "Thank you again."

Elise smiled, making herself look a hundred years younger. "Don't let me down."

She exited and Cinder stared at the spot where she'd stood for a moment before locking the door and walking to the backroom.

Dax's eye widened. "Not a bad look. Not as pretty as you are, but not repulsive by any means."

Cinder chuckled. "I'll take that as a compliment."

Dax tossed the cloak she'd given him over his shoulders and followed her to the door.

"Whoa. Where are you going?"

"I'm not letting you go to this thing alone. Your step-mother gives off some vibrations that make my inner bear twitchy. I'm not taking the chance of letting her hurt you."

"I'll be fine. I'll be with hundreds of other fae."

"I don't think that would stop her."

Cinder had to admit, it did make her feel better knowing he would be there. "Well, you can't go like that. If you're going to go, you have to go as... my brother. And for that, we need different clothes. And a different face."

Cinder grabbed him by the arm and strode out the door. "Lets go."

They raced down the alleyways and toward her house.

CHAPTER SEVEN

R ome pulled on the sleeves of his royal purple jerkin while Stil set his crown on his head.

"I hate wearing this stupid thing. It's so pretentious."

"I completely agree," said Stil. "I just wish Cinder could see you in it."

Rome's stomach turned at the thought of Cinder. He'd gone out first thing that morning to try and see her, but there'd been no answer at her house. Not wanting to catch his father's wrath, he'd headed back to the castle.

He slipped his hand into his pocket and squeezed the ring that slipped through his fingers like his hopes of marrying Cinder.

"Did you sleep at all last night?" Stil asked.

"How could I? I finally get off my rear to ask Cinder to marry me, and I can't get past her minotaur of a step-mother. Now I am forced to watch my father's spectacle continue and marry whoever is left. I've ruined what happiness I could've had in life and for what? A few more years gallivanting around? Another wasted decade, waiting to see if she would change? When in my heart I don't want her to. I want her to be who she is. Wild. Free. Powerful."

"Then go get her."

Rome's leg muscles tightened, wanting to propel him out of the castle and down to Cinder's house again. But he couldn't.

Stil shook his head and set his hand on Rome's shoulder. "I am sorry my friend. If it makes you feel any better, I'm pretty sure she is hurting as much as you are."

"Will you find her for me? Tell her I love her. Make her come here so I can tell my father, and we can end this."

"I can go, but the bell is about to ring. The competition will start in my absence. Mayhaps I will wait until afterward. Then, before the ball, I'll look, and you can tell your father then."

"Gah." Rome pulled on his hair. "By then it will be too late. Why? Why was I so stupid?"

"Because you're young." Rome's grandmother stood in his doorway.

He crossed to her and took her hands in his. "Grandmamma, please. You must stop this."

She shook her head. "I cannot. But do not fear boy. All will be well in the end."

"But grandmamma this isn't what I want. I want Cinder."

"You think I don't know that?" She laughed.

A bell tolled outside the castle and Rome sank into a

plush purple chair; his silk jerkin so tight he wanted to tear it off. "I can't do this. I can't."

"Stil would you leave us for a moment please?"

Stil nodded. "Of course your majesty."

His grandmother waited until Stil left before turning her stern gaze on him. "Roman Geoffrey I refuse to allow you to act like a petulant child. Look at you. All those things you said of Cinder you are doing yourself. Your fear of her not doing her duty. Of not doing what was required of her. Of going against the law. Well, what are you doing? Sitting here in this chair, whining about an agreement you said yes to. Is this how our country is to be ruled when your father and I are gone? By your whims? When you give an agreement but it doesn't turn out in your favor, you break it?"

He wanted to yell at her, tell her she didn't understand. That she'd gotten to marry the man she loved. That they were sentencing him to a life of pain, regret and sorrow. Problem was— her words rang true. All these years he'd cursed Cinder for doing the very thing he now did. "You're right. What kind of man am I if I go back on my word now?"

"Good. Now stand up. Fix your clothes and let's go down to greet your guests."

Lifting his body from the chair was like dragging a centaur through a muddy field. It fought the entire way. He straightened his jerkin and breeches though he had no desire to go down and meet the women waiting below. To listen to the fawning and the kowtowing and the endless parade of flattery. But it was his duty, and he couldn't go back on that.

Rome took his grandmother's arm. He stuck his hand in his pocket and squeezed the ring that hid there. If only he hadn't been such a fool.

ROME'S HEART POUNDED LIKE LIGHTNING AS HE LOOKED OUT on the swarm of females below the large picture window. Who knew there were so many eligible women in the kingdom?

"Are you sure they are all legitimate?" he asked.

"Quite sure," Phinneaus replied. "Every birth order certificate has been checked twice by myself and the magistrate."

"There are over sixty maidens down there," said his father. "And most of them are quite pleasing to look at. A few not so much but that won't matter. In the long run, it's not the color of the peach but its sweetness that keeps you wanting more."

Rome was pretty sure, even a peach needed to look appetizing before someone would want to take a bite.

His father signaled, and the bell rang once more. All the women formed a line down one side of a long purple carpet, which spanned the entire length of the upper courtyard.

"It's time for you to greet your guests," said his father.

Rome nodded, and his gaze scanned the line of women as his father, Phinneaus, and grandmother started down the flight of stairs to the courtyard.

"She's not there," said Stil.

"I know." Just saying the words made his chest tighten.

Picking Cinder out of the entire city of women would have taken him no more than a moment. He turned from the window and descended the stairs.

The large double doors were already open, and an uproarious round of applause and cheers poured in. His father took his grandmother by the arm and helped her down the steps to the courtyard as Phinneaus, Rome, and Stil followed.

Candles hung in the air. The fountain and swans continued swimming and spouting in time with a violin and flute. An extensive set of tables spanned one side of the courtyard, set up with fruits, wines, and cakes of every kind.

Stil excused himself as Rome walked with his family down the line of contestants. Some were young, some older than Rome himself. And a few looked barely old enough for him to notice even.

He donned the practiced smile he'd been taught by his mother to use when meeting people for the first time. The smile that was neither too friendly nor too smug. The smile that said, I'm happy to meet you and thank you for coming. Making people feel welcomed but not special.

A family member accompanied each girl. Father, mother, uncle. They introduced the girls and in turn, each girl then giggled, blushed or stammered before curtsying. He fought to keep from rolling his eyes and imagined the laugh that he and Cinder would have over such trifling females. Cinder would call them *zhenzen* or *malrops*. And she would be completely right. After all, how could a woman who entered a contest, only to win a prince, be anything less than a doxy?

Some of the girls he recognized from the city. Most he

did not. About half way down they came upon Olivia. She blushed as Rome approached and when Lady Sabine stepped forward to introduce her daughter, Rome cut her off.

"Livy. How very nice to see you."

The girl blushed and curtsied. "Your majesties. Your highness. Uncle Phinneaus."

"I do so hope that we will have a few moments to talk. Perhaps before the ball tonight?" Rome asked.

"She would enjoy that very much your highness." Lady Sabine put her arm around her daughter's shoulders, and Olivia winced at the contact.

He smiled. If anyone would know where Cinder was, it was Olivia. "I look forward to it," he replied, not sparing Lady Sabine a moment's glance.

Both women curtsied again, and he continued down the line.

Rome wasn't sure how his father expected him to remember even a handful of the women he'd been introduced to and he'd just started trying to recall even one of them when his grandmother stopped.

"Rome I would like to introduce you to Lady Rowena. Lady Rowena's late aunt was a dear friend of mine."

The woman gave Rome a light smile but didn't giggle, blush nor stammer when she spoke.

"It is an honor, Prince Rome." She gave a small curtsy, but her sharp green eyes never left his.

The hairs on his neck prickled. "Have we met before Lady Rowena?"

She shook her head. "I don't believe so."

The air about her seemed familiar. Her stance and the steadiness of her gaze. But he was sure he'd never seen her before. He would have remembered a raven-haired beauty like Lady Rowena.

"Shall we move on?" asked his father.

"Yes." But Rome couldn't seem to pry his eyes from the girl. "There is something so familiar about you. Are you sure I haven't seen you somewhere? In the village perhaps?"

She inclined her head. "Perhaps that is it."

"Rome." His grandmother took him by the arm. "We should keep moving."

"Lady Rowena," said Phinneaus. "It is my pleasure to meet you as well." He held out his hand but just as she was about to take it, Rome's grandmother bumped into Phinneaus.

"Oh, I'm terribly sorry," she said. "How clumsy of me. It must be the heat. Phinneaus, would you mind terribly going to get me some cider?"

Phinneaus inclined his head. "Of course your majesty." He bowed to Lady Rowena, then headed to the refreshment table.

His grandmother linked her arm with Rome's. "Come my boy. There are plenty more to meet."

She pulled him forward and over the next hour, every chance he got, he stole glances at Lady Rowena. He found that, unlike all the others, who watched his every move, she stared straight ahead paying him no attention.

. . .

99

AFTER THE INTRODUCTIONS, THREE THRONES WERE magicked out. One for Rome, his father, and his grand-mother. Phinneaus took up residence in his usual place, to the rear and right of the king's throne, where he folded his hands into his bright magenta robes.

A second row of tables draped in blood red clothes appeared behind the contestants.

The tables held small, padded placemats every foot or so down either side. The entire gathering looked on as the tables were arranged, parallel to the thrones.

Phinneaus whispered into the king's ear, and he rose from his seat and held up his hand for silence.

"Ladies and gentlemen. Our first competition will begin shortly. As you know, magick is the very essence of our world. It is who we are as a people. Therefore, the three tests will involve magick. The first will be the hardest. Only those who are able to complete the task will move on to the next round. We have set up food and drink for everyone to partake in, however, we ask that you do so quietly, so these beautiful young ladies may concentrate."

Rome scanned the gathered crowd of hopeful family members cheering on their contestant.

"How does it feel to know that so many young fae want to win your hand?" his grandmother whispered.

"Like a prize pie at the annual Faema Blessing Day sale."

His grandmother chuckled, then began to cough. She magicked a handkerchief and coughed into it violently.

"Are the herbs not helping?"

Rome flicked his fingers, and a goblet of water floated

over from the dessert table. He handed it to his grand-mother, she sipped it, and then breathed in deeply.

"The herbs are helping, just as they are meant to," she croaked. "The coughing shows me that they are. They're loosening the mold."

Rome glanced around the crowd again and found Lady Rowena's eyes glued to his grandmother. Her gaze flickered to his, and he gave her a curt nod. She returned it, then looked away.

Such an odd creature.

"As you know," his father continued. "The art of trans-mutation is the hardest, and potentially deadliest, art to master. The magick needed to change one object into another is difficult enough but transforming a live creature into something else, takes not only skill but patience and finesse as well."

Servants appeared, carrying two cages a piece. Each contained a kitten. Some mewled, some paced, and others looked out of the bars in anticipation. One by one the cages were set on the red placemats in front of the women.

"There is a kitten for each one of you," said the king. "Your first task is to transform it into another living, breathing creature of your choosing, but not a feline. A lamb perhaps, or a bird. Maybe even a snake. Whatever it is, the animal must be alive and stay in its new state perma-nently. Any that die, or change back, will not count and the contestant will be disqualified. You have two hours to complete the task. And time starts now. Begin."

The crowd looked around and whispers floated through the air. Some of the girls looked to their parents, others stared at the kittens as if they were daemons. Finally, one burst into tears and ran off, followed closely by a woman and a man.

Olivia stood near the middle of the group. She stuck her fingers through the bars to pet her kitten. Lady Rowena stood next to her and said something, causing Olivia to look up and smile. Olivia nodded, and then Rowena turned to her kitten, stuck her fists on her hips and blew the hair from her eyes.

A jolt raced through Rome. He sat forward, his eyes fixed on her. That stance. He'd seen it a thousand times over.

Stil arrived next to Rome, a plate of food in his hand.

"Do you see that?"

"See what?"

"Lady Rowena. The way she's standing."

"Yes?" asked Stil.

"Cinder does that same thing."

Stil leaned in close to Rome's ear. "I think you have Cinder stuck so deep inside you, everything reminds you of her."

Lady Rowena turned and looked at Rome, her expression blank as a piece of newly fashioned linen.

He shook his head and looked up at Stil. "Perhaps you're right."

Rome chuckled and reached into his pocket. It didn't matter the outcome today. He still planned on marrying Cinder.

CINDER STARED AT THE KITTEN AND LISTENED TO THE chatter of the other contestants.

"This task is impossible."

"How do they expect us to do something like that?"

"Why would I know how to make a kitten into something else?"

"I changed a tea cup into a doily once."

None of them sounded sure of themselves and very few even knew where to begin. It just proved her point. Fae had become lax in their magick training. If it ever came to war, they'd be dead within a day.

"I think I'm going to try for a canary," said Olivia.

"Have you ever owned a canary?" Cinder asked.

"No. But I've seen them in the market and they're beautiful."

She didn't want to insult her sister but she didn't want her sister to kill the kitten either. That would weigh on Livy's shoulders forever.

"Maybe try something simple. Something you've had as a pet or held before," Cinder offered.

Livy's face scrunched up and then her eyes widened. "I kept a pet mouse once, in my room. Until my mother found out and killed it."

Cinder remembered the incident all too well. Olivia had been inconsolable for weeks until Cinder had animated a toy mouse for her.

"A mouse sounds perfect." Cinder smiled. "Just remember to concentrate, not on what the animal is now, but what you want it to be."

Olivia nodded and twitched her lips from side to side while concentrating.

Cinder glanced around at the other contestants. Some stroked their kittens, while others stared at the animals, like they had no idea what they were. If Cinder was to do the task, as she knew she could, it would draw suspicion. Transmutation was one of the hardest schools of magick and the very first she had taught herself. She took her kitten out of the cage and picked it up, giving the appearance of trying to figure out what to do with it.

Down the line, a screech of horror rang out, then a second. She scanned the commotion to find two contestants covered in blood. A dead kitten lay in pieces in front of them and a second seemed to have exploded on them. The girls continued to shriek as servants raced in, waving their hands over the mess and cleaning it up instantly. The girls ran to their respective parents, sobbing.

"Babies," said a redhead from across the table. "They would never make a good princess if the mere sight of blood makes them squeamish."

"Maybe it's the thought of taking innocent life that upsets them so much," Cinder retorted.

The redhead narrowed her gaze on Cinder. "And who asked your opinion? From what I can tell, no one's ever heard of your family before."

"Funny," Cinder smiled. "I was just thinking the same of you."

Several of the contestants around them snickered.

"Ha, ha! I did it! I did it!" Came a call to Cinder's left.

Everyone turned to see a little white rabbit, hopping around the table.

"It's still the same color, though," someone called.

The girl scowled and put her rabbit in its cage before heading off to the refreshment table.

"I can't," Olivia moaned.

"Stop thinking so hard," Cinder said. "Feel it. Connect with it. Make the kitten an extension of your will."

"Stop helping her," the redhead snapped. "We have to do it ourselves. Helping her is cheating."

"Seems she just helped all of us," said a brunette two stations away. "So I don't think that's really cheating now is it, Drusilla?"

"Well some of us don't need help, Anastasia," the redhead shot back.

Cinder rolled her eyes.

Olivia mouthed 'thank you' and went back to her kitten.

The girls at the table were the exact reason she had no interest in court life. Rome had been oblivious to it but Cinder had always been acutely aware of the stares and snickers at her expense when he would drag her to the balls and parties his father threw.

She'd never told him of the time one of the girls he'd been dancing with *accidentally* spilled a glass of wine on Cinder's favorite dress after he'd cut their dance short to say hello to Cinder when she'd arrived. Of course Cinder had taken care of the wine with a flick of her wrist- and managed to spell the girl's shoes so she tripped over her own feet the rest of the night.

But things like that were more common than anyone realized. Cinder had borne all of it with a grimace and a touch of magick, reminding herself that the only person whose opinion she cared about was Rome's. And look where that 'opinion caring' had gotten her. In disguise, on borrowed magick, competing against the very girls who would walk on top of her as opposed to help her up if she stumbled.

"One hour remains," called a servant.

Cinder looked down the row as harsh whispers bounded around from the mounting anxiety. Their negative energy grated on her skin and the prying eyes of all the courtiers and family members had begun to make her twitchy. But above all it was the feeling of being watched by Rome that had her even more on edge.

"Breathe," Dax whispered.

She glanced over her shoulder at where he lounged against a nearby wall. He appeared relaxed but she spotted the tension in his shoulders.

"You can do this. Forget everyone else."

She blew out a breath and stretched. She knew she could do it, that wasn't the issue. The issue was doing it too fast and arousing suspicion from everyone there. But she had waited long enough and the sooner she finished the challenge the sooner she could get away from the group.

She set her kitten on the mat in front of her and rolled up her sleeves. Placing her hands on the animal, she let its life force seep into her. She located every bone, every muscle, then concentrated on the kitten's heartbeat and breathing. What did the kitten want to become?

Applause erupted from all around and Cinder opened

her eyes. Drusilla, the redhead, had a large brown owl on her shoulder. The animal craned its neck to look around-seeming as proud of itself as Drusilla did. It was surprising Drusilla hadn't chosen a peacock. It would have been much more befitting.

Olivia groaned. She'd turned her kitten from white to gray, but it was still a kitten.

"Concentrate," Cinder said. "Feel the animal's life force."

Olivia blew out a breath and nodded.

Drusilla looked down her stubby nose at Cinder, an expression of triumph on her lips.

"So sad there isn't better competition here. I had really hoped this would be hard."

Cinder paid the twit no mind and went back to her kitten. Locating the life force once more, she poked and prodded with her magick. It was all too simple. Taking an animal and turning it into a different animal. All you really had to do is connect with the animal in front of you and then imagine it as a something else. It helped if you knew a bit about the animal you wanted it to turn into, but depending on the extent of ones magick, it wasn't a requirement.

The question Cinder couldn't answer though was, what should she turn the kitten into? An owl was good enough to win if someone didn't do better. A unicorn would be fun but she had no room for a fully grown animal like that. If she intended on traveling though, it might be fun to have a ride. A fae riding unicorn was bound to attract some unwanted attention though. Even if she went to stay with the Gwyns.

An arachnoid. A giant, hairy arachnoid the size of a dinner plate. Or a basilisk. She'd love to see Drusilla's reaction to one of those. If the basilisk turned her to stone, all the better. Cinder chuckled and looked up to Rome. He watched her with great intent and her smile fell and she went back to her kitten. No, turning everyone to stone was not a good idea.

Olivia laughed. "I did it." She clapped her hands and a small mouse scrambled around the table. "Look mother! A mouse."

"Well done, Olivia," called Phinneaus.

Olivia waved to her uncle.

"Very nice, Olivia." Lady Sabine sauntered over just as the owl on Drusilla's shoulder screeched, swooped down, and grabbed the mouse- the bird swallowed it in one gulp.

"Oh no." Olivia's clasped her hand over her mouth and her chin quivered.

Drusilla giggled as the owl devoured the mouse. Anger flared inside Cinder and she thrust her magick at her kitten barely even thinking of what she wanted it to become.

With a gigantic roar the kitten stretched and grew. The contestants backed away from Cinder's kitten as all of its fur rained down onto the table revealing bright blue and pink iridescent scales. Wings spread from a serpentine back and claws gouged into the wood. The creature yawned and a puff of smoke curled from his nostrils. It opened its bright golden eyes and peered around the group.

Cinder flicked her wrist and her baby dragon lunged at the owl. The owl took to the sky and the dragon followed, twice as fast and twice as large. It caught the bird in its claws and ripped its head from its body before roaring and stuffing both pieces into its mouth.

Gasps and screams sounded from all around the group. Cinder swallowed hard at the horror of what she'd done. Fear raced up her spine. She'd let her anger get the better of her… again. She glanced around and found everyone's eyes on the dragon who swooped through the air. Everyone…except Rome. He looked like an uncomfortably warm, pompous baby in that overly fluffy white cravat and silly jeweled crown. She couldn't imagine having to wear something like that on her head every time people showed up at her door. But at that moment, not even his outfit bothered her as much as his gaze and the slightly crooked smile on his lips as he stared at her.

She would've laughed at him if she wasn't trying so hard not to be herself. Her gaze moved to his grandmother who shook her head in amazement. Cinder smiled and then turned to the dragon and whistled. Her dragon looped through the air and headed straight for her. Girls ducked and ran out of the way but Cinder held out her arm without fear and the dragon landed on it, light as air.

Whispers echoed around the group and as every eye fell upon her.

Lady Sabine's flute of ansleberb wine hung in the air an inch from her lips. Her eyes flared with anger but she said nothing. Fighting her urge to lower her eyes and look away from her stepmother, Cinder simply gave a curt nod.

"Can I pet him?" Olivia asked.

Cinder nodded and broke gazes with her stepmother.

She couldn't know. There was no way she could know the truth.

"What are you going to name him?" Olivia asked.

"I…" Cinder cleared her throat and pushed all thoughts of her stepmother from her mind. "I don't know."

"Are you going to keep him?" Olivia's eyes sparkled with wonder.

"I… hadn't thought about it. I'd just wanted to…" Her gaze traveled to Drusilla whose face had grown so red, Cinder feared she might have eaten something she was allergic to. "Do my best to offer a real competition," she finished.

Drusilla huffed and stomped off to where her parents embraced her and pet her like a prize dog.

"Thank you." Olivia squeezed Cinder's arm. "For looking out for me. No one has ever done that for me except my sister."

Dax walked to Cinder. He wore one of her father's old jerkins and breeches that she'd lengthened and tapered. The shoes were a bit too large but she'd given him two pairs of stockings. His taller and thinner fae glamour held without anyone's suspicion.

"A dragon?" he whispered, stroking the animal's ear. "Wasn't that a bit ambitious?"

The animal hopped from Cinder's arm to Dax's shoulder and nuzzled him.

"I was angered, what can I say?" She pet the animal's smooth neck.

"Be careful of that anger, lest it give you away," he replied.

She looked up at his expression to find it nothing more than jovial. He was right. If anything could cause her downfall it would be her anger indeed. She watched her dragon take to Dax as if he'd been the one to create it instead of her. An interesting development. She filed the bit of information away to talk to him about later.

A bell rang and a collective sigh sounded from the crowd.

"Time has finished," Phinneaus called.

The king stood from his throne, alongside his mother and Rome. "We would like to thank everyone who has participated. Unfortunately, those who did not finish the required task will now be asked to step away from their stations."

Close to half of the girls stepped back, into the consoling arms of their families. Half a dozen puppies, a bunny, a monkey, various birds, a dozen mice played on the table.

The king, queen mother, and Rome walked down the row of remaining contestants, complimenting each in turn.

They reached Olivia and her head drooped.

"Hello Lady Olivia," said the king. "No animal for us today?"

"She had a mouse, your majesty," Cinder blurted. "But it was unfortunately eaten by an owl."

The king nodded. "Splendid child. Your father would have been proud. I'm sorry to hear of its demise. But I'm sure it was just perfect."

Olivia's chin popped up and she smiled. "Thank you, your majesty."

Phinneaus winked at Olivia, making her blush.

The king turned his attention to Cinder and the three-foot long dragon that Dax held.

"Well, well, well, Lady Rowena. I must say, this is an impressive display. Have you seen a live dragon before?"

"No, your majesty." Her eyes flicked to Elise's.

"That is quite impressive. Quite impressive indeed." The king's gaze traveled the length of the dragon for a long minute. Cinder thought that he might ask to touch it when he suddenly spun in a circle. "Our winner! Lady Rowena."

The crowd cheered for Cinder, but every eye held jealousy and disdain. Cinder's cheeks heated at the display of attention. She crossed her feet and wished to just fade into the crowd.

Lady Sabine's eyes lit with rage and she turned to Phinneaus and grabbed his arm. He glanced down at her momentarily, before clapping for Cinder and moving forward to join the king's entourage.

"Curtsy and say thank you," Dax whispered.

Cinder cleared her throat and gave a small curtsy. "Thank you."

"Lady Rowena will be first to dance with Prince Rome tonight. After they've spent some time getting to know each other," said the king. "We encourage all of you to enjoy the current refreshments and rest before the ball. The remaining contestants will have a room of their own prepared for them in the upper halls of the castle. Those who will not be continuing are welcome to stay as well. We will have the knight's area prepared for your relaxation and enjoyment."

After a round of well wishes and chattering everyone moved to the food. Many girls asked to touch Cinder's dragon and took turns petting him. The animal seemed to relish the attention.

"Quite an accomplishment."

Cinder jumped and turned to find Rome right over her shoulder.

"I suppose," she said.

"I only know two people who might be able to pull off such magick. And only one of them is fae." He scanned her face as if probing for something.

Her heart stampeded. "Well, now I guess you know three."

He smiled. "Do we know each other? I swear I know you."

"I doubt you know my sister." Dax stepped up to the group. "Our family tends to keep to ourselves."

Rome's eyes flickered between them. "Your sister?"

"Yes. I'm Erik." Dax held out his hand.

Rome took it and shook. "A pleasure, Erik."

"If you'll excuse us, your highness." He held out his arm to Cinder. "My sister is most likely tired from such a magickal display. She should eat and then rest before the ball."

"Of course. It's wise that the next competition round isn't until the day after tomorrow," said Rome. "I'm sure most of the women will take much time to recover."

Cinder nodded and then turned to walk away. Surprisingly her magickal display hadn't taken as much out of her as she'd anticipated. She could only attribute it to Elise's royal magick. The power she possessed rivaled even Cinder's.

Dax ushered her toward the food tables and people moved out of the way as they moved closer.

"Lady Rowena? What are you going to do with the dragon?" Rome called.

Cinder turned back to him and smiled. "Keep it, of course."

CHAPTER EIGHT

Rome growled in frustration and paced his bedroom. Stil chuckled and picked a grape from the pile that sat on his plate.

"Thinking about Cinder?"

"Gah, did you see those women out there? Some of them barely possessed enough magick to make the kitten explode."

"Yes. But at least they were able to do something with it. What about the girl who ran off crying before she'd even tried?"

Rome rubbed his face. "And that Lady Rowena. Making a dragon from a kitten? Who does that?" No one except perhaps Cinder, and he wasn't even sure she was that powerful. Who was Lady Rowena? How could she possess such strong magick yet no one had heard of her?

Just the thought of having to eat at the feast with her and spend time with her was enough to send him over the edge. She looked at him as if he was nothing. And acted as if she'd been forced to attend. But for all her standoffishness, he found himself somehow attracted to her. Which bothered him even more. As if he hadn't betrayed Cinder enough.

He needed to see Cinder.

"Go to Cinder's shop, Stil. Find her and bring her here. I have to talk to her. This contest is going to drive me mad."

Stil stroked his goatee and plucked another grape from his plate.

Frustration wound Rome tight as a wet rope. "Why won't you help me?"

Stil laughed. "I'm your friend not your butler. You want someone to fetch her, send a footman. But I'm here to tell you, I know Cinder, and unless you go yourself, she is just bound to get angrier. And I know that I don't want to be on the wrong side of her angry magick."

Rome slumped against the wall. "You're right. As usual."

"Come on." Stil walked over and patted Rome on the shoulder. "I must get going. Princess Aurora of Draakland has called for me. I'll walk down to the servant's entrance with you so you can sneak out."

Rome nodded. He slipped his hand into his pocket, making sure the ring remained in there. "The dragonlands are still under attack I take it."

Stil nodded, his eyes clouded with sorrow. "Going on five years now. Ever since…" His voice cut off, thick with emotion. "I've exhausted all my resources. There is nothing new I can tell the princess. I wish the king and queen would try to fight back against the dragons. They're just too devastated– about everything. Everyone is. Except the princess. Aria would fight the dragons single–handedly if she were allowed. But her parents refuse to send any more men into the mountains to die. I go there more to keep her from doing something that will get her killed, than anything else."

They walked into the hallway, toward the stairs. The sounds of female voices and laughter floated up toward them, making Rome's throat go dry. He'd never been so nervous in his life. All the girls, looking at him like he was the refreshment table made him feel like a side of the best meat.

He squared his shoulders, and Stil laughed.

"Yeah, laugh all you want, you're a mage you can't even court a woman. You have no idea what it's like to be looked upon as a prize peacock at the market."

Stil nodded. "That is true. But what I laughed about was how fun it would be if Cinder could see how scared you were of a bunch of girls in fancy dresses."

Rome scowled, but there was no getting out of it. He walked with Stil, down to the third-floor landing, where squeals of delight met him.

"Prince Rome!"

"Rome!"

"Hi, Rome!"

"Hello, your highness."

An entire group of girls advanced on them, like a flock of ducks.

"I guess they haven't all gotten a room yet," said Stil.

Panic settled in Rome's stomach. "You know, I think I'd

better just stay upstairs for now," he whispered to Stil. "I forgot something in my room," Rome called to the group.

"Really?" asked Stil with a smile. "What? What did you forget?"

Rome ascended the staircase, taking the steps two at a time, moving away from the women. He glared at his friend over his shoulder. "My father. I promised to meet with him about… the ball."

Stil leaned on the banister. "I don't remember him saying that."

Rome shot daggers at Stil before smiling at the women. "I'll see you tonight."

"Can't wait," several shouted.

"Me too." He waved and raced to his room.

Where the hell was Cinder when he needed her? And how was it that, no matter the situation he was in, she was always able to make it better?

CINDER PACED HER LARGE ROOM. SHE'D ONLY BEEN THIS high up in the castle once before. Servants occupied the first two floors, where parties, and meetings were held. The upper two floors were reserved for special dignitaries and the royal family. She knew that Rome's room was somewhere upstairs, but she didn't remember where exactly. He'd snuck her up once when they were twelve. As soon as her father found them, he'd given her such a tongue lashing about propriety, she'd never dared the stunt again.

She bit her thumbnail and traipsed back and forth on the beautiful silver rug.

"If you don't quit that you're going to wear a hole in the thing," said Dax.

She waved her hand at him. "I could fix it in an instant."

"You should rest. You're making Alabrax nervous."

She looked over at the dragon sitting on a high windowsill, looking out.

"He sure looks nervous."

"Trust me, he is," said Dax. "I can feel it."

She stopped. "Feel it?"

He shrugged and pulled on the collar of his green jerkin. "It's strange. It's like I know what he's thinking."

She'd never heard of such a thing before. But then again, she'd never met an animal shifter either. "Is that an animal thing? Because you're a werebear?"

He glanced up at the dragon. "I don't think so. I had a connection with Adrian and the rest of the wolves, but that was only when I was in bear form. This feels... different."

She could see through the glamour she'd put upon him, the red magick that still surrounded him worried her further.

She blew out a breath and stared at the plush, fernblend colored bed longingly. Her skin prickled, like she'd scoured it with tree bark. Her eyes had begun drooping an hour ago. The blast of magick she'd used to produce the dragon had flagged her energy- more than she wanted to admit. She hadn't noticed it until they had reached the room. It was strange because usually stuff like that hit her right away.

"Are you worried about someone finding out who you are?" he asked.

"No. Yes— but mostly no. I'm worried about my sister. And that insolent redheaded doxy Drusilla. I'm worried about you and what will happen if I don't win. And what will happen if I do win. And what am I supposed to say to Rome tonight that won't make him more suspicious than he already is?"

"How can you tell he's suspicious?"

"Trust me. I know."

"All right." Dax rose from his seat and placed his hands on her shoulders. "Let's take a breath and figure these things out one by one."

She nodded and put her fists on her hips. She sucked in a deep breath and then blew it out.

"You can't worry about what happens if you win, or if you don't because those are out of your control. You can only do your best and cross those bridges when you get to them. As for Olivia, she can fend for herself. This competition isn't something you can help her with. She has to do this on her own. And as for Drusilla, she's nothing compared to you, magick or otherwise."

Cinder blew the hair from her eyes and smiled at Dax. "I barely know you, but I can honestly say, you are one of the kindest and smartest men I've ever met. You remind me of my friend Stil. I wish you could meet him. You and he would be great friends."

"Maybe, after I find out who I am I can."

"He was up there," she said. "Standing with Rome during the challenge."

Dax shook his head. "I wasn't paying attention to anything but the competition I'm afraid."

"Maybe he'll be at the ball tonight and I can–"

"Introduce us? No, Lady Rowena, you can't."

"*Posletoth.*" She stamped her foot. "I hate not being me."

"Tell me about it."

She squeezed his arm. He'd been so great to her, and she had yet to give him what he'd come to her for in the first place. "I'm sorry Dax. I'm going to help you. I promise. I'm going to find out who you are."

"It can wait a few more days. You need to save your magick for now."

"No." She shook her head. "You've been way too kind and patient already. I won't have to compete again for another thirty-six hours, and I am too wound up to sleep, so let's try."

He glanced around the room. "Here? Now?"

She pointed to the plush settee. "Yes. Sit."

Dax did as asked and Cinder sat next to him. Nervousness roiled her stomach.

"I… have an idea I'd like to try." Over the last day, she'd thought of something they could try, but it would be strange and more than a little awkward for both of them.

His eyebrow lifted. "Your tone indicates you've not tried this before."

"It's risky, but not in the way you think." Her palms grew slick, and she rubbed them together. "I want you to kiss me."

"Excuse me?" His eyes widened.

"When you kiss someone, everything else floats away,

and all you can do is feel. I have a theory that your mind will relax, and I'll be able to slip behind whatever is blocking your memories."

Dax swallowed hard and wiped his hands on his pants. "Uh… I haven't… I mean… It's been a long time since I've kissed a woman."

She tried to keep the mood light. "That's fine. The last time I kissed someone was so many years ago I don't even remember his name."

Dax licked his lips as nervousness passed over his face.

"We don't have to," she said. "I can try a different way."

"No. I think it's a good idea actually."

She cocked an eyebrow at him.

"Not like that. I mean, not like I want to kiss you." His cheeks flushed. "Not that I don't want to kiss you it's just—" He blew out a harsh breath and rubbed his face.

She laughed and patted his shoulder. "It's all right, Dax. Try to calm down. If you don't, this won't work."

He nodded, and she inched closer to him, until their knees touched. A sudden burst of anticipation stopped her as his hazel eyes searched her face. But then she raised shaky hands to his cheeks. The scruff of his whiskers tickled her palms.

He held so still, that she wondered if her touch hurt him. Looking into his eyes she saw an expression of such longing that her heart ached. Loneliness and sorrow poured over her, and the sudden desire to comfort him struck her.

She ignored the fluttering in her stomach and leaned in until their lips met. He didn't move. She pressed her mouth harder against his. His hand traveled up her arm, sending shivers down her spine. Leaning he licked the crease of her lips. Waves of desire washed over her, and she allowed him to deepen the kiss. A flood of emotions stormed her mind. Desire, need, betrayal.

Focus. You're here to do a job.

She pushed her hands up to his temples, and as he pulled her closer, she probed for the magick block on his mind. Like a large wool blanket, it coated and clouded his thoughts. She pushed it with her mind, and the web of magick melted away.

A small castle came into view, at the edge of a wood, leading to a mountain. Inside a room, Dax was shackled to a bed. A woman, with long, flowing, red hair, entered. She approached him, running her hands over his body.

"When will you give in to me? You can't hold out forever." She rounded him and kissed his cheek.

Cinder gasped and pulled away. Pain shot up her arms to her neck, paralyzing her.

"Cinder!"

She stared into space as stars floated in and out of view. Shockwaves coursed through her body, ripping and tearing at her from the inside as if she'd swallowed lightning. She fell to the floor, wanting to scream but all air had been pushed from her body.

"Cinder!" Dax loomed over her, his face frightful.

Her back arched and her diaphragm clenched as if she was being strangled from the inside out. Her vision darkened as she gasped for breath. Pounding sounded in her ears and pressure built around her like a she was being compressed on all sides. A minute passed, and her head grew fuzzy with a red, hazy shroud. She was going to die.

"Cinder. Tell me what to do!" Dax cried.

Alabrax swooped down from his perch and roared in her ear.

No. She refused to be killed because of one woman's petty jealousy. Cinder summoned all the magick she could and shoved it through her body. White hot light shot from behind her eyes and the red haze exploded in a shower of sparks. She gulped in a huge breath of air and her muscles finally relaxed. A chill swept over her body.

Dax pulled her to his chest.

"I'm all right," she croaked, sucking in another breath.

"The hell you are," he said. "You were the color of Alabrax's belly scales."

She clutched his shirt and buried her face against his chest. Her heartbeat pounded in her ears, and her muscles twitched as she tried to control the terror that still flooded her.

"That— was definitely— some powerful magick," she finally said.

Dax looked her over. "Are you sure you're all right? I could call—"

"Who?" She laughed. "I'm the only healer in the kingdom."

His eyes clouded with concern, and she patted his cheek. "I just need a few minutes to rest, and some wine would be nice."

Dax nodded and propped her against the couch. He raced across the room to the sideboard and filled a goblet with some wine. He grabbed the entire tray of food as well and brought them back to her.

"Here." He held the cup to her lips, and she took several large swallows.

He plucked a peach from the food tray and pulled a knife from his boot. He cut off a sliver and handed it to her.

"Thank you." She lifted the peach shakily to her mouth and allowed the sweetness to slide across her tongue.

Alabrax sidled up next to her and sniffed the peach. She gave him the rest of her piece, and he chewed it for a moment before spitting it out and flying back to his perch on the windowsill.

Dax smiled. "Not a fruit dragon I guess."

Cinder nodded. "I suppose not."

Dax dissected the peach, and she devoured several slices. When her heartbeat slowed, and the shaking had waned, she looked to Dax.

"Did you find anything?" His eyes held hope.

She nodded and recalled the memory of what she'd seen. "There's a small castle," she said. "In a wood that butts up to the mountains in the east."

"Wolvenglen?"

"I don't think so. It felt south of Wolvenglen. South of Volkzene. But north of the Draaklands. It's old, timeworn outside. A place that you wouldn't find unless you were looking for it."

"Is that where I'm from?" His eyes held hope.

"I doubt it. Magick surrounded the entire building, shrouding it from prying eyes. It looked as if you were a prisoner."

"Prisoner? By whom?"

Her gut clenched. "By a woman. I've seen her before, but I do not remember who she is."

Dax looked across the room as if lost in thought.

A wave of fatigue washed over her afresh. Shame burrowed inside her at her weakness.

"I'm so sorry Dax, but I think I need to lie down for a bit."

"Of course." He helped her up. "I'll keep watch, in case someone shows up. There are still several hours until the feast and ball."

Cinder shuffled to the bed and fell atop the beautiful comforter. "I'm only going to shut my eyes for a couple of minutes. Then we can talk more about what I saw and what it may mean."

He stared up at the dragon on the windowsill. "Take all the time you need."

Cinder closed her eyes and fatigue blanketed her.

"CINDER. CINDER YOU NEED TO WAKE UP." A HAND SHOOK her shoulder.

Her eyelids fluttered open, and Dax's face floated into view. She glanced around and found the light in the room quite dim.

"How long was I asleep?"

"About four hours."

"Four hours?" She jumped from her bed and bumped into him.

"Easy. Your dress arrived and shoes and some contraption- I have no idea what it is."

She looked over at the couch. A beautiful, bright blue dress lay where the settee should have been. It was so poufy she could barely see the furniture underneath.

"That is a lot of dress."

He laughed. "It took two people to bring it in."

"It's going to take three people to get me in it." She walked to the gown, surprised her legs didn't wobble. It was the most beautiful thing she'd ever seen. A shimmering, iridescent over fabric wrapped around it and up to the shoulders. Crystalline gems lit the piece up like tiny Yuletide lights. On the table stood a pair of matching shoes. They appeared to be made of the same crystalline gems. She hoped her giant feet would fit, and she wouldn't break them.

She lifted a corset from the table and tossed it across the room. "No. No. No. No, thank you. They can put me in a fluffy gown. They can make me wear shoes I'm bound to break. But I draw the line at not being able to breathe. I've had enough suffocation for one day."

A knock sounded on the door, and Dax answered it. A demure lady-in-waiting entered and curtsied to Cinder. "I've come to help you get ready, Lady Rowena."

Dax nodded to Cinder. "I'll await you outside." He held out his arm and Alabrax swooped off the windowsill and landed on him.

He closed the door behind him and Cinder turned to the lady-in-waiting. She'd never had someone help her before. Livy had played with her hair a few times but the poor child knew little to nothing of hairstyles.

"Can you do my hair?" Cinder asked.

"Of course, M'lady, but should we put your dress on first?"

"Certainly." Cinder smiled. She should know that, but having not gotten ready for anything more than a day at the shop in the last decade, she had no idea what she was doing. She only hoped it didn't show.

CHAPTER NINE

"**T**ell me Lady Rowena. What do you think of the rumors of daemons coming back to the lands?" Rome shoved a piece of turkey in his mouth and licked his fingers.

Lady Rowena looked at his hand in disgust and delicately used her fork to eat a piece of meat off her own plate.

Rome smiled. Eating with his fingers was one of the things Cinder had said she hated most about him. Which was why he did it now. Indeed all well–bred women would feel the same would they not?

He'd decided, over the past hours, to make himself as boorish as possible. Maybe if he acted like a complete barbarian he could get some of the females to drop out. Or at least, the winners. After all, gentility had been what fae were known for. And a proper fae woman would expect him to act like nothing less than a gentleman. Unfortunately for them, he was willing to do whatever he had to, burp, slurp, chirp or pass gas to turn them all away. Surely any woman with half a modicum of self respect would refuse to marry a man such as he was about to portray.

"I think what happens outside our walls is of no concern," she replied.

He let out a bark of unusually loud laughter and took a long drink from his wine. "Truly? I would have thought a Lady would be more concerned about all those who live in Fairelle."

"I don't see them banging down our gate to be let in or to help us. We live in peace. As long as it stays that way, why worry about what we can't control?"

He snorted. Cinder would never be so narrow-sighted.

She laid down her fork and folded her hands in her lap. "Did I say something amusing?"

"Yes. I find it quite humorous, since I myself am concerned with what happens in the world." He picked up a turkey leg, bit into it and let the juice dribble down his chin.

She took his napkin and handed it to him.

"Oh, thank you." He tucked it into his lap, then wiped his mouth with the back of his hand.

Her eyes narrowed. "You certainly are different."

"Different than what?" He fought the urge to grab his napkin and ask for a bowl of water to clean his face and hands.

"Different than… what I'd imagined you to be."

He leaned in close and winked at her. "So you've thought of me before then?"

She studied him for a moment. "Am I missing something, your highness?"

"Not at all." The perplexed look on her face had him almost burst out laughing. "I merely wondered if you've fantasized about me. Maybe late at night, you've wished on a star, hoping you could perchance meet me, we'd fall instantly in love, and I'd take you to be my bride."

Her eyes narrowed, and she turned away.

Rome's gaze connected with his grandmother. Her glare of disdain slapped him in the face making his spine burn with shame. He looked down at his plate and pushed a roll around with his finger.

She had no idea what all of this was doing to him. To love one person but be forced to marry someone else. No matter how lovely Lady Rowena was, or how much she intrigued him, she was not his Cinder.

He sucked down the rest of his wine and called for another glass. "So what do you like to do in your spare time Lady Rowena?"

She gave him a sideways glance as if sensing a trap. "I needlepoint and I tend to the servants for my father. He's ill and requires constant bed rest. My brother and I look after things for him. I also enjoy cooking. Baking really."

"Sounds like a full day of nothing." The words spilled from his mouth before he could rein them in. He swallowed hard, hating himself for being such a bastard.

"Excuse me?"

"I only meant, what good are those things here? Yes, you could order the servants around but why? They do their jobs just fine. You, of course, will not be allowed to cook. I do suppose here, as the princess you would get quite good at needlepoint. Or reading perhaps. There is a lot to read."

She cocked her head to the side. "If I were your wife, would we not spend our time together?"

He shrugged and gulped his wine. "Not really. I have several friends I like to see and do things with. I'd probably continue to spend most of my time with them. Or playing cards. I love to gamble."

"And drink," she mumbled.

He took another, large swig in reply. As he went to set his cup down he misjudged the distance, and it slipped, splashing onto the table.

"Your friends? You mean like the human I saw at the contest?" she asked.

"Yes. Like Stil. Among others."

"I'm surprised your father allows you to be friends with a human. None of the rest of us are allowed."

"Stil has been a family friend for a very long time and he's one of the heads of the mage school. They're trying to improve communication with the different cities. Like the Draaklands. But it wouldn't matter if he didn't allow it. I go where I want and with whom I want. Like Lady Cinder. I spend quite a bit of time with her."

Lady Rowena picked up her wine and sipped it. "The apothecary girl? I didn't realize she was a lady."

"Her father, Lord Rondell, was a good friend of my father. His advisor in fact before Phinneaus." Rome lifted his roll and buttered it.

Lady Rowena wrinkled her nose.

"Do you know Lady Cinder?"

"She seems pleasant enough. A bit outspoken for my taste. And no parentage of real distinction. I suppose that's why she isn't here." Lady Rowena smiled bright as an evening star.

Rome crushed his roll in his fist. Magick sparked off his fingers. The urge to flip the table and yell for Rowena to be removed almost overtook him. Who was she to speak so of Cinder?

Rome grumbled and shoved the roll in his mouth. He wished he knew why Cinder wasn't there. More than anything, he wanted her by his side, not Lady Rowena.

"Would it bother you, Lady Rowena, if I was to continue my friendship with Lady Cinder, if you were to win the contests, I mean," he asked spitting bread out of his mouth.

"Good friends are hard to come by so I suppose not. She's no threat to me. It would be I in your bed. I who had your name, your title, and bore your children. And as I said before, she is just a shop girl so…"

Rome's nails dug into the palms of his hands. "You would do well, Lady Rowena, to show a bit more discretion in how you judge people in the future. A wagging tongue is not often looked upon as a beneficial trait in royalty."

"Too true, Prince Rome. But then, I don't find the truth to be a wagging tongue."

Rome jammed his fork into a potato and speared it into his mouth. No one spoke of Cinder that way. No one.

CINDER WAS PLEASANTLY SURPRISED AT HOW WELL SHE HAD managed to upset Rome. His obvious distress, at her insults, showed that he did indeed care. At least to some degree. She wanted to burst out laughing, reveal herself right then and there, so he could see her joke. But there was too much at stake. Drusilla would probably be declared the winner if anyone found out this early on, and who knew where she would end up. Or Dax for that matter.

But for all her success in upsetting him, she had to admit, she'd never seen him act like such a dullard before. Yes, he enjoyed the occasional evening of ale and cards, but not in the castle and never in front of his father or other dignitaries. It wasn't like Rome to be so unmannered. The sight troubled her.

They finished their meal in silence, then stood to the side as the room was cleared for the ball. Together she and Dax watched the women fawn over Rome. Drusilla leaned on Rome's shoulder, her arm linked with his, her breast pushed up so far in her bodice that Rome's eyes stayed planted right on them.

Cinder shook her head. With him drunk and Drusilla practically stripping down right there to lay in his bed, it was a good thing she'd shown up to protect him. He couldn't even fend for himself in that state.

"Lady Rowena?" Phinneaus headed in her direction, his long red silk robes floating about him. Open in the front, his immaculately tailored breeches and jerkin peeked out from underneath. Purple and blue, they'd been woven with a subtle golden thread. And a silver sash, with a purple crest, pulled the entire ensemble together.

"I think I'll make myself scarce." Dax walked away before Phinneaus could reach them.

"Lady Rowena. It is wonderful to see you," said Phinneaus.

Cinder curtsied. "Thank you, Head Advisor."

"How are you doing this evening? Not too tired from all the magick this afternoon are you?"

She smiled. "I am glad that I shall have tomorrow to recover."

He inclined his head. "You are too modest my dear. Your dragon today was nothing short of spectacular."

"You flatter me."

"And you've never seen a live dragon before?"

"I haven't."

He shook his head and smiled, revealing pearly, straight teeth. "Remarkable. I'd love the opportunity to speak with you more about how you did that."

Butterflies swirled in her stomach. "I... would be honored." She curtsied.

Music began from the magicked instruments in the corner, Rome appeared out of the crowd and headed straight for her. From the sway of his gait, it was evident that he'd had more than enough wine.

He stopped in front of her, his eyes glazed. Without a word, he held out his hand, and her heart fluttered. She slid her fingers into his and he led her out onto the floor. His arm slipped solidly around her waist and though her hips barely touched his, through the layers upon layers of fabric, her body lit up at the contact.

When he pulled her tight, she caught the faint scent of his cologne and inhaled. He stepped forward and whirled her around the floor. All around, people stared at them. The women with bitter expressions of envy. The men with lusty, greedy leers. All of them wishing they were on the floor, dancing at that moment.

Around and around they twirled, until Cinder thought she might collapse from dizziness. She was so glad she'd left the corset sitting on the couch.

Rome didn't meet her eye through the entire dance. Instead, he looked over her shoulder, a magnificent, if not somewhat lopsided smile planted on his handsome face. Even so, Cinder couldn't keep her eyes off him. She relaxed into his rhythm, allowing him to lead her across the floor and back again, something she'd never done before. In the past Rome had always complained that she was leading when they danced. She hadn't meant to, it was just her nature. So keeping vigilant and staying subordinate to his guidance took extra concentration.

The music finally ended, and everyone clapped. She sucked in air, as he let go of her, not realizing how light-headed she'd become.

"I think I could use a breath of fresh air," she said.

"So could I." His eyes darted between the gathering throng of females who, no doubt, hoped to be his next dance partner.

He took her arm and escorted her through the ballroom to the balcony on the far side of the castle overlooking Ville DeFee. Cinder breathed in the scent of her city. Flowers and fruit. Stone and silk. It would ever be the smell she associated with home. No matter where she went or how long she was gone. The smell would linger with her forever.

It had been years since they'd stood together on that

balcony overlooking the city. Balls and festivals had all but ceased in his mother's absence. She glanced over at where he leaned heavily on the railing staring outward. She wondered if he was looking for her below. Trying to see her apothecary to see if the lights were still on. Had he thought about her at all that day more than their conversation at dinner? If he knew she stood right beside him, what would he say? Cinder breathed deep and sighed. He'd probably chastise her for entering the contest without permission.

Below, candles flickered, suspended in mid–air to light the streets. The large golden city gate separated them from the rest of Fairelle. Her thoughts traveled back to what Rome had said about the daemons and others in Fairelle that they were in the midst of trouble. She'd heard Stil speak of it before, but she'd never really thought of it coming to their walls.

If what Rome had said was true, those ornately carved gates wouldn't hold back what awaited them on the other side. Not with the little magick they had left.

Without a word, Rome grabbed her around the waist and pulled her into his arms. Cinder stood too stunned to move.

"I've waited all night to do this." He crushed his lips to hers.

The shock all but had her frozen on the spot. But as his tongue coaxed her lips apart, she melted into him and kissed him back. She'd waited forever for him to kiss her like that. For him to hold her in his arms. For him to want her.

Rome broke away and kissed across her cheek to her ear. "Why don't we go someplace private," he whispered. His hand snaked around, and he grabbed her rear. "It's obvious your magick is far superior to anyone else here. We'll be wed before the end of the week. Why wait? My room is just upstairs."

Cinder blinked several times. "Are you inviting me into your bed?"

He kissed her again. "Why not? Then you can see exactly what you will be getting when you win me."

Cinder tried to process what was happening. He leaned in to kiss her again and she pushed away from him, stumbling back. "You sir, are a brazen rake. Do you think that I would just fall into your bed?"

He chuckled and ran his hands down her bare arms. "Come now. I'm sure you've heard by now of my... proclivities."

Cinder's throat went dry, and she wrapped her arms around herself. "No. I'm afraid I haven't."

He licked his lips, and his hooded eyes scoured her body. "You were right Lady Rowena. You will have my name, and you will have my title, and you may yet bare my children, but you will never have my heart. And you will rarely have my bed. That is unless you don't mind sharing. I do so love a group." He gave a leering smile that made her teeth ache.

All playfulness was stripped away. Rome reached down between his legs and adjusted himself. Cinder gasped without thinking. Heat flushed up her neck and anger swirled inside, sending magick pounding through her veins.

What the hell was going on with him?

"I think I shall retire for the evening," she said through clenched teeth. She turned to go, but he stepped in her way.

"But we were just getting to know each other." He ran his hand up her arm again, and she slapped it away.

She stepped into his space, making him back up. "Touch me again and I'll make sure it's the last time that hand feels anything." She stepped around him and searched inside the ballroom for Dax.

"So, I take it you'll not be returning to the contest then?" he called.

"I wouldn't dream of it." She located Dax, being hung on by Drusilla, and strode toward him. "I've had enough for one night."

Drusilla looked around the room.

"He's out on the balcony," Cinder said. "And he's already waiting for you." If Rome wanted to act like a troll. She would treat him like one.

CHAPTER TEN

Cinder and Dax gathered their things and slipped out of the castle by the servant's entrance; a bit too close to midnight for her liking. She practically ran the entire way she was so infuriated by her interaction with Rome. She'd never, not once, seen him act like that. Especially toward a lady. She thought his treatment of her might make her cry, but surprisingly she found that her anger burned too bright for sadness or embarrassment to take root.

They'd barely made it to the alley behind her shop, when her glamour dissolved. Dax walked into the shop, ducking, so Alabrax didn't hit his head. Cinder scanned the alleyway, making sure they hadn't been followed or watched and then stepped inside the backroom.

Dax walked to the hidden room and opened the door.

"What are we going to do with Alabrax?" she asked. "We're not going to be able to keep him in here for long."

"It's only for a few days. He'll need to feed and spread his wings, but he's still young."

Cinder nodded. "Well, I suggest you wait until everyone is home from the ball before letting him out."

"I will."

Cinder's shoulders sagged. The emotional and physical toll of the day slammed into her like an ogre. "I better get home before Lady Sabine arrives. I'll come in the morning to check on you."

He nodded and yawned. "Be careful."

She gave him a warm smile and remembered what she'd seen in his mind. "You too."

"Cinder? Are you all right?"

She turned back and sighed. "I don't think so."

"You're going to stick this out aren't you?"

Was she? Was she going to stick it out after seeing this side of Rome? A side she'd never seen before. Knowing he would bed any fae he thought wanted him?

No. She couldn't do it. Standing back, watching the man she loved get pawed at by every maiden in the country was one thing. Seeing him destroy his character was quite another.

Cinder lay in bed when Lady Sabine and Olivia returned home, thirty minutes later. She listened to her step-mother chastise and berate Olivia for everything under the Fairelle moon. From her performance and attitude, to eating too much, then to not forcing herself on the prince more…

"We've been in that castle more than all of those other

girls combined. Hell below, he was at our doorstep just yesterday."

He had been? Cinder hadn't known that. What had Rome been doing at her house?

"I'm sorry mother."

"Yes, you are. You have no idea what it means if you don't win this, Olivia. What it means for me, especially."

"I'll do better tomorrow mother. I'll win. I promise."

"You'd better." The door to Lady Sabine's room slammed shut. Followed by a softer shut of the door across the hall.

Cinder wanted to go to her sister and console her, but as much as she loved Olivia, one thing was for sure, her babying was only a hindrance. If Olivia somehow won, she'd have to stand on her own two feet, or be torn apart by the other contestants. Either way, her poor sister needed to do it on her own for once.

"CINDER!"

Shisa! The sun was up. She threw her dress over her sleeping gown and raced down the stairs without brushing her hair.

Lady Sabine sat at the table with Olivia. "What is going on with you? You act as if you were the one out late, winning contests and dancing with the prince."

Cinder's limbs dragged due to overexertion and lack of sleep. "I'm so sorry, Livy. I'll get you something to eat right away." She rushed into the kitchen.

"Olivia? I'm the Lady of the household. Not Olivia."

Cinder had no time for her stepmother's insulted feelings this morning. She needed to get Dax; then she had to go to the castle to meet with Elise.

She flicked and swished her fingers at everything in the kitchen but the pull on her magick was like blades to her nerves. She bumped into the counter and steadied herself. Too much. She'd been doing too much.

As the fire lit, she put the kettle on the stove by hand. Eggs cracked into a pan and Cinder carried it to the stove as well. A knife cut several slices of bread, and they floated to the stove top to warm.

She poured tea into two cups and carried them out to Olivia and her stepmother. Heavy purple bags puffed Olivia's eyes like ripe plums.

Lady Sabine sipped her tea and then shoved the cup back at Cinder. "It's weak."

"I'll make some more."

Lady Sabine waved her off. "Don't bother. Wait. Can I take it that since you still reside here that you sent the human away as I instructed?"

Cinder nodded and looked away.

"Good." Lady Sabine stood. "I have a headache. I'm going to my room. You go make sure the shop is open today." She stood and moved up the stairs, her body swaying in a rhythmical, hypnotic motion.

Cinder wanted nothing more than to go back up to bed herself. But she didn't have the same luxuries her stepmother had.

She walked to the kitchen, plated the food and headed back to sit with Olivia.

Livy's head hung like a limp ragdoll.

Cinder forced a cheerful smile. "So tell me everything," she said, setting the plate in front of her sister.

Olivia poked at her egg yolk with a fork and then shrugged. "Not much to tell. We competed. Some girls failed some didn't." She broke the yolk and it spilled over her plate. She looked up and a small grin spread across her face. "The ball was unusual."

"What happened?" Cinder scooped her egg onto her toast and bit into it.

"Well… the winner, Lady Rowena, got to eat and dance with Rome. They didn't look like they got along very well, though. Mother said that she was the most ungrateful girl ever. But to me, it seemed like Rome was giving her a rough go. Then, after their first dance, they retired to the balcony, but a few minutes later she rushed in, very upset, and left with her brother."

Cinder barely managed to choke down her toast. "Really? That is unusual."

Livy nodded. "Yes, but it was after Lady Rowena left that things took an even worse turn."

A pit grew in Cinder's stomach. She wasn't sure she wanted to know what had happened but she couldn't stop from asking. "Worse how?" She tried to keep her voice even and uninterested.

"First, Rome danced and flirted with every girl there. Including me, which was strange because he's never so much as looked at me before. Second, he drank everything he could get his hands on, got into an argument with his father, and eventually had to be carried out."

Cinder's mouth fell open. "He didn't."

Olivia nodded. "I didn't realize he was that big of a drinker."

"He isn't." When she'd left, she'd had no idea he would react so badly. Acting like that would destroy his reputation forever— not that trying to sleep with other women around was bound to win him any awards in chivalry. Her gut twisted with the memories of how he'd kissed her and tried to get her to bed him. She'd thought he cared about her, but at the drop of a hat he'd been ready to sleep with a woman he didn't even know.

"Well, the only person he was even remotely kind to after she left was me. But all he did, the entire time we danced, was ask about you." Olivia raised an eyebrow.

Cinder blinked rapidly, and she bent close to Livy. "He… he did?"

Olivia smiled. "How can you not see the way he's always felt about you?"

"I'm sure you're quite wrong about that. Rome and I are friends, nothing more."

Olivia shrugged and grabbed the jar of marmalade. "Well, he didn't seem like just a friend when he showed up the other night with flowers in his hand."

Cinder's fork clattered to her plate. "Flowers?"

Olivia's gaze moved to the staircase, and she fell silent for a minute. "Mother said you were sleeping, but I think she just wanted me to talk to him. He was quite upset when you couldn't come down. I found the flowers in a pot outside the next morning. I'm sorry I didn't say anything before now but… well… I thought it would be fun to be a princess. To get out of this house and away from Mother. But I realized last night that is never going to happen for me. Even if I did win and married Rome, I'll never be rid of her."

Cinder grabbed her little sister and hugged her tight. Poor Livy was right. Cinder could leave any time she wanted. Wash her hands of her stepmother and just run away. But no matter where Livy went, no matter what she did, Sabine would follow her and drag her back.

Livy sniffled and then let go of Cinder. She gave her a genuine smile. "You'd like Lady Rowena. She's so much like you. She helped me turn a kitten into a mouse even."

Cinder returned Livy's smile. "She did?"

"And then when this total snot named Drusilla had her owl eat my mouse, she made a dragon and the dragon ate the owl."

"That must have been quite a sight."

"I really hope that if you can't marry Rome she does. I think she'd do a good job of putting him in his place like you do."

Livy turned back to her eggs and began eating them with gusto.

Cinder's feelings were a mix of confusion. It made no sense. Rome had come to see her, yet he'd tried to sleep with Rowena. He gotten drunk and in a public argument with his father. What was he up to?

She frowned. It wasn't like Rome. Wasn't like him at all.

. . .

CINDER UNLOCKED THE SHOP, WALKED IN AND A SCREECH from the storeroom greeted her. She set down her bag, then knocked on Dax's door.

He opened it looking haggard. "Thank Osmus you're here. I can't get him to be quiet."

"Did you take him out last night?"

"Yes, but I think it just made things worse. He shouldn't be like this. He should be tired and sleepy."

Cinder looked in the room. Alabrax blinked at her, and then hissed.

"Stop that," Dax called.

She waved her hand at the dragon, and he yawned, curled into a ball, and went to sleep.

"That should buy you a few hours at least," she said. "But, he's not going to be able to stay here very long. I can make a potion to put into his water that will make him less active if you'd like."

"That would probably be wise. At least, until I leave."

"You can go anytime, Dax. I've told you everything I think I'm going to be able to. If you want to find your past, you need to go to the abandoned castle."

"I'm not leaving until things are settled for you. Besides how would it look if you suddenly showed up without family?"

"It would be all right- considering I'm not even sure I'm going back."

A sharp knock on the outer door pulled her attention. "I better get that. There's a basket of food for you on the counter."

Cinder pressed down her white overdress and pulled on

the sleeves of her blue dress as she walked to the front door. Through the window she caught sight of a royal tunic and a head of coppery hair. Her heart leaped and her belly flopped at the same time.

She unlocked the door and opened it. "Prince Rome."

He held out a bouquet of flowers, full of sungolds and purple hearts. The smile that played across his face was wider than she'd seen him use in a long time.

"Well, are you going to take them?" he asked.

She took the bouquet and walked to the counter. His demeanor gave no indication that they'd fought just days earlier, or that he'd been a fall down drunkard the night before.

"How are you this morning?" he asked.

"I would say better than you, but you seem to be mostly recovered from your night of heavy libation and celebration." She whisked the flowers into a vase and then turned to catch his eye.

His smile fell, and he rubbed his neck. "You heard that did you? From Livy?"

"My sister was awash with all kinds of news this morning."

He closed the door and crossed to her. "Cinder that wasn't me, you have to believe me. I didn't want to do it, but I figured, if I could come off as horrible, maybe some of the girls wouldn't come back."

She fluffed the flowers. It sounded plausible, but still, very unlike him. "And what about the winner? Do you want her to come back?"

He grabbed her hand to stop her. She looked up into the eyes that she'd grown to love, and all she saw was pain.

"Cinder you have to know that none of those other women mean anything to me. They aren't the one I want to be with." He stared at her again, the way he had days before, and the truth of his words warmed her.

"Truly?" she managed.

He rounded the counter and surrounded her in his muscular arms.

She rested her hands on his chest. He'd asked Lady Rowena if she'd dreamt about him before, and had she told him the truth, the answer would have been yes. She had dreamt of him before. And she'd dreamt of this moment before as well. But now, in reality, she could not believe it was happening. It shouldn't be happening. He knew better than to toy with her emotions.

The scent of his cologne filled her nostrils.

He pushed a curl from her forehead. "I love you Cinder. I've always loved you. I never wanted anyone else. I've been a fool to wait this long to tell you."

His words almost made tears flow from her eyes. Decades. She'd waited decades for him to say those words. And now that they hung in the air between them, fear crept up her spine, like an icy shard of reality. Her heart begged her to give in. To say she loved him too. To let him sweep her away from her life of pain and loneliness. But... she couldn't.

He leaned in to kiss her but just as his lips were about to touch hers, she pressed a finger between them. Her heart told her to stop living in her head, but for the first time in her life, her head won out.

"And what about Lady Rowena?" she asked. "The one you attempted to entice into your bed last night?"

His brows knit together. "What?"

"Lady Rowena. I'm told she's pretty with brown hair and green eyes. You kissed her didn't you? And asked her to go to your bed?"

"Cinder... I–"

"Did you really think no one would see or hear that? That I wouldn't hear about it?"

His eyes widened, and guilt laced his features, making her stomach sour.

"Cinder, it's not what you think."

"So, you didn't ask her to sleep with you?"

"I did, but I didn't want to." He leaned in to kiss her again, but Cinder stepped out of his grip.

She crossed her arms over her chest. "All right then. Explain it to me. Explain how you love me, but you invited a lady of the court to sleep with you? Explain how you were ready to ruin her reputation and possibly her opportunity to marry another, should she lose the contest– but you didn't want to."

He blew out a harsh breath. "I said those things to push her away. To get her to quit the contest. You didn't enter so I've been doing everything I can to stop the bloody spectacle. I don't want her. I want you. I came here because I want to marry you." He pulled a blue stone ring from his pocket. "Yes. I want to marry you Cinder. I love you. I've always loved you. I was stupid."

Her mind spun until she couldn't think straight. He wrapped her in his arms again and kissed her forehead.

Then her cheek. "Marry me," he whispered. He kissed her soft on the lips and her knees almost buckled. "Marry me."

The word 'yes' clung to her tongue, waiting to be uttered. She wanted to say it. Every last inch of her body wanted her to say yes… But she couldn't. It wasn't right. It wasn't fair. If she said yes now, every fae in the kingdom would hate not only her, but Rome as well. Being hated herself was one thing, but she couldn't do that to Rome. If they hated him, it would tear their city apart. It would tear him apart.

She pushed away from him and shook her head. "I can't. I don't want to be your way to escape what your father is putting you through. I know you don't wish to marry a stranger, but I don't want to be the reason every fae in Ville DeFee hates you and turns on your family. You made a commitment. You agreed to the contest. You must do your duty."

His brow knit together and he stared at her for a moment before laughing. "Did you just tell me I needed to do my duty?" He held up his hand. "Wait. Are you telling me no?" The tone of disbelief in his voice didn't suit him.

Her heart crumbled, and she sucked in a breath to cover a sob. "Yes. I am telling you no, Rome."

Heated sparks flashed in his eyes. "I have dozens of women begging and competing to marry me but I come here to ask for your hand, and you say no. And then, you of all people, want to lecture me about my duty? You who considers herself above just about every law in this land. You who couldn't follow the rules if it meant saving your life. You, who once told me that the only duty you had was to your own heart?"

The air of superiority that flooded off him caused anger to prickle her skin like fire sparks.

"You thought I would just say yes, after you promised every female in this kingdom, a chance at winning your hand?"

"I only did that because I thought you would enter the contest."

"But you knew I couldn't."

"When has that ever stopped you before?" he yelled.

She opened her mouth to protest, but he held up his hand.

Pain planted on his features and his eyes clouded. "I do love you, and I know you love me, though you are too damned stubborn to admit it. And yes, it's true, I asked Lady Rowena to my bed but not because I wanted to sleep with her. Like all the rest of those vipers, draped in fancy silk dresses, I was trying to offend her; to get her to leave. I was doing what needed to be done and damn the consequences. I followed my heart for once. I did it for us. To be with you. You, of all people, should understand that."

Saying the words threatened to crush her. But someone needed to act like an adult and for the first time in their relationship, she was the one. "Rome, I do understand. It's you that doesn't. You aren't thinking with your head right now or acting like yourself–"

"No. I'm acting like you."

She shook her head and dropped her gaze. Her heart plummeted to her toes. "And therein lies the problem. You aren't me. You're you. You don't see it, but I'm trying to help you. To be the person you need me to be at this moment. The fae you've always wanted me to be. The one who puts the fate of the kingdom first."

"Truly? Then I suppose you don't know me at all Cinder. Because if you did, you'd know that that's not the woman I want. I want the woman who thinks for herself and takes me on her adventures."

She'd never seen him so selfish before. Everything he ever did was for the greater good. "Don't you see what would happen if I was that woman now?" A sob crept into her voice. "You'd marry me, yes. And you'd love me, for a while, but eventually, when the weight of your father's crown sat on your head, and you found yourself alone in every possible way, save having me, you'd hate me for it. And with how much I care for you, I cannot do that to you."

He slipped the ring back into his pocket. "Then I have your answer."

She reached for him. How could he be so blind and not see the wisdom in her words? "Rome, I'm—"

The bell rang, and a young couple walked in. Spotting Rome they bowed low.

"Your highness."

Cinder swallowed hard wanting to kick herself in the rear.

"I should probably go," he said.

She fought back tears. Her eyes traveled to the young couple. "I suppose you should."

Cinder mustered the courage to keep from kissing him and telling him, she would marry him. A thousand times over, yes.

And so she did what she'd been taught to do. She curtsied and donned her most humble expression. "I wish you the best in your contest tomorrow, your highness."

The anger that rippled through Rome made the air around him shimmer.

He bowed to her and headed for the exit. "Good day, Lady Cinder."

The door slammed with such force, it shook the windows and Cinder flicked magick at them to keep them from cracking.

She brushed a tear from her eye and shoved a smile on her face as she looked at her customers.

"How may I help you this good morrow?"

ROME STORMED THROUGH THE STREETS, IGNORING EVERY bow and curtsy as he passed. How could Cinder have reacted the way she had? His mind raced with anger as his head pounded in pain. She'd turned him down.

He couldn't remember much of the ball after Lady Rowena had stormed off, the wine had taken care of that. But what he did remember was the feeling that he was nothing more than a name. Every woman he'd danced with had smiled and preened and looked around as if she'd already married him. He didn't want a wife like that. How could his father think someone like that would be best for

Ville DeFee? Magick or no magick, nothing was worth being married to a woman of no substance. Pretty eyes that held no real intrigue. A mind full of parties and gowns and how to decorate a nursery but nothing of consequence. Nothing to converse with him about. To keep him on his toes. Nothing unexpected. Just the dull day in and day out of existing without living. That was not the kind of woman he wished for. He wanted the kind that followed her heart, when she wanted and how she wanted. Just the way he'd professed to be to Rowena.

He stopped walking. Just as she'd done today in telling him no. He shook his head making his brain rattle and his eyes burn. He really had drunk too much the night before.

He should have known that it wouldn't have been easy to get Cinder to say yes. In all the years he'd known her, how had he been so daft as to think she would have giggled, clapped her hands and fallen at his feet. He was such a dolt. Everything she'd said had been the truth. And she was simply doing exactly what he loved her for. Being herself. Forging her own path. And hell, keeping him on his toes with the unexpected. He chuckled and gripped the ring. He wasn't giving up.

Rome continued forward and caught sight of the shut city gate. The sun glared off it making his eyes burn. He shielded them with his hand. Over a dozen guards barred the way. His brows drew together. They never closed the gate during the day. The farms needed tending. He strode to the gatehouse and the captain of the guard looked up from a parchment.

"Your highness."

"Why is the gate closed?" Rome asked.

"I'm not sure, highness. This parchment came from your father an hour ago, requiring that we let Phinneaus and a group out and close the gates for the day. We aren't to open them again until after sundown."

What was his father up to?

Rome headed for the path up to the castle, but he found his gaze continually drawn to the gate.

ROME ASCENDED TO THE HIGHEST TOWER OF THE CASTLE. He stopped at the outer door and tried the handle. It lowered, but when he pushed, it didn't move. He shoved his shoulder into thick planks and the door squeaked but barely moved. It had been ages since someone had been in the tower.

He tried again, and the door gave way, causing him to fall to the dusty floor. Getting to his feet, Rome coughed at the scent of ash and dust. He brushed off his clothing and looked around. He'd only been in the small room, that housed a giant brazier and old mirror, once. Before his mother had died, she'd brought him up to see across the lands of Fairelle. His chest squeezed at the memory of his mother. She'd been so much like Cinder. Brave, strong, kind.

He stepped around the brazier, to the other end of the room, where the entire side was made of glass- from floor to ceiling. He looked out past the wall of Ville DeFee toward the groves and fields. His stomach roiled at the height and he covered his mouth. He didn't want to vomit all over the windows. He burped and swallowed hard. He couldn't remember the last time he'd had half that amount of alcohol. If it had been any other day, he would have gone to Cinder for a tincture to cure the headache and nausea. Little chance of her helping him now though.

He drew in a breath and looked out at the fields. A dozen or so workers moved through the groves, methodically, sprinkling small droplets of something onto each plant.

Rome watched them for more than an hour, trying to figure out what they were doing, but in the end, he could see no difference in the crops, so he headed back to his room to sleep off his hangover.

"Rome?"

He turned at the sound of his name. "Grandmamma. How are you feeling today?" He planted an uncomfortable smile on his face.

"Better. The cough has subsided some."

The news filled him with relief. He didn't want to think about anything happening to her, not for a long while.

"Let us sit and have tea together," she offered.

With how his day had gone so far, the last thing Rome wanted to do was sit and have tea. But who knew. In a few days he could be married to a woman who'd protest him having tea with his grandmother. Not that it would matter, but one thing the past day had taught him was, not to put things off.

"Sounds wonderful." He bowed and took her arm.

They walked together to her room where she rang for tea. He plopped onto her couch and tried to settle his thoughts.

"Quite a day yesterday." His grandmother sat next to him.

He rubbed his head. "That's one way of putting it."

"I heard you enjoyed yourself at the ball last night. Perhaps a little too much?"

He looked over, and his stomach flopped. He hated disappointing his grandmother. But her look was one more of curiosity than scrutiny.

"I... wasn't my best. That is for sure."

"And why is that? I found Lady Rowena to be most lovely."

Rome blew out a harsh breath. "Lovely yes. The right one? No."

Rome dug in his pocket and pulled out the ring he'd tried to give Cinder. He set it on the table and stared at it.

"That's beautiful."

There was a knock and his grandmother waved the door opened. A maid entered, set down the tea tray, then left. His grandmother flicked her fingers and the tea poured into the two dainty cups.

"It was for Cinder," he finally said. "She couldn't enter the contest. Not that she would have." Dark sadness tipped into his heart. "I've loved Cinder since we were twelve. I was stupid to wait to tell her. I just kept hoping..."

"That she'd change?"

He nodded.

"Rome, you love her for who she is and for what you know she can yet become. But you cannot force it upon her."

"It doesn't matter. I asked her to marry me today, and

she said no." He leaned forward and covered his face with his hands.

"Does she not love you as well?"

"Oh, she does. But for once she's doing what she ought to do, instead of what she wants. Which is ironic, as I am finally doing what I want and not what I ought. I don't care what anyone thinks. I want to marry her and only her. But she said, if she agreed to marry me now, it would turn the entire kingdom against our family, and I'd end up hating her."

"She is most likely correct in that assessment. Our people are fickle and proud. Not a good combination."

"But it's more than that. She's angry with me for something stupid I did last night."

"Just one thing?" His grandmother raised her eyebrow and chuckled. "There is not much a man can do that love, time, and apologies cannot fix. What did you do that was so terrible?"

He looked up. "I asked Lady Rowena to my bed."

His grandmother spat her tea out and began to cough. He clapped her on the back several times and she set down her cup.

"You what?" she croaked.

"I didn't mean it. Truly I didn't. I was trying to get her to drop out. I want them all to drop out. I only want Cinder. Not someone who wants me for my title."

"And Cinder found out…"

"Apparently her younger sister heard and told her. And she told her I was a drunken cod. Grandmamma, what do I do now?"

His grandmother sat deep in thought for several minutes.

"First, you drink that tea. It won't be as good as one of Cinder's remedies, but it should help with your pounding head. Next, you apologize to Lady Rowena."

"What?" Rome picked up his tea.

"Apologize to her. Tell her the truth and leave it at that."

"But how will apologizing to Lady Rowena help me with Cinder?"

His grandmother shrugged. "I'm not saying it will. It's the right thing to do, though."

If he'd been in his right mind, he'd have had the idea himself. He didn't really want to be known as a mule-headed dung beetle by everyone in his kingdom.

"And what do I do about loving Cinder?"

"Unfortunately," said his grandmother. "I believe Cinder is correct in her assertions." She laid her hand on Rome's. "Tomorrow, at the contest, take your time with the contestants. Look deeper. Not all of them are as shallow as you make them out to be."

Rome nodded and sipped his tea wishing it was something stronger. He was going to need help apologizing to Lady Rowena.

CHAPTER ELEVEN

The next morning Cinder awoke, having gotten less than three hours of sleep. Between tossing and turning over the plight with Rome, and her stress about Alabrax, who'd only grown increasingly more restless during the past day, she could barely concentrate on anything else. She dragged herself from bed and headed down to fix breakfast for her stepmother and sister. Doing everything by hand took longer, but it also took less magick, and she was going to need all the magick she could muster.

The challenges were bound to continue being daunting. Not that she was even sure she wanted to stay in the competition. What was she thinking? She couldn't just rid herself of the glamour at the end and expect everyone to accept her cheating. And she couldn't marry Rome as Lady Rowena. She could take off her Lady Rowena persona and just let her disappear, but to what avail? Wouldn't the runner-up just take her place?

Cinder hung her head. What had she gotten herself into? She didn't know. But one thing she was sure of, no matter what was going on between Rome and herself, she had promised Elise she would win the contest. And she wasn't going to let Elise down.

TWENTY MINUTES LATER, SHOUTING ABOUNDED AS HER stepmother ordered Olivia about. Cinder shook her head and stared at the plate of food she'd made her sister. Everything on it, except the fruit, would be nixed by her stepmother. She waved her hand over it. The plate shimmered and the food appeared to be no more than a grapefruit and a boiled egg.

Cinder set her stepmother's plate in front of her. She turned it once, sniffed it, then began to eat. After the first bite, Lady Sabine looked over at Olivia's plate and nodded. Cinder placed her hand on Olivia's shoulder and gave her a pointed look. Olivia's brow furrowed and she picked up her fork.

"Start with the grapefruit," said Cinder. "They're sweet this morning."

Olivia stabbed a piece of fruit and put it into her mouth. Her eyes widened and then she smiled slightly.

"Thank you, Cinder."

"Hurry up," said Lady Sabine. "We don't have time for you to waste. We need to get you dressed."

"I need to go as well." Cinder looked over at the clock and headed back to the kitchen.

"And what is so important that you need to head off so early this morning?"

Cinder stopped at the sound of her stepmother's words. Damn. When would she learn to be more careful? Being two people was not something she'd be able to keep up much longer.

"I… just want to make sure the shop is open before the contest starts in case anyone needs anything."

She glanced over her shoulder, and her stepmother studied her as if preparing an insult. Cinder wanted to rush back out to the table and wipe the smugness from Sabine's face. To tell her stepmother the truth. Not hold her tongue and not pretend to be happy with serving and cooking and slaving to keep her stepmother in good company. To tell her stepmother that Rome had proposed to her. Her. The worthless stepdaughter of no value.

"You need to help Olivia. No one is more important than your sister."

Cinder's gaze landed hard on her stepmother. "I whole-heartedly agree."

Lady Sabine's eyes flashed, then she waved her hand, dismissing Cinder.

Cinder strode out the back door. Leaning against the wall she sucked in several deep breaths, refusing to cry, but tears slid down her cheeks anyway. What was wrong with her? Why hadn't she told Rome yes? Married him and let things play out. Mayhaps things wouldn't have turned out horribly. More than ever, it was evident she wouldn't be able to stay in that house.

A trickle of fear mingled with excitement. It had been

the only home she'd ever known. First with just her and Papa, then Lady Sabine and finally, Olivia. She knew every crevice, every creaky stair, every missing stone.

The back door opened, Cinder swiped at her eyes and put a smile on her face. Livy stared at her feet.

"Mother said I need to get ready."

Cinder nodded. "Of course."

Olivia bit her lip and reached for Cinder. The two embraced and Cinder kissed the top of her little sister's head.

"Promise me you'll do your best day," Cinder said. "Not for her, for you."

Olivia nodded. "I know Rome wants you."

Cinder pushed a dark curl from her sister's face. "If you win, you have a fabulous time. You deserve it."

"If I do win this thing, I'm taking you with me," she said. "I won't leave you here. I promise."

Her sister's sweetness struck Cinder to the core. "If you win, your mother will go with you."

Determination crossed Olivia's face tugging down the corners of her mouth. "Not if I can help it."

THIRTY MINUTES LATER CINDER THREW HER CLOAK AROUND her shoulders and reached for the doorknob. Like tiny needles Lady Sabine's nails dug into Cinder's arm, stopping her. She turned to find her stepmother's face a mask of anger.

"You think you're so witty. You think I don't see what you're doing?"

Had she let something slip about being in the contest? "I'm sorry?"

"I see the way you fawn over Olivia. Pretending to be her friend. Pretending to be the one who cares about her the most."

Cinder's spine snapped straight. "I do care about her the most."

"You're just trying to put a rift between Olivia and myself. You're afraid she's going to win the contest and leave you in that obscure little shop while she and I go off to the castle to live as we deserve. But know this. You are a nobody. A nothing. A—"

Cinder jerked from her stepmother's grip. "I am not nothing. And I'm not nobody. I am the daughter of Lord Rondell. It's true that I may not know who my mother was, but that doesn't make me any less than I am. And whether you like it or not I am Lord Rondell's daughter. Yes, I am afraid she's going to win and go to the castle but not because I'd be left behind, but because you will go with her. If Livy were to leave me here, I'd be overjoyed, as long as it meant she'd be safe from you."

Lady Sabine's eyes glowed like embers. "You better be careful Cccccccinder. You have no idea who you're meddling with."

All the words she'd never said piled up inside her, like a stack of parchments ready to bury her. "You think the only thing I know how to do with my magick is heal people, make your food and clean up your messes? You have no idea what I'm capable of."

Lady Sabine's nostrils flared, and her eyes narrowed. The look on her face was deadly.

"Don't tessssst me girl. You won't like what happens if you do."

Cinder stood her ground, even though a chill raced up her spine. "I'm not afraid of you."

"You should be," Sabine hissed.

A set of light footsteps descended the stairs behind them.

"Mother, I'm ready."

Lady Sabine's eye twitched, then she looked away. Cinder seized the moment and fled out the door. Sabine's malice and threats dogged her every step as she rushed past stores and shops each sporting a banner of the house they hoped to win the contest. Heart pounding, blood bursting in her veins, she ran toward the apothecary. She'd endured Sabine's anger, orders and demands for decades. Every snub, every insult, every glare of disgust. She'd smiled and curtsied and endured them all. Biting her tongue and complaining to Stil and Rome. If she'd said everything she wanted she'd have told Sabine she was vile. A terror to behold. That no matter how much magick she used on her face her insides rotted like a walking corpse.

Something about the woman was off. The way she moved. Her pattern of speech when she got angry.

Cinder's footsteps slowed, and for the first time, she wondered if Lady Sabine was even fae.

Cinder passed a dress shop and then stopped short. She stared at the storefront. Next to a beautiful blue gown very similar to the one she'd worn the night before hung a family crest. She smiled and covered her mouth. Lady Rowena's family crest hung in the window for all to see. Cinder spun around and found several other shops with the Rowena crest as well. They were rooting for her. Her.

Cinder continued on slowly marking each shop with the Rowena crest. To her surprise more than half the shops on her street were on her side.

She shook her head and looked to the sky for the first time in a long time.

"What do I do mother?" she whispered.

A light breeze caressed her face and she closed her eyes allowing everything to float away. The sun shone down on her body warming her to the core. She smiled and hugged herself.

A cart bumped her leg and Cinder turned.

"Sorry Cinder," said the baker rolling sweets and buns down the street. He reached in his cart and pulled out a pastry shaped like a dragon.

Cinder thanked him and looked down at the blue and pink puff pastry that resembled Alabrax almost exactly. She stared at the dragon and courage swelled within her. She knew what she needed to do.

Biting into the pastry she strode toward her shop. She had to get herself and her sister away from Sabine.

"You're going to be late," said Dax.

"I got held up." Cinder hurriedly set down her cloak.

"Someone has been knocking on the front door for five minutes."

"Yes," said a voice from the back door. "I have."

Cinder spun around to find Rome's grandmother standing in the doorway.

Her cheeks flushed with heat as she looked to Dax. "Your majesty, I'm so sorry, I–"

The older woman waved her hand. "You need to hurry. There's less than fifteen minutes until you need to be at the gate."

The older woman stepped inside the backroom before closing the door and pulling down the shade.

"Uh… I'll just go in the other room." Dax headed for his secret room.

"Nonsense," said Elise. "I'll do you right after. I'm assuming you're her brother?"

Cinder and Dax exchanged a look.

"Come, come now. Don't act so surprised. I'm much aware that my grandson isn't the only fae in the kingdom with friends of other races. Once upon a time, there were several human families my husband and I were close with. So wait your turn," she ordered.

Dax gave a slight bow. "Yes, ma'am. Your highness… Your majesty… ma'am."

Cinder held her hand up. "Wait."

"You're quitting?" Elise's hard-set eyes bore into her.

The words stabbed Cinder to the core. "I want to continue. I do. But I can't watch Rome destroy himself and his reputation. I can't stand by while he makes a fool of himself."

Elise crossed her hands in front of her and stared at Cinder. "And how do you think we can save him? By giving up on him? By letting his father win? By allowing some power grubbing *moptrap* win his hand in a contest?"

Cinder swallowed hard and searched for words.

"Why do you think I came to you in the first place? I came to you because I knew Rome had feelings for you. Actual feelings. And I came to you because my son is wrong. The royals of Ville DeFee are the weakest magickally. It's you who are the strongest. You who will decide the fate of Fairelle if war comes to our door. I've seen your strength. I've seen your stubbornness, and that is what will keep us alive. Not silly headed girls in pretty dresses they can't afford."

Rome's grandmother flicked her hands over Cinder's face and arms. The beautiful teal dress was still growing down Cinder's arms when the older woman grabbed Cinder's hands.

"You can choose to come or not, Lady Cinder, but as for me, I will do my part to make sure you have everything you need."

Elise's magick flowed up Cinder's limbs like water. Soothing her aching heart and speaking peace to her mind.

Elise pulled away and beckoned Dax forward. "Now, I'm pretty sure I remember what you looked like yesterday. Honestly, I don't think most people will notice any difference one way or another." She stuck the tip of her tongue out of the corner of her mouth and clapped her hands in Dax's direction. His human appearance morphed into a thinner, fae version of himself.

"Wonderful." Elise looked Dax over, then her stern gaze landed on Cinder once more. "I must get back, but I look forward to seeing you out there today, Lady Rowena. I surely hope you do not disappoint me."

Cinder curtsied, and her fairy grandmother left without another word. She stared at the backdoor. Elise was right. This wasn't about her; it was about all of them. She'd started this rebellion, and she needed to see it through. For all of them.

"Before we go." Cinder pulled a vial from her pocket. "Put it in Alabrax's water. It should put him out until we return."

Dax took the vial and headed for his room. Cinder looked herself over in the mirror.

She took a deep breath. She had to set things right.

CINDER MADE IT TO THE GATE AS THE OTHER WOMEN WERE lining up.

"What's out there, do you think?" One asked.

"Something harder than yesterday," replied another.

"I heard they brought in an army from the north," someone squeaked.

"Well, I heard that it has something to do with the crops," replied another.

"Hi." Olivia slid next to Cinder in line and plucked at her bodice. "It surely is warm this morning."

Cinder stared for a moment before composing herself. "Good morning, Lady Olivia. Yes, it is warm."

A red glint caught Cinder's eye and she noticed the red stone necklace that Olivia wore. It was Sabine's. Now that was cheating, but she doubted her sister knew what the necklace did. Cinder didn't even know. But Sabine hadn't given it to Olivia for adornment, that was for sure.

"What a beautiful necklace. Where did you get it?"

Olivia touched the stone at her neck, making it glow. "My mother gave it to me this morning. Isn't it beautiful?"

"Quite," Cinder replied.

"And expensive as well." Lady Sabine slid up next to Olivia and Cinder's hands clenched tight.

"Well, introduce me to your friend Olivia." Lady Sabine smiled at Cinder.

"Lady Rowena, this is my mother, Lady Sabine Rondell."

Sabine held out her hand to Cinder. "Pleasure. You're the one who conjured the baby dragon, did you not?"

Cinder shook the tips of Sabine's fingers. "I did."

"Such a remarkable piece of magick for one so young."

Olivia looked at her shoes.

"Lady Olivia did quite well herself," Cinder replied.

Olivia gave Cinder a weak smile.

Lady Sabine twirled a lock of Olivia's hair. "Yes…" she mused. "Well, I'm sure my Olivia will give you a run for your magick today, Lady Rowena. She's been practicing very hard."

"I hope she does," Cinder replied. "Lady Olivia is a most welcomed opponent."

Lady Sabine turned Olivia to face her and began fiddling with Olivia's clothes. "Now remember what I told you."

"Yes, mother."

"Don't let anyone or anything, distract you." Her eyes slid to Cinder.

"Yes, mother."

"And most of all, remember the consequences if you do not win today."

Cinder's gut pulled tight as a grapevine.

"Yes, mother." Olivia's voice was barely a whisper.

Lady Sabine smiled, fluffed her daughter's hair, then walked away. Olivia stared after her mother for several seconds, until a bell tolled.

"What did she mean by that?" asked Cinder. "What happens if you don't win?"

Shame flooded Olivia's face. "If I lose, she's sending me to live with my grandmother Morgana."

Cinder grabbed Olivia's hands. "I won't let that happen, all right?"

Olivia's eyes widened. Her mouth opened and then closed again as she searched Cinder's face. Olivia nodding vigorously and opened her mouth again. Cinder's gaze moved to the stone necklace which grew brighter the longer she held Olivia's hands. Cinder dropped her little sister's hands and stepped away quickly. The glowing dimmed and Cinder cleared her throat.

Her cheeks heated as several of the other girls looked on. "I mean. I'll do everything I can to help you today, Lady Olivia."

Olivia nodded again but continued to stare at Cinder. Cinder fought the urge to say more, but with so many people around she had to keep her composure.

Cinder glanced up to find Phinneaus staring down at

them from his perch high upon he castle wall. She quickly faced forward, heart galloping. She needed to stay focused. She couldn't be too familiar with Olivia. Someone would suspect something if she was.

"LADIES, AND LADIES," SAID ROME'S FATHER.

Every eye turned upon the king, Rome, his grandmother and Phinneaus as they stood high upon the ramparts, over-looking the scene.

"We thank you, once again, for coming out today for our celebration."

Rome scanned the crowd. The number of contestants was half what it had been the day before. No more than thirty women remained. He looked from face to face, hoping, by some miracle, he would see Cinder, but the tight knot in his gut told him she wasn't there.

"Do you see Lady Rowena," said his grandmother. "She looks quite lovely today."

"You should keep your eye on my niece, Olivia. Today she is sure to impress, your highness," interjected Phinneaus.

"Hmmm..." Rome didn't care about Lady Rowena, except to apologize to her. And Olivia was a sweet girl, but it was Phinneaus' other niece that Rome had his sights on. Bloody stubborn Cinder. Her words from the day before still hurt, like a thumb pressing into an open wound. But his determination was set. He didn't care what she'd said. He loved her, and he was going to prove it. After the ball tonight, he was going to go to her house and demand to see her, Lady Sabine be damned. Then he'd profess his love again and make her see reason. Together with his grandmother at his side he would then make his father see reason and after his father, the entire kingdom. He didn't care if they hated him. Didn't care if they didn't want him. Didn't care if they floundered in their own self-righteous indignation. All he cared about was being with Cinder. If he couldn't have her at his side, not all the wealth in the treasury was worth a thing.

His mind had been made up the night before after talking it through with Stil. Even if it meant he had to leave Ville DeFee to be with her, he would do it.

"...And so, today you will be tested with nature," his father continued. "Outside these gates each of you will be given a section of our fields to replenish. You'll have one hour to conclude your test."

His father waved his hand, and the giant gate creaked opened.

"Good heavens," said his grandmother. "Your father really has gone too far this time."

Outside the gates every field in the valley spread out. Not a stalk stood straight. Not a vine spiraled toward the sky. Not a fruit held a natural color. Every single plant had grown black and sickly looking. The apple trees stood barren where only the day before they'd been flush with pinks and greens and yellows.

The ansleberry bushes shriveled flat against the dirt instead of being round with plump fat blue berries.

The kingdom's entire livelihood sat in ruin on the fields of Ville DeFee. Their produce brought more money to the kingdom than any other export they had. Rome looked on in horror at the lengths his father had gone to.

"If these girls can't fix the crops, we'll have a serious problem on our hands," said his grandmother.

Rome shook his head. "Then let's hope they can."

THE GASPS FROM THE GROUP HIT CINDER'S EARS BEFORE SHE saw what was outside the gates. Whispers started like the buzzing of a hornet's nest.

"What's going on?" asked Olivia.

"I don't know." A knot formed in Cinder's stomach.

"Here. Here. Here. Here." A guard held small silver cards and handed them out to the women in turn as they exited the gate.

Cinder and Olivia stepped up, took their numbers, then got their first look at what lay before them. The entirety of their food supply had been killed.

"Oh my goodness," said Olivia. "Our food. All of our food."

Cinder grabbed her hand. "Breathe deep. As long as everyone does their section, we'll be fine. The king wouldn't have done this if he didn't know how to bring it back."

The words were sound but even Cinder wasn't sure she believed them. Rome's father had done many foolish things in his time but this went beyond foolishness. It was downright reckless.

Together they walked to their quarter acres of land and surveyed the damage.

"What could have caused this?" asked Olivia.

Cinder crouched down and touched one of the diminished corn stalks. It held a greenish-black tinge to it, but the stalk wasn't dried out. She touched the soil and found it still damp.

"It's not bugs," she mused.

"Maybe a weed abater?"

Cinder shook her head. "They'd be shriveled and dead."

"Why are you working together?" Drusilla stormed over.

"Is it a crime to talk?" Cinder retorted.

"This isn't a collaborative event. You can't both get the prince. But you can both get disqualified if you're caught cheating."

Cinder rose and stepped closer to Drusilla. "You should mind your own business. That is unless you want me to call my dragon to help show you some manners."

Drusilla slammed her fists on her hips. "Fine, assist the baby trying to figure out what killed the plants. It doesn't matter. We all know she has no real magick anyway. And in the end, Prince Rome is mine."

Cinder's fingers twitched with the desire to throw an ugly spell on the stupid git. "Drusilla, you may look like you have noble blood and you may smell like you have noble blood but at the end of the day, Prince Rome would rather wed a toad than a stuck up, half magicked doxy like you."

Drusilla sucked in a breath and her cheeks turned to flames. Magick twitched around her fingertips and Cinder raised her hand, producing her own magick.

"Do you really want to battle this out? I've been taught

spells that you could spend the next fifty years working on and you still wouldn't be able to decipher."

"I highly doubt that from a girl whose family no one seems to be able to trace."

"Maybe that's because we've spelled everyone we come in contact with to forget they've seen us." Cinder stepped closer to Drusilla, a smile planted on her lips. "Or maybe it's because they're all dead."

Drusilla blanched and though she continued to try and put up a good front, Cinder saw the terror in the girl's eyes.

"Forty five minutes remaining," called a guard.

Drusilla turned on her heels and headed back to her section of the field.

Cinder watched the girl go, knowing she was dangerously close to showing her true colors. She needed watch herself.

"She's right," said Olivia. "I should do this on my own."

Before Cinder could reply, Olivia walked back to her section of crops.

Cinder's heart broke at the sight of her little sister. She couldn't let Livy fail. Who knew what would be left of Olivia if she didn't succeed.

CINDER SPENT MOST OF THE HOUR TESTING HER SECTION OF corn. From root fungus to blight she wracked her brain for any spell that might have caused the plants to wither. The bell tolled, letting them know that there were only ten minutes left to the challenge. Cinder glanced around. Not one girl had fixed her crops. What happened if no one succeeded?

She plucked a piece of greenery from her corn stalk. A silver liquid oozed out of the tear in the leaf. Cinder touched the liquid and rolled it through her fingers. She lifted it to her nose and sniffed. Blood.

Startled she threw the foliage to the ground and wiped her hands on her skirt. Poisoned blood. She quickly ran down the list of creatures she knew with poisoned blood. Vampires, Werewolves, Daemons... no. Dragons, nereids, centaurs... no. Cinder sucked in a sharp breath. No. Not poisoned blood. Pure blood. The purest magickal blood there was.

But it wasn't possible. How in the world would they get some? And why abuse such a beautiful creature?

Cinder spread her fingers and wiped them over a corn stalk. It shimmered, then the color returned to its leaves, and they fanned out, bright and emerald as they should have been.

Damn whoever had done it. As soon as the contest was over, she was going to find out, and make sure they paid for such a desecration.

She curled her magick in tight, then spread it out over her crops. The plants shimmered and slowly came back to life. The use of so much magick pulled in her veins, making her light headed.

The bell rang. Five minutes. She ran to Olivia and grabbed her by the arm.

"Unicorn blood. It's unicorn blood."

Olivia's eyebrows drew together. "I... I don't know what to do."

"You can't cleanse it. It's pure already. Too pure for the plants. You need to corrupt them. In corrupting them, the unicorn blood will cleanse and strengthen them. Making them better."

Olivia shook her head. "I don't understand."

"It's all right. You don't have to. You just need to kill the plants."

Cinder glanced around at the other frantic contestants. They'd begun to gather in groups, throwing random magick at the crops.

"I... I don't know how." Tears welled in Olivia's eyes and she glanced over her shoulder toward the gate. "M... mother's going to send me away."

"No." Cinder grabbed Olivia's hand. "She isn't."

Cinder pulled all of her magick tight inside. Visualizing every single plant in Olivia's section, she threw her hands out with Olivia's just as the bell rang. Magick burst from Olivia's fingertips in a spray of bright red light, flying over the entire valley.

She cried out in fright and grabbed onto Cinder. The magick drained from Cinder quicker than water from a broken spout. Cinder's vision blurred and then her knees buckled. As if the magick had been sucked out of her by a giant straw she went completely numb and her entire body began to shake.

"Cinder. Cinder are you all right?" Olivia's face swam in and out of view.

"I'm... Lady Rowena," she managed.

Olivia shook her head. "I see through your magick. I know it's you."

Cinder shook her head and tried to get to her feet, but fell to the ground once more. The red stone necklace at Olivia's throat pulsed with life. For a split second she swore she saw her own white magick floating and swirling inside the red gem before it disappeared and the stone went dark.

Cinder clutched at the necklace trying to pull it from Olivia's throat. She needed to get it off her sister.

Livy grabbed her hand. "Stop, Cinder. You're going to break it."

All around gasps sounded. Bleary-eyed Cinder turned and looked over the valley. They'd cured every single plant.

Rome, his father, and grandmother all headed down to the gate.

"Are you sure this was a good idea?" his father asked Phinneaus, for the fourth time in an hour.

"I took care of everything myself, your majesty."

"What exactly did you do to the valley?" he asked.

Phinneaus clapped the king on the shoulder. "It's an old family spell."

As the gate opened, there was a bright flash of red light, which made Rome cover his eyes.

"What was that?" he asked.

His grandmother shook her head. "I don't know."

The gate pushed open, and they looked on as every

plant in the valley sprung back to life. The crowd that had gathered cheered and clapped.

Rome strode out to meet the collection of contestants who stood both baffled and nervous.

"*Voonda*! You all did it," the king cried. "Amazing."

"No," came a voice from the back. "It was her." Someone pointed to the left. The women moved away leaving only Olivia and Lady Rowena standing in front.

"She did it." Lady Rowena pushed Olivia forward gently. "She fixed the entire valley."

Olivia looked back at Lady Rowena, conflicted.

"Really?" said the king. "The whole valley?"

"I... I..." Olivia's cheeks flushed.

"No," someone shouted. "She cheated!"

"Cheated?" asked the king. "How did she cheat?"

Lady Drusilla, strode forward, head high, proud as a phoenix.

"I don't know," she said. "But right before the valley exploded with magick, Lady Rowena was holding her hand."

Rome's gaze shifted to Lady Rowena. Her face was waxen and pale and a bead of sweat trickled down the side of her hairline. She trembled and swayed on the spot like she was about to throw up.

"Is this true, Lady Rowena?" the king asked.

"I merely comforted the girl before she undertook such an enormous spell. Nothing more." She wiped at the sweat with the back of her hand and her eyes connected with Rome's.

A niggling of recognition hit him. Something he couldn't place his finger on, but was there nonetheless.

"Do you have any proof?" the king asked.

Drusilla looked around the group. "You all saw it right? You all saw what happened. It was Lady Rowena's magick combined with Lady Olivia's that fixed the plants. They cheated and did it together."

The group shook their heads and murmured disagreement.

Phinneaus stepped forward and put his arm around Olivia. "My niece doesn't lie. If she says she created the feat, then she did."

The unsettled look on Olivia's face didn't miss Rome's inspection.

"Lady Rowena, did you help Lady Olivia?" asked the king.

Rowena pulled herself up as tall as she could. "I did not."

"It's settled then," said the king. "Lady Olivia is the winner. She will dine with Prince Rome tonight at the feast."

The crowd erupted into cheers except for Drusilla who stormed off cursing like a bar wench.

Olivia didn't smile either as her cheeks flamed. Lady Sabine rushed to her daughter's side, hugged her tight, then whisked her away.

The rest of the women and onlookers headed toward the castle as well, but Rome's gaze stayed fastened on Lady Rowena. Her brother moved to her side and put his arm around her waist, holding her up. He said something, but she shook her head, and they stood for a moment, neither moving. Her brother smoothed her hair and his arm flexed from the way Rowena leaned on him heavily.

He'd only seen one other be that taxed before. When Cinder had mixed her magick with Stil months previous. She too had used so much magick that she'd barely been able to stand, much like Lady Rowena's current state.

Rome looked at his father and grandmother as they headed for the castle and then made his way toward Rowena and Erik. "Are you feeling all right, Lady Rowena."

She stiffened and straightened as best she could, pushing from her brother's chest. She gave him a polite smile and inclined her head. "Yes. Thank you, your highness. Just a bit winded is all."

"Can I get you something? A healer perhaps?"

"No!" The words came out harsh, and Lady Rowena cleared her throat, then threw on a weak smile. "What I meant to say was, I'm sure I'll be satisfactory after I eat and take a nap. I forgot to have breakfast this morning and in this warm weather I'm just feeling a bit overexerted. Quite embarrassing I must admit."

His eyes locked on her brother's and Rome extended his hand. "Rome. I'm sorry, but I've forgotten your name."

Her brother shook Rome's hand. It was surprisingly strong for a fae and he could swear it was heavier than it appeared. "Erik."

"Ah yes, that's right." Erik was quite tall for a fae and broad as well, something Rome had missed earlier. His deep brown eyes stared at Rome unblinkingly, sending an uneasy feeling through Rome's gut.

"I really should get my sister to her room," Erik finally said.

"Of course." Rome waved them on. "But before you go. Lady Rowena, I wonder if I might apologize for my behavior the other night. I was not quite myself, and it was uncalled for."

She licked her pale lips. "Yes, it was quite uncalled for."

Rome bowed. "My sincerest apologies to you and your brother."

Erik nodded. "Apology accepted. If you will excuse us."

"Yes, yes. Again, I'm sorry. Please, go. See to Lady Rowena."

The brother and sister headed to the castle; with Erik practically carrying Lady Rowena, she leaned on him so hard. She was strong, of that there was no doubt. Proud as well. But what he didn't understand was why she was lying. Anxiety mixed inside Rome and a million questions sprung to mind. He wanted so desperately to rush after Rowena and question her at length. What had happened in the field? Why was she so shaky? What was her connection to Olivia? And why hadn't she wanted to be tended to by a healer?

Of all the questions that swarmed in his mind one question had been answered quite clearly. Olivia may have won the challenge, but she wasn't the one who healed the fields.

CHAPTER TWELVE

R ome stayed in his room the rest of the day, trying
to piece together what had happened outside the
gate. The magick done had been a tremendous
effort. He only knew two of people capable of pulling off
such a feat. But neither had been out in the valley that
morning.

By the time he was readying for dinner, he was positive
Lady Rowena had performed the magick- and he was ready
to confront her about it. What he didn't understand was,
why she'd helped Olivia. That too was a question he was
determined to get answered.

HE SAT AT THE HEAD TABLE, OVERLOOKING THE REST OF THE
dining hall. Olivia and her mother sat at the table next to
him. It took every ounce of restraint Rome possessed to

keep from asking Lady Sabine why she had not allowed Cinder to attend the banquet.

He scanned the onlookers for Lady Rowena and found her clustered amongst her brother and several other eligible men from the kingdom. For some reason the sight of her with so many eligible suitors made jealousy prickle through him. As if sensing his gaze she glanced Rome's way and gave him a curt nod.

She wore a pretty pink frock with a matching flower in her dark hair. Her coloring had returned but fatigue burdened her eyes.

"So, Rome," said Lady Sabine. "How are you enjoying the competition so far?"

"It's quite eye-opening." He looked to her and then back at Lady Rowena, who had gone back to pushing food around her plate.

"I'm sure it is. To see so many young women, vibrant and youthful, all vying for your hand in marriage. But my Olivia was quite incredible today, wasn't she?"

"Indeed." He looked to Olivia and smiled. "Livy is a sweet girl."

Olivia blushed and looked down at the table. Lady Sabine pushed her fingers under Olivia's chin and tipped her head up.

"Tell me, Livy," said Rome. "How is your sister? I haven't spotted her at any of the competitions. Surely you don't have the apothecary open."

Lady Sabine's nose twitched at the mention of Cinder. "Unfortunately yes. We do what we must to help those in need. Just because we are fortunate enough to be part of this competition doesn't stop others from falling ill I'm afraid. I offered for her to come with us, but Cinder said she couldn't possibly turn her back on her customers. Not even to come watch her half sister. Personally I think she's just jealous that she was not allowed to enter the contest."

Olivia's gaze darted to the corner of the room and then back to Rome.

"Have you not seen her lately? I know she was most distressed to hear that you'd stopped by the other night, but she didn't get to see you."

Was she? She hadn't seemed upset by it the last he'd spoken to her.

"We spoke, yes. Unfortunately, our parting words were not ones befitting old friends."

"Cinder has always had a wicked tongue and a nasty temper," said Lady Sabine. "I blame myself for indulging her so much as a child. Her father, rest his soul, and I would have done better to put our foot down a bit more."

Chills ran up Rome's arm, making his hair stand on end. He knew all too well the kind of indulgences Lady Sabine had offered Cinder in her upbringing, and none of them had benefited Cinder in the least. He wondered for a moment if the woman actually believed the words she spoke, or if lies just rolled off her tongue like poison, in hopes of infecting all those within earshot.

"Cinder has never been anything but kind and generous to me, mother," said Olivia. "She works hard at the apothecary to keep us fed and clothed, giving of her own magick each and every day without a word of complaint. I only wish I was half as good a person as Cinder is."

Lady Sabine's eyes flashed, but she tittered. "Oh, my dear sweet child. I am glad that I've been able to shield you from the worst moments of your sister's temper. I'll be even gladder when you win this tournament and we move here, away from her."

Rome choked on a piece of meat and had to gulp several swallows of water to get it down. Olivia smacked him on the back lightly.

He cleared his throat. "So, you would want to live here? In the palace?" he croaked.

Lady Sabine gave a broad smile. "Well of coursssse. I'll have grandchildren that need to be loved and cared for. Don't you agree, Prince Rome?"

Lady Sabine's occasional speech impediment set Rome's teeth on edge.

"My mother raised me until her death," he replied. "And then my father and tutors took on the job."

Lady Sabine's smile cracked a fraction before she turned back to her food.

It was a lie of course. His mother and grandmother had raised him, but he wasn't about to tell Lady Sabine that. Not that he'd ever marry Olivia, but if he did one thing would be made quite clear – Lady Sabine would *not* be living in the castle. If it was up to Rome she wouldn't even be residing in Ville DeFee. The entire kingdom would be a better place if he could just throw the vile creature out the city gates and tell her never to return. But that was not his place.

. . .

ROME AND OLIVIA SAT IN SILENCE FOR THE REST OF THE meal. A million questions whirled in his mind about Cinder, filling him to the brim, like an over poured cup. But with Lady Sabine so close, there was no way for him to ask the questions that had been bombarding him all day.

By the end of dessert, Rome could take no more. When the servants cleared the tables, he hurried Olivia onto the dance floor.

"So tell me," he said, as he twirled her around. "How did you find out what had been used to kill the crops?" Rome kept a pleasant smile planted on his face and looked amongst the crowd for Lady Rowena but she was nowhere in sight.

"Oh they weren't killed," she replied. "They were cleansed."

He glanced at Olivia. "Cleansed?"

"Someone sprinkled unicorn blood on them." Olivia smiled.

All feeling drained from his body. Unicorn blood? That was treacherous demon magick to use such a sacred animal's blood. No one had even seen a unicorn in over a hundred years. In the war with the daemons they'd all but wiped out the last herd using the blood for their foul magick. How could his father allow such a thing?

Rome turned Olivia and they headed the other direction. Again he looked for Rowena but couldn't spot her. "And... and how did you figure that out?"

"I... well... I... uh..." Olivia's face drooped and she scanned the crowded room. "Lady Rowena told me."

Rome stopped dancing. He knew it.

Another couple bumped into them, and Rome led Olivia from the floor. He needed answers.

They walked out a side door, to the balcony overlooking the city. Olivia rushed to the railing, sucking in deep gulps of air.

"No. No. No," she whispered to herself. "I shouldn't have said that. She'll kill me for telling." Sobs wracked her for several minutes before Rome joined her and offered a handkerchief.

Rome looked through the door to the dance floor and several of the contestants peered out at him. He waved and then magicked the door shut in their faces.

Finally Olivia regained control of herself. "I'm sorry, your highness." She blew her nose into the small white cloth. "I didn't want to do it. I didn't mean to lie, but she made me."

"Lady Sabine?"

"No." Olivia shook her head. "Lady Rowena. My mother said she would send me away if I didn't win today, so Lady Rowena helped me. She let me take credit, to save me."

"But why, Olivia? Why would Lady Rowena do that for you? Do you know her? Are you friends?"

Olivia bit her lip. Her eyes darted all over the balcony and finally inside the ballroom where the guests continued to dance. She shook her head. "It's not my place to tell. You have to ask her yourself."

Yes. Answers were exactly what he wanted. "I think I will."

Rome marched back to the door, leading to the ballroom, and opened it. He leaned to the guard on the right side. "Find Lady Rowena and bring her to me please."

The guard nodded and stepped down to the dance floor. Rome closed the door again and walked back to Olivia.

He took her squishy hand in his and kissed the back of it. "I would never let you be sent away, Livy. I promise you that. Neither would your sister. Cinder loves you. She would do anything to protect you and keep you—" He stopped. *Hands on her hips, she blew her hair from her eyes.* His heart raced, and a trickle of recognition flowed over his mind. Stupid. How could he have been so stupid? The way she'd treated him. Her anger at how he'd treated Lady Rowena. The reason he hadn't been able to locate her. Why he hadn't seen her in the crowds, or at the dinners. It was because she'd been there all along.

"Cinder."

Olivia's eyes grew wide. "I... I..."

Rome squeezed Olivia's hand tightly. "Lady Rowena is Cinder, isn't she?"

Olivia's gaze moved to the door. "I should go. If mother hears me—"

Before Rome could protest, Olivia dashed across the balcony and around the corner, to a set of steps that led down to the floor below.

Lady Rowena stepped onto the balcony at the same moment, and she scanned the area. "Where's Lady Olivia?" Her gaze hardened and she advanced on Rome. "What did you do to her?"

Rome held up his hands. "Nothing. I didn't do anything." He nodded to the guard, who closed the door to the ballroom. "I swear. Livy is unmolested and left of her own accord."

Could it be? Could this beautiful woman, with dark hair and a tan complexion, that looked nothing like his Cinder, actually be her?

Lady Rowena nodded and planted her hands on her hips. "Was there something you wanted your highness or did you just call me out here to gape at me?"

"No... I..." It was her. It had to be. How had he been so blind? The mannerisms. The way she moved. The way she was able to work his nerves so easily. Even her tone of voice matched that of Cinder. He'd been blinded by what his eyes saw and hadn't listened with his heart. It's why he'd been strangely attracted to her all along. The infuriating way she dismissed him and her words at dinner together, all of it had been a ruse. A way to throw him off track so he wouldn't suspect. And she'd almost made it. She'd almost succeeded. If only she hadn't helped Olivia. It was her one weakness and her greatest asset at the same time, always had been. Her kindness toward those who couldn't help themselves.

What he wanted to do was kiss her. His Cinder. No wonder she'd been so angry with him. She hadn't just heard about what'd happened with Lady Rowena; she'd seen it first hand.

"I wanted to apologize again for my behavior," he finally said.

"Not needed. You apologized already." Her eyes narrowed. "Aren't you supposed to be spending time with Lady Olivia tonight?"

He needed to keep his wits about him. "I was, but she said that you might be able to clear something up for me."

"And that would be…"

He took a step closer. "She said you were the one who discovered how to cure the unicorn blood."

Lady Rowena's licked her lips. "She told you that, did she?"

He took another step. "And how did you even figure out what it was that had infected the plants?"

Her eyebrows furrowed. "I broke off a leaf and saw silver liquid dripping. It smelled like blood."

He stepped closer still and she backed up a step. "What's the matter, Lady Rowena? You weren't frightened of me the other night."

Her expression grew angry. "Who said I'm afraid of you?" She blew a stray hair from her face.

There she was. Rome stepped closer and Lady Rowena stepped back. They continued their dance until she bumped into the castle wall.

"What are you doing?" she demanded. "You just said you were sorry for the other night. Was that a lie? If you toy with me again, I'll have you know, I won't be so kind this time. You've seen what I am capable of."

He stepped into her space, his body inches from hers. Upon closer inspection, he could see it. All the ways Lady Rowena resembled Cinder. The way her hair lay to the same side when pulled up into a comb. The way she batted her lashes, three times, when she got excited. The scent of mint and jasmine that followed her from her apothecary. Even the small bow in the curve of her upper lip was the same. Little things. Overlookable things– for someone that hadn't known her as long as he had.

He raised his hand to stroke her cheek, and she shied away.

"What are you doing?" Her voice came out as a shallow whisper.

He ran his knuckles down her face to her neck. Then he leaned in and sniffed her hair. Her breasts heaved against her bodice as she sucked in a ragged breath.

"Cinder," he whispered in her ear. "I know it's you."

"You... you mistake me for someone else, sir. Maybe you've had too much to drink again."

"Cinder." His voice came out more commanding. He kissed the pointed apex of her ear, then pulled back to lock eyes with her. "Take off the magick so I can see you."

Her eyes glowed with fear. "I... I'm not her."

Rome slipped his hands around her waist and drew her close. She stiffened but didn't protest. He leaned in and brushed his lips against her cheek. "The glamour is a good one. But I know the feel of you. The smell of you. Your soul. I see you in there, behind the façade. Show me."

"I..." Her breath caught as he licked down the side of her neck to her exposed collarbone.

His body responded to the salty taste of her skin. He kissed over the hollow of her throat. "Show me."

She tangled her fingers in his hair, making his arousal spike. He wanted her. Needed her. Cinder.

She drew his head up and went to kiss him, but he pulled away.

Her hooded eyes were pools of desire.

"Let me see your face," he said again. "Your face. Not this mask you've created."

Conflict battered her features for a moment, and then the air around her shimmered, and the image of Lady Rowena fell away.

"Rome." His name died on her lips as he crushed his mouth down on hers. Her tongue swirled with his, and he grabbed onto her. She was his. The one he'd always wanted.

He ran his hands up her sides and over her breasts making her moan in his mouth. He wanted her. He needed her, but she pushed him away.

She glanced around. "Not here. I can't be seen."

He grabbed her hand and pulled her along the balcony to a set of steps by the edge. He was ushering her down when a rustle of leaves caught his attention. He looked over the balcony and saw no one, but the hairs on his neck prickled just before he continued down to the room below.

CINDER'S HEART THUNDERED AS ROME PULLED HER INTO A study, and then opened a secret panel and dragged her down a dark, narrow corridor. Her heels clicked on the floor, and she tripped in the dark.

"Come on," he said.

"I dropped my left shoe." She searched around in the pitch black, but Rome slid behind her and helped her to her feet. He backed her into the wall and planted his lips on hers hard.

Tremors of desire lit her body up like candlelight.

"*Melway Yanzeer*. Forget the shoe," he said. "I'll buy you a castle full of shoes after we're married."

Married. He still wanted to marry her.

He locked his fingers in hers again, and they took off, albeit slower this time. At the end of a hallway, Rome turned, counted thirty steps, then patted the wall. There was a small click and a passage opened into a dark green room with gold accents.

He helped her through the opening and closed a portrait behind them. He barely gave her time to look around before he spun her and wrapped his arms around her again.

"This is your room," she said.

He kissed her. "Yes."

"It's different than I remember." Nervousness lodged in her stomach. "What if someone comes in and finds me here?"

He flicked his fingers at the door and it locked. "They won't."

He kissed her again, the scent of his cologne making her knees shake.

"Cinder I want you. I want you here in my room. In my bed. In my life. Forever."

She swallowed hard. She wanted this too. Gods knew she wanted this. Wanted him. Wanted to be his.

"Say it. Tell me you'll be my wife." He held her face in his hands.

As Lady Rowena, she'd won both of the first two contests. There was no one else that could take her place as the winner. Everyone else had been disqualified in the last round when they'd failed to complete the task. Technically the contest was over. He had the right to choose her.

"Yes."

His lips crushed hers again, and his hands traversed the back of her dress. He unlaced the top, and she ran her fingers over the buttons of his doublet, undoing them one by one. He threw his coat to the floor and stripped off his tunic. Cinder finished with the ties on her dress and stopped. Her gaze raked up and down his lean, muscular torso. How long had it been since she'd seen him without a shirt? Was she ready to see more? To have him see more of her? All of her?

He stalked to her and cupped her face. Kissing her gently he pushed her gown off her shoulders. If she was going to stop him, now was the moment. Instead she slipped her arms out of her dress and let it fall down to her waist. It caught on her hips, and Rome shimmied it to the floor, leaving her wearing nothing but her pantaloons. The cool air pebbled her skin and made her shiver.

Rome flicked his fingers and the logs in the fireplace lit.

Cinder smiled to herself, she'd taught him that trick.

His hands skimmed up her legs to the flat of her stomach and back up, over her breasts, making them tingle. He kissed her again as his large warm palms molded over her breasts pinching her nipples and making them stand at attention. Desire shot straight to her core and she wanted nothing more than to feel his hands all over her body.

She licked her lips as he picked her up and carried her to his bed. He pulled back the deep green comforter, and she slid between the soft sheets. She trembled, and fought the urge to shield herself from his eyes. She'd never gone this far before. Never been naked with a man before, or in one's bed. She'd never done any of the things they were about to do. She hoped that she didn't disappoint him.

Rome opened the drawer of his nightstand and pulled out the beautiful, light blue diamond ring. Without a word he slipped it on her ring finger, then kissed it.

"You're mine now," he said.

Cinder flicked her fingers, and a golden band appeared on Rome's hand. "And you are mine."

He slid in beside her, his body looming next to hers. He caressed her breasts, in turn as he kissed down her throat. She moaned as vibrations spread across her body. He ran his tongue down between her breasts and then sucked one into his mouth.

Cinder grabbed onto his hair as his palm skimmed between her legs and he rubbed her through the thin fabric.

"Rome." She could barely get his name out through the jumble of emotions and sensations rushing through her.

He kissed down the side of her neck. "Yes, my sweet."

She wanted to make sure he knew. That he understood what they were about to do.

"Rome, I've never…"

"I know." He kissed her mouth again, his fingers rubbing her most sensitive spot. "That is what makes this all the more delicious. I will be your first, and your last. Together we will learn and explore everything about each other. And only I will know the secrets your body holds."

She grabbed onto his shoulder and moved against his hand. She wanted him to show her the way. To explore everything fantasy they could possibly entertain. To know him in a way that no other fae ever would. To be his in every way.

Desire spread through her like a warm bath. It branched out and settled in her core, making her body hum.

She rubbed at him through his breeches. He dropped his head to her neck and groaned.

"Cinder. I've wanted you for so long."

"Years," she whispered.

"Decades."

She untied his breeches and pushed them off, setting him free. He lay long and hot against her hip, then rolled over and kicked off his pants. She peeled her bloomers from her skin, and he covered her body with his.

He kissed her lightly as his fingers trailed down to her core and rubbed at her skin. He kissed her and rubbed at her until her body grew slick and then slowly he dipped his fingers inside her. Cinder's back arched, and her eyes shut as a flood of need crashed down on her. This was what she'd always wanted. To love and be loved by Rome. Her soulmate.

He removed his fingers and pressed his hard length against her. She stiffened instinctively.

"Relax." He kissed her forehead, her eyelids, and her cheeks, and she willed her body to unwind. He pressed against her harder, moving slowly, building the friction between them. She concentrated on his breathing and let her legs go slack. Slowly he circled her, kissing her throat and licking up to the apex of her ear. With small, gentle thrusts he inched his way inside her until she shuddered and then he was in.

"Are you all right?" His eyes found hers, full of desire mingled with concern.

"I'm fine." She kissed him, and he began moving again. His body pumped and kneaded against hers in a beautiful, seductive rhythm.

She dug her nails deep into his back muscles, and he quaked. His head fell to her shoulder, and he rocked inside her faster.

"Cinder. Oh my Cinder."

A tremor of desire skimmed her skin. He said her name again and within seconds his rhythm increased and he called to her so loudly, she feared the entire castle would hear.

She covered his mouth with hers as he cried out and his body shook above her. He tensed all over, his breath halting before starting again a moment later.

His kisses languished on her mouth as his rhythm slowed, then stopped. He brushed the hair from her face, a bead of sweat trickling down from his hairline.

He looked deep into her eyes and smiled. "I love you, Cinderelle Gillece."

"I love you too, Roman Geoffrey."

He kissed her again, and then rolled onto his side, pulling her to him. They lay in each other's arms for several minutes, neither one speaking. After decades of loving him. Helping him. Spending time with him. It had all been worth it. Waiting for him had been worth it. He held her close and ran his fingers up and down her arm. She wanted nothing more than to have him inside her again but in that moment she suddenly became self-conscious of what they'd done.

Wetness slicked her legs and she looked down. Embarrassment flooded her, and she flicked her hand. The sheets cleaned themselves in a flash of magick.

Rome chuckled. "Cinder, my sweet. You don't ever need to be embarrassed with me. We've loved each other too long."

"I just..." She wasn't sure what to say. She'd known what would happen the first time, being a virgin, but it was still humiliating.

He tipped her chin and kissed her, running his tongue over the seam of her lips and coaxing them apart. "I love that I was your first."

"My only."

He smiled, and his hand moved down her body to slide between her thighs once more.

"Then let me show you what we have to look forward to, for the rest of our lives."

Cinder shuddered, grabbing onto the sheets. He rubbed circles around her sensitive nub making her moan. She fought to thinks straight but all she could think of was his body inside hers again.

"Rome. What are you doing?" she panted.

"Showing you what you did for me." His head dipped, and he flicked his tongue down her neck and over the swells of her breasts to her nipples. Tingles skittered across her flesh, and her skin puckered. He pulled her ripe bud into his mouth and bit it playfully.

She raked her fingers through his hair as a nexus of

pleasure centered in her core. She pulled his hair hard and growl of pleasure escaped his chest.

"Cinder, I want you again."

She nodded, unable to do anything more.

He slid inside her, warm and slow. Her body arched to meet his and he planted his hips on hers. He cradled her neck with his palm and pulled her breast back into his mouth. A slow, steady rhythm built between them. His body slid down over hers, rubbing and sending shockwaves of pleasure up her spine. Her thighs warmed, and tingles skittered up the insides of her legs.

She entwined her legs with his and gripped his firm backside. Lifting her pelvis she pulled him into her, harder and deeper. A pulsing need grew in her core. Soon Rome had to release her breast and grab the headboard for support. Their bodies moved quicker as the pulsing wound tightly inside her, like her magick.

"Cinder." He kissed her hard. "Melt for me. Let yourself go."

She relaxed her mind and concentrated on her body. Rome kissed her again and something inside clicked. Her muscles pulled tight and then everything drifted away except the cry in her throat and the waves of ecstasy that flooded over her, drenching her in utter bliss.

Rome called her name as again he came.

Completely spent, she pulled his lips to hers and kissed him hard.

He was hers. All hers.

ROME CRADLED CINDER IN HIS ARMS AND COVERED THEM both with his sheets and comforter. He skimmed her arm with his fingers, unable to believe that she was finally in his bed.

He thought of all the wasted moments, days, years he'd spent alone without her in his arms. He'd been a fool. But every moment with her, moving forward, was one to be cherished. He'd never waste time with her again.

"Rome." She swirled his light dusting of chest hair through her fingertips.

He hugged her tighter. "Yes, my darling."

"We uh… I mean, you didn't…" She cleared her throat.

He chuckled and lifted her chin to kiss the tip of her nose. "If I'd known how coy and shy taking you into my bed would make you, I'd have done it ages ago."

She bit his rib making him jump.

"I didn't what?" He laughed.

"Use anything. Cover yourself."

His laughter died away as her words struck him. "Uh… well, no. I mean, it's not like I do this every day."

She looked up into his face, her eyes a mask of concern. "What if I get pregnant?"

He shrugged. "Tomorrow we'll be wed, and no one will know the difference."

"What if your father won't allow us?"

He smiled. "It doesn't matter what he wants."

"And why is that?"

"Because we have a fairy grandmother on our side."

CHAPTER THIRTEEN

Cinder rolled over and felt the spot next to her, but it was empty. Glancing around she found the fireplace still lit and a small tray of food waiting on a table, but no Rome.

She stretched and yawned. Where had he gone? She scratched her head and patted down her unruly curls, feeling more refreshed than she ever had, despite the little sleep she'd received. Laying back down and buried her face in his pillow taking in the scent of his body. She spotted the large diamond ring on her finger and smiled. She was his, truly his.

They'd spent hours making love and even more talking about and planning for the future. They'd made contingencies for everything. They both agreed that the contest was no more and though she'd cheated to get in, she was the winner at that point. But even if his father didn't agree with that assessment the contest was null and void and Rome was free to marry who he wished- and he'd made it plain to her that no matter what it took he would not be bullied by his father any longer.

She'd rarely seen Rome that assertive before and for the first time she saw that he truly would make a great king if he continued to be both judicious and follow his heart. In that way she was grateful for the contest. He'd learned from it, and so had she.

The large portrait on the wall in the sitting area swung inward and Cinder sat up and smiled.

"I thought-" She stopped short as Phinneaus stepped into the room, carrying her shoe.

Cinder gathered up the covers in a vague attempt at modesty and scanned the room for her dress.

Phinneaus spotted her. "Niece, I came as quick as I could."

Niece? Never once had Phinneaus called her niece.

Guilt and embarrassment heated her skin as she fought to process what was going on. "Where's Rome?"

Phinneaus set her shoe on the coffee table and gathered up her clothes.

"With his father. He told the king everything. His Majesty is most pleased. He, Prince Rome, and the queen mother are preparing for the wedding as we speak."

Cinder blew the hair from her face and watched Phinneaus as he picked up her pantaloons and walked toward the bed. "Pleased? Really?"

Phinneaus gave her a broad smile. "Yes. When he learned what you had done, and the lengths you had gone to so you could be with the prince, he knew that he'd been wrong, and you were meant to be with Rome. No one can deny the power of your magick. The Queen Mother herself stood up for you on your behalf."

Rome had gone to his father without her? She supposed that was best, but why hadn't he, at least, let her know he was going? Probably because he knew she'd insist on going with him. Again he was making very wise decisions.

Phinneaus set Cinder's clothes on the bed. "I'm sending word to your stepmother, and I'm sure she and Olivia will be here to meet you within the hour, up in the bridal tower."

She stared at Phinneaus, trying to grab ahold of the words being spoken. She was to be wed. The ceremony was already being prepared. There was so much for her to do- "Bridal tower?"

"Surely you've heard of it? The highest tower in the castle? It's reserved specifically for brides and their family. It hasn't been used since Rome's parents were wed. A beautiful room that overlooks the entire kingdom."

Phinneaus walked to the other side of the room and looked out the window. "It's such a lovely day for a wedding," he said.

Everything moved faster than she had anticipated. She'd expected to wake and spend the morning with Rome, then possibly go see his grandmother and finally his father. She'd expected a bit of a fight and then the afternoon awaiting the king's decision and possibly by that evening another frank discussion with the outcome hopefully being in their favor. But none of that was happening. Instead she was being shoved out of bed and into the bridal tower.

"Tell me," asked Phinneaus. "How did you figure out the crop challenge?"

With him looking out the window Cinder took the chance of getting dressed. Cinder slipped on her chemise, then grabbed her dress. "By the smell."

"The smell?"

She slid her dress over her head and reached behind her to try and lace it up as much as possible. For the first time she wished she had someone to help her. She gave up trying and flicked her fingers at the back of her dress. The laces did themselves as she sucked in a deep breath.

"I know what every poison, mushroom, and mold in Fairelle smell like. But the leaves didn't smell like any of them. They smelled like blood."

Phinneaus chuckled. "Ingenious. I knew you were the one."

Cinder straightened her dress and tugged it into place. She finally stood and flicked her fingers over the dress smoothing it down. "The one for what?"

He peeked over his shoulder, then walked toward Cinder. "Why, the one from the prophecy of course."

"Prophecy?"

Phinneaus threw her a broad smile that reminded her of too much of Sabine. "Didn't your father teach you the lore of Fairelle?"

"Well, yes, but..." She wracked her brain remembering the words of the prophecy. "I'm not the one from the prophecy."

"Of course you are." Phinneaus wrapped his arm

around Cinder's shoulder. "Now, come on, we must hurry." He took her arm and led her to the picture passageway.

Cinder's head spun. Too fast. It was all moving way too fast.

"Why can't we use the hall?" she asked.

"Because Prince Rome could be anywhere and we don't want him seeing you before the wedding."

She slid from his grasp trying to figure out how to keep a hold on the situation. "I think mayhaps I should wait for Rome and speak to him before I go."

Phinneaus' face contorted into a pout. "But the Queen Mother is already awaiting you with her dressmaker and the royal jeweler. We have a scant amount of time to get this all pulled together, my dear. You don't want to keep everyone waiting do you?"

It was happening. Really happening. She was getting married. To Rome. Why was she fighting it? What did it matter that it was happening faster than she anticipated, it was happening. It was what she'd been dreaming of for decades. "No, of course I don't. But I should get my shoes."

"Don't worry about them. We'll have beautiful new ones made for you within the hour." Phinneaus took Cinder's hand once more and urged her through the hole into the darkened passage.

She flicked her fingers, lighting the dozens of sconces on the walls. It was a clean stone hallway that went on for a great length. Phinneaus closed the portrait and the opening sealed shut and blended completely into the stone wall.

She followed Phinneaus as he led her away from Rome's room and down into the depths of the castle.

The stale air grew thick around them and a niggling of anxiety traipsed over her. What if the king had only consented to their marriage because he too thought that she was the one from the prophecy.

"Remind me again, what the prophecy says. It's been so long since I've heard it," she said.

Phinneaus took Cinder by the arm at a fork in the passage and proceeded in a different direction than she and Rome had come from the night before.

They took a turn and Cinder lit more sconces.

"Let me see," said Phinneaus. "After the first, the second the third, the enemy will pull back. They'll work in the dark, with the fae they'll hide and await their moment of attack. Advantage they'll take, of the weak and the proud, and all goodness they will destroy. Until the one girl, who answers to none, catches them in their ploy."

Cinder's mind churned the words over and over in her head. That couldn't possibly be her. "But I don't know anything about an enemy," she said out loud.

"You will. I'm sure, in time, you will. And when you figure it out, you'll save us all."

Cinder's gut twisted. Marrying Rome was one thing. Saving all of her kingdom was quite another. She wasn't sure she was ready for such a thing.

They came to a dead end; Phinneaus opened a panel and stepped out. He held out his hand for Cinder and she took it, shielding her eyes from the bright morning light. They stood in a narrow hallway where the stone showed many years of dust and neglect. She looked around unable to place where it was she stood within the castle.

"Are you sure this is the way?" she asked. "It looks like no one has been up here in ages."

Phinneaus laughed. "Well, of course, no one has been up here in years. The last bride was Rome's mother as I said."

A slight breeze chilled her skin as it blew through the hallway. Cinder rubbed her arms. They must be high up for it to be so cold. She walked to a nearby window and looked out. For the first time she saw the mountains behind Ville DeFee. They stood tall like giant centennials protecting the kingdom from the rear, but also feeling like they were closing in around her.

Her breath caught and suddenly it became hard to breathe. She leaned on the window for support. If she went up to that room and put on a white dress and married Rome she'd be the princess. But not just the princess, the one that everyone expected to save them from evil. Being princess was one thing. Being a savior was something else entirely.

Phinneaus started up a long winding staircase and looked back when she didn't follow him. "Are you coming, my dear? I'd hate to break with tradition."

"I… I think maybe I need to take a minute to think this all through."

Phinneaus walked back to meet her. "You want to marry Rome don't you?"

"Yes," she admitted vehemently.

"Then what's to think about? You didn't disguise yourself and win the contests only to give your virtue to him, and then back out, did you?"

"No. Of course not. It's just… What will everyone

think? And what if you are wrong? What if I'm not the one from the prophecy that everyone is expecting me to be? How can I possibly save the kingdom from destruction when I'm... just me."

"It doesn't matter what they think. The others were disqualified last night when you were the only one who was able to complete the task." Phinneaus smiled and squeezed Cinder's arm. "It's over. You won. And as for being the one from the prophecy, I shouldn't have said that. I was just very hopeful for you. I didn't mean to cause you distress. Besides everything is fine with Ville DeFee. No one is knocking down the gates. There are no wars that we've been alerted to. It could be years or even longer before we are affected by what might be happening in the world of men." He stroked her cheek and then kissed it. "Now come on. Let's get you ready." He ascended the circular staircase again and was soon out of sight.

He was right. It could be years, decades even before the prophecy came upon them. Maybe by then the real girl would be found.

She was being ridiculous. It was pre-wedding jitters that's all. She was nervous and letting her mind run away with her. She wanted to marry Rome. That was what she wanted. They'd decided the night before that together they could get through anything, even if it meant having to leave the kingdom to be together. If that was true then surely they could deal with anything else that might be thrown their way.

Curiosity burrowed in Cinder's gut as she gazed at the staircase. She squared her shoulders and shook her head.

She needed to let all doubts go and focus on what she truly wanted. To be Rome's wife.

Striding to the staircase, she followed Phinneaus round and around until her legs grew wobbly from lack of breakfast and a night in Rome's bed. Higher and higher they ascended.

"Just a few more steps," Phinneaus called.

Cinder made it around the last bend to find him standing by an old wooden door.

"What did you say was the purpose of this tower?" she panted. "To make a bride pass out?"

Phinneaus chuckled and opened the door, allowing Cinder to step inside.

"It is the highest tower of the castle. The brazier in the center is to warn the kingdom of danger. But, as the bridal tower, it is so every Princess-to-be can look over the entire land and see what it is that she's working for before she marries."

Cinder's muscles burned from the hike and she sucked in several deep breaths trying to slow her heartbeat.

She walked to the enormous floor to ceiling window and looked out. Ville DeFee. Every street lay below her. Every house. Every building. The array of colors dazzled in the sunlight. She picked out the route to her shop and her house. She followed a child as they skipped past the brewery and the baker's shop. She gazed out to the fields, lush with fruit once more and watched the workers pluck and pick and cut.

She smiled. All of it would be hers in just a few short hours. Once she and Rome were wed she would no longer have to worry about money, or Lady Sabine, or overusing her magick. She would be able to spend her days helping people, and studying the ancient tomes in the royal library, and in bed with her husband. She ran her hand over her belly and wondered if their love making had already begun to root inside her.

She imagined setting up a nursery and tending to their children. Reading to them, teaching them magick, watching as they grew and learned and became strong like their father. Many children. Six, maybe seven. With four sons and three daughters. And Livy would be there with her. Helping her, by her side, and completely out of reach of Lady Sabine.

A niggling started in the back of Cinder's mind and she turned and looked about the room. Phinneaus had said that Elise and several others were waiting for her already, but dust and cobwebs blanketed everything in the space. And no one else was around. A warning bell sounded in her mind, not unlike the warning brazier in the very room she stood. Something wasn't right.

Phinneaus watched her with great curiosity. She honestly couldn't remember the last time she'd seen him so quiet.

She wracked her head for something to say. "The unicorn blood challenge was clever. How did you get the king to agree to it?"

Phinneaus' chest puffed up, and he brushed a speck from the sleeve of his blue robes. "He didn't know what I planned. The whole thing was my idea."

She lifted an eyebrow. "Was it?"

Then it had been Phinneaus who'd killed the unicorn.

That kind of sacrifice was more than illegal in Ville DeFee; it was grounds for banishment. Dark magick was the most horrific of offenses to the fae. Anyone caught using dark magick was feared that they may turn into a dark fae and they were cast out immediately. And one couldn't get much worse than killing a unicorn.

He nodded, tucked his hands deep into his robe and walked around the perimeter of the round room. "You see, in the beginning, I was aiming for Olivia to sit on the throne, but the poor girl just doesn't have it in her. Your magick, however, is unmatched in this kingdom. It was my sister, Sabine, who kept me from coming to you earlier. But now that you'll be the princess I'll be able to spend all the time in the world with you. Teaching you, mentoring you, helping you to fulfill your greatest potential."

"Like you tried to do with Olivia, by giving her the red stone necklace." Cinder swallowed hard. She hadn't meant for the words to come out of her mouth.

He smiled. "That wasn't me who gave her the necklace, it was Sabine. But see how clever you are, you even figured that out."

Cinder tamped down the fear and anger that bubbled within her. All these years she'd looked to Phinneaus like a surrogate father figure and friend. He'd been kind to her when even her stepmother was not. But the vibe that he gave off now had her on edge. Something didn't add up. Could she have been wrong about him all these years? Had it all been an act, a betrayal worse than the pain and disdain Sabine had heaped on her? Was he really worse that

Sabine? Vying the whole time behind the scenes, waiting to take it for himself?

She tread a thin rope with him. She still had no idea why he'd brought her to the tower or what he even wanted from her, save his ludicrous idea of mentoring her. She needed to keep him talking. Get him to incriminate himself.

"And what does it do exactly? The red stone necklace?" she asked.

His face lit up like a child with a shiny bauble. "The red stones themselves are conduits for magick. Created by a mage, they hold magick within them and amplify it when needed."

It explained why she'd felt like the stone had sucked away all of her power when she'd touched Olivia in the field the day before. And why she'd seen her magick swirling inside the stone. The stones were powered by magick.

"So a mage made the stones?"

"My brother, Rasmuss."

She glanced around, looking for a way out, besides the door that Phinneaus barred. "And where does the magick come from? The magick in the stones?"

Phinneaus' brows furrowed. "We used to have a source. A girl we kept safe in a tower. But she was released a few months back."

Flint. Zelle.

"But now that I have you, I'll be able to break the prophecies once and for all. And with your magickal abilities..." He held his hand out to her. "Join me Cinder. Let me show you what real magick can do when taught in the ancient forms of power that my family holds knowledge of."

Cinder's ribcage squeezed around her lungs like a vise. It was true. It had all been an act. He'd never cared about her. Never worried for her. Never wanted anything more than to use her. She'd been a fool to believe that he'd wanted anything more from her than her magick.

At least Sabine was horrible to her face; but Phinneaus, he was worse than Sabine. He was the pet snake that you thought you knew when in reality he was just waiting for the precise moment to show his fangs and strike the hands of those who had cared for him. Phinneaus had betrayed her. He'd betrayed them all. He had fallen so far. He'd become a dark fae.

Anger at his betrayal burst through Cinder. She threw her hands out and bright lime colored light shot from her fingers. Phinneaus whirled out of the way as her green light turned to ropes and hit the wall with a thud. She thrust her hands out again, and blue sparks morphed into shards of ice. Phinneaus disappeared, and the shards impaled the wall where he'd just stood. She spun around, and he blew a bright pink powder in her face.

"*Agnauseautum.*"

Cinder coughed and her vision blurred. Her knees buck-led, and she hit the ground. The room spun and she fought to get to her feet, but her legs refused to obey. Like wobbly noodles they gave out and she fell again. She sucked in air and coughed out pink dust. Panic scratched up her neck as she tried to pull on her magick to cleanse her body, but nothing happened.

"My sister said you wouldn't turn to our side, but I

wanted to prove her wrong. With you on the throne, we could have turned the tide in our little war."

Cinder tried to focus. She had to get away from him. She drew her magick in tight and thrust her hands out at him but no magick released. Her arm dropped to her lap like it had been made of molten lead. She struggled to raise it again. Phinneaus drew close and knelt next to her pushing her arm back down as if it weighed nothing. Phinneaus's face swam in and out of view as he eased her to the floor and she coughed and sputtered fighting to stay conscious. Her mouth open to spew curses at him, but no words formed.

"Pity. You really are a beautiful girl. And I cared for you, I really did." He stroked her cheek and then sighed. "But no matter. If we can't get you on our side, then we'll just have to settle for using your magick instead. After all, having you out of the way is almost as good as having you with us."

He stroked her hair and then bent in and sniffed it before kissing her forehead.

A scream bubbled up her throat but no sound came out. A tear squeezed from her eye. Rome. Where was Rome? Where was Stil? Where was Dax?

"Sleep," said Phinneaus. "It will make everything so much less painful if you sleep." He waved his fingers at her and a stream of red magick floated toward her and then, everything went black.

Phinneaus stared at Cinder's unconscious form for a moment. She was strong, possibly stronger than even Zelle had been. Her magick would fund their campaign for years to come. He stroked her hair, maybe in time he might even be able to sway her to their side. But at the moment he had to get her somewhere safe.

He walked to the old worn mirror in the corner and pushed the stone atop its frame. The surface wavered and shimmered like a pool of water.

"Morgana's hideaway," he called. The mirror zoomed and raced past door after door until it connected with a room. He smiled. She always left the mirror on, in case of emergency.

Phinneaus walked back to Cinder and plucked her slender body from the floor. She really was quite exquisite. He walked to the mirror and stepped through the surface. He held her tight as the magick squeezed them from all sides and propelled them forward until they stumbled out of the mirror and landed in a large bedroom. The smell of sex and mold filled his nostrils. Morgana rarely used the hideout anymore, except for the occasional tryst but her scent still clung to every surface.

Since the run in with Zelle and Cutter, she'd kept to her castle, north of the Draaklands, waiting to see what would happen next. But that didn't mean she didn't expect her children to continue their pursuit of breaking the prophecies. Oh no. Her talons grew tighter with each one fulfilled.

Terona had failed to keep a hold on the vampires, and her stupid human pet, Lillith, had allowed the werewolves to reunite with their mates. Rasmuss had failed to keep Zelle in the tower, and Morgana herself hadn't been able to stop Cutter and Zelle from going back through the rift. Three prophecies had been fulfilled, but they ended now with the Fae.

Phinneaus hoped that draining Cinder's magick would be the one thing that could buy him favor with his mother. And possibly get Sabine out of his hair– forever. If he could do that, he would become the favorite son, not Rasmuss and Morgana would be eternally grateful. Phinneaus smiled.

He moved to the bed which had seen more nights of sex than nights of absence. Laying Cinder on the crimson colored comforter struck him with a strange sensation. The desire to kiss her raced over him. To feel her creamy skin laying against his. To taste her magick and pull it inside. He took a step and then stopped short. No. There was no room for affection. No room for compassion. What he did, he did for his family and his people. There was too much riding on his success to be sidetracked by a pretty face.

Rushing forward he grabbed the metal shackles from the corners of the bed and fastened them around her wrists.

His eyes raked over her form and smiled as memories bombarded him and a wave of desire had him stiffening at the sight of her.

He was going to enjoy his time with her. So much more than he had with her mother.

CHAPTER FOURTEEN

Rome climbed the stairs, back to his room, unable to keep the smile from his face. He'd stood up to his father and to his delight, his grandmother had as well. By tonight the entire kingdom would know that he had chosen a bride, and the contest was over. It was a win for everyone.

He knocked on his bedroom door, then entered.

"Cinder?" He stepped inside and glanced around. "Cinder?"

He frowned, shut his bedroom door and headed for the bathing room. "Cinder?"

Nothing in the bathing room had been touched. He crossed back to the sitting area. The tray of food sat right where he'd left it for her.

Maybe she'd wanted to get home and break the news to Olivia. Of course. They'd both agreed that Livy was to come to the castle first thing and Lady Sabine was to be left for the time being in her house. Cinder would no doubt need him to extract Livy from her mother's clutches.

Rome walked out the door and down toward the side of the castle. He descended to the kitchen and spotted the cook.

"Has anyone, other than servants, left by this exit this morning?" he asked.

"Sorry highness. Not a soul. I've been here since before sun up."

A wash of fear melted down Rome's back. Cinder would never leave through the front door to be seen by everyone within and without. The cook must be mistaken. Cinder would have taken precautions to disguise herself before leaving. He strode out the door and headed down the walkway leading to town. He wasn't about to let her face her step-mother alone.

FIFTEEN MINUTES LATER ROME KNOCKED ON CINDER'S front door. He waited anxiously until Olivia opened the door.

"Rome." She gave him a small smile. "Can I help you with something?"

"Good morning, Livy. I've come to help Cinder."

Olivia's brows furrowed and she glanced around the street. "Cinder? I assumed she was with you," she whispered.

A chill swept over his skin. "She was, but... I thought she came home to fetch you."

Olivia shook her head. "Mother was furious when she

awoke this morning to find Cinder hadn't made breakfast. I told her Cinder had gone into the shop early today, but honestly, I haven't seen her."

Rome swallowed hard. It was fine. Nothing. She'd probably just gone to the shop to check on things. No big deal.

Rome smiled at Olivia. "Thank you. I'll try there next."

"Rome." Olivia's eyes filled with trepidation. "Please let me know that she's all right when you find her."

"Don't worry. I will."

Olivia closed the door quietly, and Rome took off for the shop. With very step his anxiety ratcheted up another notch and he fought to keep his composure as every villager bowed and curtsied in his presence.

The walk seemed to take twice as long as it should have, and by the time he arrived he could barely keep it together. Stepping up to the front door he found it locked. Fear crept over him and lodged at the base of his neck. He rounded the building and tried the back door. It was locked as well.

The uneasy feeling he'd gotten in the castle doubled. For as long as he'd known Cinder she'd always been at home or her shop. And during business hours, she was never not at her shop.

Rome banged on the door, and the window rattled. "Cinder!"

A screech rang out from inside that chilled Rome's veins. He flicked his fingers at the lock, and it clicked open.

"Cinder? Cinder!"

Another screech floated from the storeroom. Rome stalked toward it, but was met by nothing more than boxes and crates of supplies. He spun in a circle, trying to think. A crack of light peeked out from under a back section of wall.

Of course! Cinder's playroom. Rome strode to the wall and banged on it.

"Cinder!"

A roar emanated from inside but no one spoke. He ran his fingers down the length of the wall until he found the hidden latch and pulled the section open with shaky fingers. Please let her be all right. Please let her be all right.

He peered inside and stopped. The human Dax stood in the middle of the small room, with the dragon Cinder had created, wrapped on his shoulder.

Smoke streamed from the dragon's nostrils and his throat warbled as he hissed.

"Easy," said Rome.

"May I help you?" Dax asked.

Rome's eyes fixated on the dragon. "I'm looking for Cinder."

"She hasn't been by yet. Have you tried her house?"

"Yes. She hasn't been there either."

Dax's brows knit together. "That doesn't sound like her."

"It's not. She stayed the night at the castle, and when I went to fetch her this morning, she was gone."

Dax nodded but said nothing.

"I know she was Lady Rowena," Rome said.

"My toth. Finally." Dax blew out a low breath. "I left the ball without her. I wasn't too worried since I'd last seen her go out on the veranda with you but when she didn't stop by first thing this morning I grew a mite bit concerned."

Rome nodded. "You're Erik. The brother."

Dax shrugged.

"Something's wrong," said Rome. "She wouldn't just disappear."

"No." Dax scratched his chin. "She wouldn't. I can help you look for her trail if you want."

"How?"

"I'm a werebear. Take me to the last location you saw her and I'll see if I can sniff out where she went."

A werebear? Was that even possible? Questions swirled in his mind but he forced himself to focus on the task at hand. Cinder had gone missing. If Dax could help...

Rome didn't like it. It would mean taking Dax into the castle. Who knew what his father would do with that news. But if something had happened to Cinder, Rome would never forgive himself. He had to take Dax's help.

"All right," he said. "But the dragon has to stay here."

"Easier said than done," said Dax. "Cinder gave him a sleeping potion, but it's all gone."

Rome snapped his fingers. "A sleeping draft may be the one and only thing I know do how to make correctly."

He raced to the front of the store and grabbed several herbs, ground them into a powder and mixed them with a bottle of mead he found in the storeroom. He poured it into a bowl and set it on the floor.

Dax looked at it. "That's not the way Cinder made it."

"This is my own secret recipe. Trust me, it works. Even for dragons."

Dax dragged the bowl to the small table the dragon had set up as a nest and placed the bowl on it. The dragon hopped from his shoulder and sniffed the liquid before guzzling it down. It'd barely finished when it wobbled on its feet and yawned.

Dax pulled the bowl away, and the dragon curled into a ball.

"How long will it last?" asked Dax.

"Two hours, maybe a bit longer. I made it strong but who knows with a dragon?"

Dax nodded and threw a cloak about his shoulders. "Let's go."

ROME AND DAX WALKED THROUGH VILLE DEFEE WITH everyone bowing and shouting well wishes his way. Rome could barely manage a few curt nods in thanks, with how unsettled his nerves were. They ducked through the servant entrance and raced up the stairs to Rome's chamber. Inside, Dax threw off his hood and took a deep breath.

"This is your room."

"Yes."

Dax sniffed again and his eyes darkened as he turned his accusing gaze on Rome.

"I didn't ask you here to judge our actions. I love Cinder and want to make her my wife. Last night she said yes and this morning my father agreed."

Dax nodded and walked around the room slowly, taking everything in.

"Someone else has been here."

"Who?"

Dax shook his head. "It's a familiar scent, but I can't place it." He picked one of Cinder's shoes up from the floor then turned, picking the second one off the table. "She couldn't have gone far without her shoes."

Rome's mind churned. Something about the shoes. The shoes... her left shoe.

"Wait!" Rome strode to Dax and took the shoes from his hand. He stared at them, and then his gaze went to the portrait in the corner. "Cinder dropped her left shoe in the passageway last night. It shouldn't be in here."

He threw down the shoes, rushed to the portrait and pulled it open. One sconce inside burned low. Dax came up behind him and sniffed the air.

"They went this way." He pushed past Rome and sniffed again. He turned to the left and headed down the passage. "Her scent is no more than an hour or two old."

Rome's gut twisted with every turn they made. They twisted and moved deeper into the castle. To a passage that even Rome hadn't explored. Finally, Dax reached a dead end and pushed a section of the wall open. They stepped out into the upper hallway leading to the warning tower.

"There." Dax pointed to the old winding staircase.

"But that's just the old alert tower. There's nothing up there but a brazier for lighting in an emergency."

"I'm telling you, the scent leads this way." Dax ascended the stairs, taking them two and three at a time.

Rome raced to catch up. Why would Cinder be up in the tower? And whom had she gone with?

Dax threw open the door and stepped inside with Rome following.

It was the same as it had been days before when he'd looked out at the valley. Except...

"The dust has been disturbed."

Dax touched something on the floor. Pink dust covered his fingers. "Damn."

"What?"

"I've seen this dust before. A mage used it to blind my friend." He scanned the floor. "There was a scuffle." He scooted several feet to the side and ran his hand over a large patch of wood that had been cleaned. "Someone lay here."

Rome found a pile of green rope slumped against the wall. "Cords."

The two looked about the room and Dax's gaze lit on an old wooden mirror in the corner.

"Ah, shite." Dax walked to the old mirror and stared at it.

"What? That mirror has been here forever," said Rome.

"I bet it has."

"What happened here? Where did they go? How the hell is it going to help us find Cinder?" He shook his head. "I knew I shouldn't have asked for your help."

"Will you shut up?" Dax said.

"Excuse me?"

Dax's gaze connected with Rome's, then he reached up and pushed a red stone in the corner of the mirror frame. The surface shimmered and a hallway appeared full of doorways.

"Holy mother," Rome exclaimed. "What... What is that?" And how had it gotten into Ville DeFee?

"A magick mirror." Dax turned to the surface. He studied the mirror as if looking for something.

"Well, how can it help us?" asked Rome.

"I'm not sure it can. But it's how Cinder left this tower."

Rome shook his head. It didn't make sense. "I don't understand."

Dax looked over his shoulder at Rome and then stuck his hand to the surface of the mirror. It shimmered and swam like a pool of water. Then Dax's arm disappeared up to his shoulder.

Rome gasped.

"*Toshma Famea!*"

"Like I said, magick mirror." Dax pulled his arm back out and scratched his cheek for a minute. "Flint Gwyn," he called.

"Excuse me?"

The mirror vibrated and zoomed, then stopped and went dark.

"It's a good thing I gave the mirror back last month when I ran into Gerall," Dax said under his breath. "Flint!" Dax called. "Flint!"

There was a rushed set of footsteps, and several babies cried out. The picture changed, and a beautiful face with purple eyes and pearly hair came into view.

She smiled. "Dax!" She looked over her shoulder. "Shhhh… You woke the twins. Wait, let me find Flint."

Rome blinked several times, trying to understand what he was seeing. A human woman carried her mirror into another room and then down a set of stairs.

"Flint," she called. "Flint it's Dax!"

She turned the mirror, and Rome saw four men sitting at a table in a grand eating hall. They all rushed forward at the same time.

A tall blond grabbed the mirror and stared into it. "Dax? Where are you?"

"Erik," said Dax. "It's good to see you. And Hass and Ian as well."

"Let me through. Let me see him." A large man with shaggy dark hair and red glasses pushed through the crowd and grabbed the mirror. "Dax."

"Flint." Dax's hand hit the frame of the mirror, and he leaned on it heavily.

Flint Gwyn. The one who'd come to ask Cinder for help the half a year before. His large face loomed in the mirror but his eyes were different. Under the red glasses they were scarred and seemingly sightless.

"Where are you? What's wrong? You found another mirror?" asked Flint.

"I'm at Cinder's. She's been taken I think," said Dax. "I tracked her up to a tower in the castle, but the trail ended at this mirror. You don't know a way to find out where this mirror went last, do you?"

Flint looked at the others and then shook his head. "No."

"Dammit."

"Do you need us to come?" asked Erik.

"No," Rome chimed in. He didn't need all of them storming the gates of Ville DeFee.

"Prince Rome," said Flint.

"I need to do this quietly. We don't know who took Cinder or why. If you lot come down here and start asking questions, who knows what will befall her."

The brothers mumbled between themselves, and then Erik nodded.

"All right. We won't come now. But if you need us for anything, we're there."

"I owe her a great debt," said Flint.

"As do I," said Dax.

"Did she help you regain your memory?"

"No, but she gave me a direction."

It amazed Rome that all of them were willing to drop everything to rush and help Cinder. Friendships between humans and fae hadn't been that strong in hundreds of years.

They were wasting time. "We should go," said Rome.

Dax nodded. "I'll contact you as soon as I can."

"Dax," said Flint. "It's good to see you."

Dax nodded. "You too, my friend."

Dax pushed the red stone, and the image faded.

"All right," said Rome. "Now what?"

Dax licked his lips. "I have an idea, but you aren't going to like it."

CHAPTER FIFTEEN

C inder woke and tried to sit up, but couldn't. Her eyes flew open, and she whipped her head from side to side. She'd been shackled to a bed. Fear trickled down her spine like ice water.

A stuffy, dusty room surrounded her. Tall wooden walls lined with beautiful paintings surrounded her. Pillows and covers of crimson silk dripped from the large wooden bed. The pungent odor of magick and sex clung to every surface.

Where the hell was she? Wait. She scanned the room, and her eyes stopped on an ornate golden mirror with a giant red stone at the top. She'd seen this place before. In Dax's memories. This was where he'd been kept prisoner. But how had she gotten here?

"Help! Help!" she screamed.

Silence emanated for a minute, but then footsteps approached and the door swung inward.

Phinneaus.

"Ah, you're awake. Marvelous." He sat on the bed next to her.

"Rome is going to kill you," she spat.

Phinneaus laughed. "I'm sure, if he ever found out I took you, he would. Which is why I'm going to make sure that never happens."

"What do you want with me?"

"Well, to start with, I'm going to take all your magick. Like I told you before, our previous source got away. So we need a new one. I'm not sure if your magick is as powerful as hers, but we'll soon find out."

"*Ala cha marona pew.* I'll never give you my magick."

He ran his hand down her leg, and she kicked him away.

His gaze raked over her body. "You don't have to give it to me. I'll just take it. Among other things. Just like I did with your mother."

Cinder's heart pounded. "You... knew my mother?"

He nodded. "She was a beautiful and powerful woman, just like you as it turns out. I loved her from the moment I saw her, as a lady-in-waiting to Rome's mother. But she spurned me and picked your father instead. I warned her that he'd ruin her, but she wouldn't listen."

Cinder swallowed hard. "What... what was her name?"

"Shantella Vondmere."

Shantella Vondmere? Cinder wracked her brain. Where had she heard that name before?

"See, her grandmother was married to the king. But she died in childbirth. Then the king remarried and the baby girl was raised by an aunt or someone. The new queen gave birth to Rome's great grandfather. The lines get a bit muddled after that, but on your side, your great grand-mother married and had your grandfather along with several other children. Your grandfather had three daughters. All three were ladies in waiting, to various women of the court. And then your mother was made lady-in-waiting, after her family died tragically in a house fire. It's ironic really. Rome's mother had substandard magickal blood. Whereas your royal bloodline, can be traced all the way back to the very first fae. Prince Verdagan. One of the original four brothers who called the Djinn. It's why your magick flows so abundantly. Though I must say, I've not seen any as great as yours in hundreds of years."

"What happened to her?" Cinder swallowed. "My mother."

He snorted. "Oh, she came to me in tears. Said she was pregnant, and your father refused to marry her. Ruined she didn't know what to do. I offered to marry her. You wouldn't have been my blood of course, but I thought I wouldn't care. I'd have had her, and that's what mattered. She wanted to wait. So, I brought her here for her period of confinement."

"Didn't anyone miss her?"

"Yes, actually. Rome's mother. She was ready to rip apart the countryside, looking for her best friend. I was a lesser member of the court back then, but I still had access to the castle. A few well-placed amnesia spells fixed any thoughts of looking for your mother."

Cinder stared at Phinneaus. She'd known him almost her entire life. And yet it appeared, she didn't know him at all.

"We waited until you were born and I took one look at you and knew you were special. Even then I could feel your power."

His expression grew dark and his eyes hard. "One night, when I was sleeping, your mother ran to your father. He took you both in and decided to marry your mother after all. I couldn't have that. It wasn't fair. After all I'd done for her. Helped her, loved her. So I brought her back here. She came down with influez and I refused to return her to your father to be treated. With all of the magick I possessed, I could not heal her somehow. Mayhaps she died of a broken heart. I will never know."

She fought the anger and terror that flooded her veins and left her as cold as the bottomless sea. "And you left me with my father." She barely choked the words out before her throat dried like the sand.

"What good was a baby to me without her? There was no way for me to look after you properly. So I sent for my sister, Sabine. She was supposed to love you. To raise you, to teach you our ways. But she was even more vain and selfish than your father. Rebuffing you and insisting on birthing a child of her own instead. I had to secure our place in the palace and on the throne, it was paramount. So, after several years of letting Sabine play house as a dutiful wife and mother, I positioned myself within the castle. Your father had to go. It was the only way I'd be able to slip into his spot as an advisor, and eventually get you or Olivia on the throne."

He stared at her through soft eyes as if looking right through her. "I had hoped it would be you and me forever,

Shantella. I would have proven who you were and placed the crown on your head myself. If only you'd not gone back to Rondell. Together we could have ruled the world."

A gleam of madness cracked his smile and she knew he was no longer seeing her. Fear trickled down her body leaving her head pounding and unable to concentrate.

"What are you going to do to me?" She could barely make the words come out of her mouth for fear of the answer.

Phinneaus pulled his hand back and blinked several times. "Something neither of us will enjoy I'm afraid. But, I can't let you leave. If you and Rome marry, it will be the end of my kin."

DAX RAN BACK THROUGH THE STREETS TOWARD THE apothecary. Rome had gone to get them a pair of horses and Dax needed to grab his things before they headed out. He wouldn't be coming back anytime soon. As soon as Cinder was safe, he had his own problems to solve.

He ran to the apothecary, threw open the door and stopped. Olivia stood in the backroom. Her eyes widened when she spotted him, and she backed up, bumping into the workbench.

"I'm not going to hurt you," said Dax. "I just need to get a few things."

"You're going to steal from my sister?"

"No. I just need to get my things."

Olivia's brows furrowed.

"Let me show you." He scooted around her slowly, careful to keep his hands up. He headed into the storeroom, then to the secret room. He pried the door open and stepped inside.

Alabrax unfurled his wings and yawned. Olivia squeaked behind him.

"Is that—"

"It's the dragon Cinder created."

"He's been here this whole time?"

Dax grabbed his bag and shoved his extra tunic and breeches into it. "Don't worry, he's coming with me."

"Is… is my sister in trouble?"

Dax stopped and turned. He didn't have time to waste but the poor child looked as if she might burst into tears if he didn't say something. "I don't know. But don't worry. I'll get her back safely. I promise."

Tears formed in Olivia's eyes and her head bobbed up and down. Damn. He hated seeing her in such distress, but he had no time to console her. Not if he wanted to fulfill his promise and get Cinder back.

Dax put out his arm and whistled. Alabrax jumped to his shoulder, his powerful claws digging into Dax's flesh through his cloak. He headed for the door and Olivia backed into the storage room.

"Please," she begged. "Bring my sister home."

He nodded and pulled up his hood. "Do what you can to stay calm. And what ever you do, don't let your mother know that you know Cinder is missing."

Olivia swiped the tears from her cheeks and nodded again.

Dax stepped into the alleyway and Alabrax took to the sky. He watched the dragon spiral higher and higher above the buildings. He signaled Alabrax and the dragon looked down at him. Their gazes connected and Alabrax roared and flew out of sight. All around people stared up at the dragon whispering and running for cover. Dax stared straight ahead as the pathway cleared. He ran flat out for the city gate.

"BUT, I DON'T UNDERSTAND," SAID ROME'S FATHER. "Where are you going?"

"I told you. Cinder was taken. I'm going to get her back." He reined in his horse as well as the steed beside him.

"You said you don't know where she is."

"No," said Rome. "I don't. Which is why I need him." He pointed down the street to Dax, who raced toward them.

"Why don't we just call for Stil and see if he can locate her with a spell?"

"There is no time. No one I know has more powerful magick than Cinder. To kidnap her someone would either have to be extremely powerful, or even more lucky. And I don't think luck had anything to do with it."

Dax stopped beside the steed and nodded to Rome before mounting the horse.

"Who is this?" demanded the king.

"A friend." Rome turned his horse around. "Open the gate!"

"I don't like this." The king grabbed his reins.

"Let the boy go," said Rome's grandmother. "You've done enough already. It's Rome's duty to go and get her."

"You're my only child and the heir to the throne. If something happens to you–"

Rome's patience waned. "Then I guess you'll have to find a young new wife to bear you more sons. As for me? I'm going to get the only one I want." He spurred his horse, and it galloped through the gates with Dax at his side.

They took to the trail between the fields and headed for the edge of the forest surrounding Ville DeFee.

A roar caught his attention and Rome looked up. Cinder's dragon sailed overhead.

Good. They were going to need help.

CHAPTER SIXTEEN

D ax whistled, and Rome slowed his horse. They'd been riding for close to a half hour into the woods past the valley.

"Where do we go?" asked Rome.

Dax looked up and whistled again. There was a screech, and then the dragon dove from the tree branches down to where they sat. Dax pulled an apron from his satchel and held it up to the dragon's nose. The dragon sniffed it and his eyes connected with Dax's.

Rome looked on, and a wave of goosebumps raced over his body. There was something different about Dax. A magick he hadn't noticed before. Not fae magick, but something else. Something... darker.

"Find Cinder," Dax said.

The dragon sniffed the apron one more time, then took to the air, heading northeast through the trees.

They followed the dragon for the next hour out into the human farmlands, south of Westfall.

"If we want help, Westfall is where we will get it," said Dax.

There were only two of them and though he and Dax were strong, he didn't know that they'd be strong enough on their own.

Rome nodded.

They headed north and within the hour, came to a stop in front of a giant manor house. The dragon circled overhead. He swooped and roared then barked and soared east.

"What's wrong with him?" Rome asked.

"He doesn't want to be here. He wants to go east."

Dax pulled his horse up to the front and hopped to the ground. He hurried to the large door and knocked.

The door opened and a petite redhead, carrying a chubby baby, peered out.

"Dax!" She pulled him into a one-armed hug.

"Scarlet."

The woman yelled over her shoulder. "Jamen! Erik! Flint! Dax is here!"

Even from outside Rome could hear the pounding of footsteps heading for the entrance. A tall blond, an even taller, dark haired man, and a shorter, dark haired man, rushed out and pulled Dax into a group hug.

Rome's chest squeezed at the sight. He had no brothers, nor cousins, nor even friends beyond Cinder and Stil. What would it be like to be hugged in a group so close?

"Is it Cinder?" asked Flint.

Dax nodded. "We're not sure what we're getting into."

"Give us five minutes." The brothers moved back into the house without so much as a glance in Rome's direction.

The beautiful woman with flowing white hair came to the door and threw her arms around Dax's neck.

He chuckled and kissed her head. "Zelle."

"It is so good to see you," she said. "Flint has been crazy with worry. As have I."

"I'm all right," he said. "Went to stay with the fae."

Her brilliant purple gaze connected with Rome's. "You must be Prince Rome." She released Dax and headed for him.

"Yes," was all Rome could manage. He'd never seen a woman that looked like Zelle before, and he got the distinct impression she wasn't all human.

"I'm Zelle. Cinder provided the magick that released me from my prison. My husband and I are in debt to her."

The sound of horse hooves approached from the rear of the manor house.

"If there is anything I can do," said Zelle. "Anything at all. Please do not hesitate to ask."

Rome nodded. "Thank you."

Erik, Flint and Jamen approached on horseback.

Zelle hugged Dax once more. "Watch out for my man."

Dax chuckled. "I always do."

He mounted his horse just as the dragon roared. Every eye lifted to the sky.

"Holy–"

"Where did that come from?"

"Easy," said Dax. He whistled and the dragon turned

and swooped toward him. "This is Alabrax. Cinder made him."

"Made him?" asked Jamen.

"We can discuss it on the way," replied Rome.

Erik nodded.

The dragon hovered in the air in front of Dax, making his horse paw at the ground.

"Find Cinder," Dax commanded.

The dragon took to the air and the brothers shook their heads.

"My toth!" said Flint. "He leaves us for a less than a year and comes back with a pet dragon of his own."

Rome had had enough of pleasantries. Every second they wasted, sitting and talking, was one more minute who knew what was happening to Cinder. He kicked his horse and the animal leaped forward. He wasn't going to sit still one minute longer.

CINDER ROLLED OVER AND VOMITED ONTO THE FLOOR. Phinneaus rubbed her back, making her want to rip his arm from his body and feed it to him.

Her limbs shook with strain, and her muscles ached with fatigue. Over the last several hours he'd sucked magick from her body like siphoning water from a bucket.

"It's always worse the first few weeks," he said. "But after that, it will get easier. I promise."

"Get away from me," she spat.

"Now, now, don't be that way. You are doing this for the

greater good. Just think, back in Ville DeFee, healing potions, herbal remedies, and fungus infections wasted your talents. But here your magick will be instrumental in the destiny of Fairelle. With your magick powering us and mixed with Rapunzelle's magick, we'll be unstoppable. And I will finally get the respect I deserve, at my mother's side, instead of being left rotting for decades babysitting my sister and the throne."

Cinder flopped back on the bed, and Phinneaus wiped her mouth with a piece of cloth. She stared at him for a minute before his words clicked. "You're the one who infected the queen mother."

He frowned, then shrugged. "I didn't know who it would infect. Honestly, I had hoped it would be the king. He's been harder to manipulate than you could imagine. I figured, if I could get Rome on the throne, unmarried, it would be easier. But then the queen mother got sick, and you started her treatment, and the king had the entire tomb magickally scrubbed for fungus, and that was the end of that."

"So what? You're just going to keep me prisoner here and drain my magick forever?"

He ran his finger down her cheek. "You look so much like Shantella. You have her spirit too. Perhaps, given time…"

"I'll never care for you Phinneaus. And just like my mother, you'll never have me." A small surge of magick coursed through Cinder. She'd only have one shot, but she couldn't waste time overthinking it. She had to act now before he took everything she had.

She flicked her fingers at Phinneaus, and he flew across

the room, crashing into the wall. His head hit the stone with a crack, and he slumped to the floor.

Cinder's heart thundered and she held her breath waiting for him to rise and assault her again or knock her out, but he didn't move. A thin sliver of hope swelled within her. If she didn't get out of there before he woke up she'd never get a second chance.

The thick iron shackles burned into her wrists. Scabs had already formed where they touched her skin. She tugged against them, digging the metal deeper into her flesh. The scabs opened, and blood oozed from the wounds. She pulled on her right wrist, and it slid slightly downward. She pulled again, but her thumb stuck tight in the cuff's embrace. The iron seared her skin and the smell made her stomach roil. She pulled on her wrist but her thumb stayed firmly planted against the metal.

She laid back on the bed and gulped in a deep breath. She didn't want to do this. She did not want to do this. She looked over at Phinneaus and then back at her hand.

If she wanted out, it was going to hurt. She bit the inside of her cheek and pulled as hard as she could against the cuffs.

THEY'D BEEN RIDING FOR HOURS IN AN UNKNOWN FOREST. An eerie silence had fallen over the place over the past hour. The deeper they got the less and less they heard. Like a blanket had been placed over that section of the forest even the atmosphere grew heavy and oppressive. Though it should only be late in the afternoon darkness had crept in around them blocking out most of the light.

The thick leafless trees grabbed at their clothes and slowed their progress almost to a crawl as the wove between the trunks one by one.

The longer it took them to travel, the higher Rome's anxiety rose. Alabrax had even stopped flying. Instead, he hopped from tree to tree continuing to lead them on.

Dax and Flint had taken the lead, talking for most of the journey, occasionally joined by Jamen or Erik. But Rome's nervousness about Cinder left him in no mood to chat. Several times he wanted to yell at them that this wasn't a leisurely stroll they were taking; it was his wife they were trying to save, but he bit his tongue and reminded himself that it had been Dax that had helped Cinder all week long in the contest.

He remembered the way Dax had held her up on the fields when she was ready to collapse. He knew deep inside that Dax cared for Cinder and he, as well as the Gwyns, had left all they knew to risk their lives to save her. So though their progression remained slow, they were all aiming for the same goal. To bring Cinder home safely.

"I've been here before," Dax announced.

"Do you remember it?" asked Jamen.

"Perhaps. Just a feeling, more than anything, but I know I've been here. We're close."

Alabrax screeched, and the men pulled their horses to a stop.

"What is it?" asked Rome.

Dax looked up at the dragon, then shook his head. "Not sure."

They dismounted, and Rome tied his mare to a tree. He and the Gwyn brothers gathered around. Alabrax swooped down and hopped onto Dax's shoulder.

"Wait here." Dax continued forward, slowly making his way through the trees. Every fiber in Rome's body twitched and screamed to keep moving, but he waited beside the Gwyns.

Minutes passed and finally Dax returned.

"I found it."

"Are there guards?" asked Erik.

"None that I can see but that doesn't mean it will be easy getting inside."

"Magick?" asked Rome.

Dax nodded. "Most likely."

"Well let's get to it then," said Flint.

The men grabbed their weapons and trudged through the mucky ground. Dax stopped them a hundred yards beyond the horses. Rome came around his shoulder to find a large, dilapidated castle, choked with briars and thorns. The windows were cracked and shattered, and the front door had been completely overrun with the twisted and gnarled roots of a burban tree.

"How do we get in?" asked Erik.

"There's a door around back," Dax replied.

"Why go that way?" asked Jamen. "We could cut through to the front door with ease." Before anyone could speak he took several steps toward the entrance.

"Jamen don't!" Dax called.

"I'm just going to check it out." He motioned for them to wait and the hairs on Rome's neck stood on end.

"I don't think he should–" Rome barely got the words out before a shimmering light flashed in front of Jamen and he disappeared.

"Dammit!" Flint raced forward, but Dax and Erik grabbed him, pulling him away.

"No," said Erik. "We can't risk losing you too."

"Where is he?" Flint yelled.

"Inside," said Dax. The brothers both looked at him. "There are holding cells in the basement."

Erik studied him for a minute. "You have been here."

Dax nodded. "I'm remembering bits and flashes. Pictures in my mind but not in order and nothing too clear. But I remember the layout of the place."

A scream emanated from inside the castle somewhere.

"Cinder!" Rome raced around the side of the ruin to find another side entrance.

The brothers called his name as he raced onward, rounding a crumbling tower. He spotted a small servant's entrance and ran for the steps that descended into the ground. A snap of magick made every hair on his body stand up, and then a defining crack resounded. A strong pair of arms pushed him out of the way, and Rome hit the ground– hard. He turned to see Dax standing right where he had just been. Rooted to the spot, a bolt of blue magick coursing through his body.

Flint and Erik rushed forward. Alabrax swooped to a ledge above Dax's head and screeched.

"Stop!" Rome hopped to his feet. "Don't touch him or

it'll hit you too." He wracked his brain for something to do and remembered a spell Cinder had taught him. He focused his magick and waved his fingers toward Dax. The blue light dissipated and Dax crumpled.

Alabrax dropped to the ground and nudged Dax with his nose. Flint and Erik moved close, and Flint turned Dax over.

"Is he dead?" asked Erik.

"No. But he'll be feeling the effects of that for quite a while," replied Rome.

"We need to get him somewhere safe," said Flint.

"I'll find Cinder," said Rome. "You two take care of Dax."

"No." Erik got to his feet. "I need to find my brother."

"I'll stay with him." Flint took off his traveling cloak and lay it over Dax's prone form.

"If you get in trouble. Holler," said Rome.

Flint looked to Alabrax, who took up position by Dax's head and nuzzled his neck. "I think we'll be good."

"Here." Erik handed Flint a sword. "Like Rome said, holler if you need us."

Flint nodded. "Get them out of there."

Erik joined Rome. "Come on."

CINDER STRUGGLED FOR BREATH AS PHINNEAUS PRESSED HIS forearm into her throat, his silky robe covered in blood. With his free hand he tried to wrestle the knife she'd found under a pillow from her grip. She pushed it toward him but with her right thumb broken and her strength all but spent, she fought just to stay conscious. Her magick and energy were little more than frayed threads and her air supply cut short. Specks lit in her vision and her head began to pound, but she refused to give in. She'd rather die than live as a magick slave.

"It doesn't have to be this way Cinder," said Phinneaus. "I can be good to you. Take care of you. Love you."

The cold, stone floor dug into her shoulder blades and hips causing them to ache from the weight of his body pressed into hers. She needed to change tactics. Her strength wouldn't last much longer. Suddenly she dropped the knife, grabbed his forearm with her good hand, and pulled it into her mouth, biting down hard. He let out an inhuman roar and punched her in the face.

Pain exploded through her face and blood gushed from her nose. She let go of his arm and blood dripped into her mouth. She blinked rapidly, trying to clear her vision. Planted her hand in the middle of his chest, she shoved with the little magick she had left. He flew off her, landing at the foot of the bed. She gulped air into her lungs, choking on the blood and spitting it out again.

Cinder rolled to her knees, grabbed the knife once more and pushed to her feet, cradling her right arm to her stomach. Her vision blurred, and the room tilted like a windmill as the smell of iron filled her nose. Blood dripped down her dress and landed in fat droplets on the floor. She fought back the nausea that threatened to consume her as she struggled to her feet, as he got to his.

"Just like your mother." Blood soaked the sleeve of his

robe and dripped down to his hand from where she'd bitten him. "I'd hoped for better from you Cinder."

His long golden hair hung in disarray around his body. His usually gentle features had taken on a more angular appearance and his eye, no longer kind, blazed at her with a fiery anger.

She swayed and bumped into a chair behind her. She spit blood on the flood and heaved in a heavy breath. "You'll never have me Phinneaus. I'd rather be dead."

His broad smile revealed a row of sharp, pointed teeth. "I can arrange that as well." He ran at her, quicker than she would have thought possible. She raised her arms to protect herself as he tackled her onto a chair. She slammed into the wood and her head whipped backward. Every muscle in her body ached as she pushed against him trying to get him off.

"There's only two ways out of this Cinder. Consent or die." Blood sprayed from his mouth and coated his pointed teeth.

Cinder screamed and Phinneaus let out a slow hiss as the door to the bedroom flew open. She tried to clear her head and process what she was seeing. "Rome."

He raced into the room and threw Phinneaus to the floor, punching him repeatedly in the face.

A moment later two more men ran in. Gwyns. What were the Gwyn brothers doing there?

"Rome!" Erik pulled Rome from Phinneaus' unmoving form. "Rome, enough. It's over."

Rome backed away and they all stared down at Phinneaus who lay on the floor eyes wide and vacant. Rome stepped away further and Cinder caught sight of the silver handled knife that protruded from Phinneaus' chest.

Cinder looked down to find her left hand covered in blood. She'd killed him. She'd killed someone. No, not someone, Phinneaus.

Erik knelt at his side and felt for a pulse. Finally he stood and turned to Rome. "He's dead."

"But... all I did was hit him. I didn't stab him."

Jamen moved to Cinder's side and knelt. His face had gentled since she'd seen him last. He picked a scarf from the floor and wiped the blood from her hand. She looked on as a hollow chasm gaped wide inside of her seeping her insides in a dark numbness.

He pushed the hair from her face. "Hey, Pretty Princess."

"Hello, Handsome."

Rome scrambled over to Cinder and pulled her into his arms. "Cinder." He kissed her head, and then her cheek. Her eyes stayed on Jamen who gave her a tight knowing smile.

Rome pulled her face to his and kissed her lips. She winced and pulled away.

He sat back and scanned her face. His eyes steeled as he touched her bruised cheek. "Look what he's done to you. By the gods if he weren't already dead I'd kill him."

"I'm all right." She tried to push her hair from her face again, with her good hand, but it shook so badly she could barely get it to hold steady.

Erik offered Rome a handkerchief, and Rome dabbed at the blood on her face.

"I think your nose is broken," said Erik.

The throbbing that radiated through her skull had already told her as much. She raised her hand to her face, but Rome pushed it away.

He lifted his fingers to her nose.

"No thank you." The words came out louder than expected. "I mean. I'll heal it. You have no training. I don't want to end up looking like a troll." She chuckled making her chest scream in pain. She was pretty sure aside from a broken nose and finger she had broken at least a rib or two as well.

Rome snorted. "How little you believe in me."

"I saw what you did when that poor dog that broke his leg. He never walked correctly again."

"I was fifteen," Rome protested.

"And your healing hasn't improved since then."

The Gwyn brothers chuckled.

"Well, at least let me stop the bleeding," Rome said. "That I can do."

She sighed and nodded. Wisps of white magick fluttered off his fingertips and up her nostrils. A moment later the pain lessened, and the bleeding stopped.

She nodded. "Where's Dax?"

"Here." Dax hobbled in, sword in hand, leaning heavily on Flint. "Are you all right?"

"I'll be good as I ever was after a few days sleep."

"What happened?" asked Erik. "Why did he kidnap you?"

"He was crazy. He'd been in love with my mother. That and he said he needed my magick. He used a jewel on his armband, hidden under his robes, to drain me."

The brothers all shared a look. Jamen crossed to Phinneaus and pushed up his sleeves revealing a large golden armband with a red stone in the middle.

"Like Zelle," said Flint.

Eric dropped to his knee and turned Phinneaus' face, then lifted his lip. "Same fangs as those I saw in the mirror back in Tanah Darah."

"Like Terona's, before we killed her." Jamen reached up and ripped the jeweled bracelet from Phinneaus' arm and handed it to Erik.

"This must be her place," said Flint.

"No." Dax shook his head. "This isn't Terona's place. Or Phinneaus'. It's Morgana's."

"Zelle's mother?" said Flint.

Cinder snapped her fingers. "That's who I saw in the vision. Lady Sabine's mother. I knew I recognized her."

Rome helped Cinder to her feet, and she shuffled toward Dax.

"If that's true," said Flint. "Then Lady Sabine is a daemon."

The words slapped Cinder. A daemon. A thought struck her, and she squeezed Dax's arm. "You're remembering."

He looked down at her and nodded. "Not everything. Not yet."

She smiled, making her face ache all the more. "You should stay here. It may help."

"No," said Flint. "What if someone comes back?"

"I don't think they will," replied Cinder. "Phinneaus said

this place hasn't been used in a while. I believe that's the only reason he felt safe coming here."

"Even so," said Flint. "I don't want Dax staying."

Dax moved out from under Flint's arm and looked at his friend. "I knew from the moment I awoke in Wolvenglen Forest hunted by vampires, none of this was going to be easy or without danger. But I need to know who I am and where I came from."

"Even if it kills you?"

"Even if it kills me."

Flint stared at Dax from behind his red glasses. "Then I'm staying as well."

Dax shook his head. "Zelle needs you. Your children need you. This I must do alone."

Erik and Jamen gathered around Dax and put their hands on his shoulders. "You're never alone," said Erik. "You're forever a part of our family, whether you want to be or not."

Dax chuckled, and the group hugged, then parted.

He turned, and his eyes fell on Cinder. "Thank you for this. I'm sorry you were hurt in the process."

She stepped forward, and he hugged her too. "If you need anything, send Alabrax. I'll come right away."

"We all will," said Flint.

Rome wrapped his arm around Cinder. "We need to get you home." He went to pick her up, and she pushed him off. "What are you doing?"

He glanced around the group. "Uh… I was going to carry you?"

She cocked an eyebrow at him which cost her painfully. "Do I look like a damsel in distress?"

He scanned the men for help, but they all looked away. His eyes narrowed, and he straightened his shoulders. "Yes."

Before she could protest further, he swooped her into his arms. She opened her mouth to complain, but he kissed her. Her cheeks flushed with heat.

"Rome—"

He kissed her again, and she pulled away.

"Are you going to kiss me every time I try to say something?"

He beamed down at her. "If you plan on protesting while I carry you out of this place."

She opened her mouth again, and he leaned in, but she pressed her finger to his lips.

"Give a fae a break," said Jamen. "Be the damsel in distress for once."

The Gwyn brothers snickered.

"That'll be the day," Flint muttered.

"*Oya Malenta*. Fine. If it helps your faehood, then carry me. But just know I can walk perfectly well on my own."

He cocked a sexy grin that made her heartbeat skip. "Of course you can darling."

Rome carried her, through corridor after corridor, and the longer he walked, the more she leaned into him as fatigue overtook her.

She wrapped her arms around his neck, and he looked down at her. She pulled his mouth to hers. Their lips met, and then their tongues swirled together. Every inch of her warmed from the contact.

His eyes were hooded with desire and she caressed his cheek.

"Thank you for coming after me," she said.

"For you, I'd go to the ends of Fairelle and back."

She smiled. "I like that."

CHAPTER SEVENTEEN

It took Cinder forty-eight hours to heal physically from what had been done to her and almost another week for her to begin to process mentally. Between her depleted magick, her wounds, and the knowledge that she'd killed Phinneaus, she'd never felt so dispirited. Tiredness and sorrow, bone deep, settled inside her, and she had to will herself just to leave her bed. He'd betrayed her, used her, and tortured her. And she'd killed him. She hadn't meant to, but there it was. She was alive, and he was dead.

Through it all either Rome or his grandmother was by her side. Surprisingly, during their hours together, Elise told her the truth about her mother, as if the amnesia spells Phinneaus had cast had died with him. It both elated and devastated Cinder to find that what Phinneaus said was true.

Both Elise and Rome had both done their best to

convince Cinder it was not her fault Phinneaus was dead, yet in her heart a small tear still bled at what she'd done.

All the while Cinder recuperated in Rome's rooms, the kingdom of Ville DeFee went on in ignorant bliss. But the castle did not. The king was in a state of distress over what Phinneaus had done to them all. The murders, the spells, the kidnapping. It was Rome that had to step in to keep things together. He'd spent hours talking with Cinder, to find out what she wanted done about the conspiracy against her. He was in favor of having Lady Sabine hanged. His father wanted her banished, but Cinder helped them come to a compromise.

By the eve of the seventh day, a buzz had begun around the castle. People were starting to wonder what had happened with the competition. Where was the prince? Where was Lady Rowena? Had it all been a ruse?

Cinder sat eating a piece of toast with some tea when there was a knock on the door. She called for it to open and the king stood in the doorway.

Cinder leapt to her feet, then curtsied. "Your Royal Highness."

The king advanced and lifted her. "Please, Cinder. You don't need to bow to me. Let us sit." He motioned her back to her seat on Rome's golden colored couch.

She sat and noticed a butler standing in the doorway, holding a silver chest.

"How are you feeling?" the king asked.

"Better every day, thank you."

He stared at her and nodded. His gray hair looked whiter than she remembered and the creases in the corners of his eyes cut deeper. But she saw Rome's future in every inch of his face.

"We went through Phinneaus' rooms and came across a silver chest that I think belongs to you.

Her eyes traveled back to the butler. "To me?"

The king motioned the servant forward, and the butler set the chest on the table before bowing and walking out.

The ornately fashioned chest was beset with light green gems, forming a pattern of plants and herbs. Her heartbeat quickened at the sight of it.

"It's beautiful, but I'm afraid it isn't mine." Her eyes stayed glued to the top.

"It was your father's. Apparently he left it in the care of the royal treasury. Phinneaus must have happened upon it and took it. I'd like to say for safe keeping, but now I believe his motives were not pure."

A chest... from her father.

"Have you opened it?" she asked.

The king looked at her sadly. "I have."

Her gaze moved back to the box.

"I came to apologize to you Cinder, for my part in how you've been treated since your father's death. Rondell was like a brother to me, and I should never have allowed you to be treated so poorly. But you must understand—"

"I do," she said. "You were protecting your people. You did what you thought was best." She looked up at him. "I only hope you now know there is a better way. All fae must become equal if we are to stay united. It only took a few people, whispering in our ears, to almost tear us apart.

Imagine if an entire army arrived. We can't survive without each other."

The king nodded, then the door opened, and Rome entered.

"Father."

The king stood. "Rome." He stared at the chest for a moment, then sighed. "I'll leave you two."

Cinder smiled. "Thank you."

He left without a word and Rome crossed to her. "You're up. Are you feeling better?"

"Much." She threw him a smile that she didn't quite feel all the way. It was better to not burden him with the feelings she still dealt with pertaining to Phinneaus' death. He held her through hours of tears and continued to hold through nights of terrible dreams. At the moment, it was all she dared ask him to do for her. The rest she would have to figure out on her own.

He hugged her tight and kissed her on the head. Her eyes stayed on the chest.

"What's that?" he asked.

"I believe it's my father's writ of lineage."

"Truly? Where was that found?"

"Amongst Phinneaus' things."

Rome shook his head. "After all these years. I wonder why he kept it."

"To use when needed, I suppose."

Rome reached for it. "Should we open it?"

Trepidation flooded Cinder's body. Part of her wanted to tear the thing open and see what her father had said. What his last wishes had been. Had he thought of her at all?

Had he left everything to Sabine after all? Were there words of kindness for her in there? Or had he finally left her a letter telling her how much of a burden she'd been her whole life?

"We could wait," Rome said gently. "There's no rush."

"No." She needed to know. Whatever it was her father had put in the box, she needed to see it. It was the only way to truly move on and look to the future. No matter what was in there, it was her past. And Rome was her future. That's all there was to it.

She took Rome's hand, and together they opened the lid of the chest.

CHAPTER EIGHTEEN

R ome stood in the middle of the throne room,
next to his father, and grandmother, decked
from crown to shoes, in his royal attire. The
three waited in silence. Contestants and their families
packed both sides of the throne room like barrels of apples
waiting to be bought. Most of the girls looked dejected,
several looked bored and a couple, including Drusilla
appeared to genuinely believe something wonderful might
happen for them. Only one family remained unaccounted
for.

Minutes passed and then a set of heels clicked on the
floor, and all eyes shifted to the back of the chamber. Lady
Sabine and Olivia entered and halted, where both women
curtsied. Olivia glanced around nervously but Lady Sabine
held her head high and strode forward, a smile planted on
her face. When she reached the edge of the crowd, she curtsied low again and waited.

"Lady Sabine," said the king. "I thank you and your daughter for joining us."

Sabine stood and pressed down the folds of her overly bright, overly full dress. "It is our pleasure, your majesties."

"How have you been?" the king asked.

Lady Sabine's eyes darted around the room. "Very well, your majesty, thank you."

Rome's fingers twitched with anger. Both Cinder and Phinneaus had vanished, yet she stood there as if everything was normal. How heartless could the woman possibly be?

"Truly?" asked Rome's grandmother. "Why, Lady Sabine that surprises me greatly. Both your stepdaughter and your brother go missing for, what has it been? Over a week now, and you act as if you never knew them."

Lady Sabine licked her lips. "Oh, well, yes, there is that. I didn't want to burden you with my own troubles. I sssss-simply meant that both Olivia and I are doing well. We are of course very distresssssed about both Phinneaus and Cinder."

Olivia took a step forward and curtsied. "Your majesty. Do you have word of my sister? Do you know where she might yet be?"

"I do," replied Rome. "And be well advised, Livy that she is indeed safe."

Olivia broke into a smile and tears rimmed her eyes. She choked back a sob and composed herself again before speaking. "Thank you, highness. That is a great relief."

"So Lady Sabine, you knew nothing of where your brother and Lady Cinder were?" asked the king.

Lady Sabine donned the wide-eyed appearance of

someone truly concerned. "No. I'm sorry I didn't. But they are both safe so—"

"Cinder is safe," said Rome. "I cannot say as much for your brother."

Lady Sabine's eyebrows drew together and her smile faltered. "I... I don't understand."

"I think you do." Rome stepped down from the pedestal and walked toward the awaiting crowd. It was why they'd been gathered. They needed to have witnesses to the forthcoming pronouncement. Others of status who would carry the words forth and make sure that every fae in the kingdom knew the truth of what had happened.

"We have been betrayed," said Rome. "The prophesies have begun, and in recent years, have drawn closer and closer to our borders. Enemies attempted to undermine and break us as a people, but know now that they've been thwarted. Their reign of terror ends this day."

"Your highness—"

Rome cut off Lady Sabine. "You, Lady Sabine, are accused of high treason against our people."

Lady Sabine's spine snapped straight. "Treason? And who accuses me of such?"

"I do," said Rome. "You and your brother Phinneaus conspired and killed Lady Shantella Vondmere, mother of Cinder Rondell, and great granddaughter of King Georgeus, a descendant of Prince Verdagan himself. You also killed my mother, Queen Aleta, then your husband, Lord Rondell. You and your brother then conspired against the kingdom of Ville DeFee to overthrow the king and place yourselves on the throne. You and your family killed a sacred unicorn and used the blood in the competition for my hand in marriage. You used a blood stone to fortify Olivia's magick and cheat her into winning the contest. And for these gravest of crimes you are to be sentenced to death."

"It's not true," Lady Sabine screeched. Her gaze fell upon the king. "Your majesty I have ever been a faithful servant and loyal subject. Where is the proof of my crimes?"

"Here." Cinder entered carrying the silver chest.

The crowd gasped, then bowed low as she walked down the purple carpet, a gold circlet adorning her head and a mulberry silk dress train trailing behind her. Only a small scar across the bridge of her nose remained of her torture at the hands of Phinneaus. The one thing that neither she nor his grandmother had been able to fix. Even so it did nothing to diminish her beauty. Her picturesque, golden hair had been plaited down her back, and the color had finally returned to her cheeks after many days of rest. Just seeing her set Rome's heart thundering. He knew she still bore the pain of having killed Phinneaus and he wished more than anything he could take that guilt from her, but he allowed her her moments of pain and silence. When she was ready she would confide in him he was sure. But as it was he gave her what she asked for. His strength, his love, and his patience.

Lady Sabine's eyes flashed with anger.

"Lady Sabine," said Rome. "May I introduce Princess Cinderelle Rondell. My bride."

Olivia broke into a smile and ran to hug her sister. Cinder wrapped her arm around Olivia.

"I'm so glad Rome found you," said Olivia.

Cinder kissed her sister's forehead. "So am I."

CINDER NODDED TO ROME, AND HE STEPPED ASIDE TO JOIN Olivia.

"What proof do you have in that box?" Sabine spat.

It amazed Cinder- though it shouldn't have- that her stepmother continued to hold such a haughty air, considering the position she was in. She had to know there was no getting out of what she'd done. No escape from what awaited her.

Cinder opened the lid to the silver chest. "My father left this for me, in the royal treasury."

"Then why hadn't it been found before?" asked Lady Sabine.

"Because Phinneaus hid it. And it was only found after searching his room."

"Then it is Phinneaus who is the master of these crimes, not me. Why is he not here to answer for what he has done? Where is Phinneaus. I want to see him," Sabine demanded.

"He's dead." The detachment Cinder felt from those words almost had her believing what he'd done to her had no lasting effects.

Lady Sabine swallowed. "Dead?"

"He kidnapped me," Cinder continued. "He kidnapped me, shackled me and stole my magick."

Hushed whispers traveled around the room.

"But before he died, he told me what he had done. To my mother. To my father. To all of them."

Cinder stepped close enough to Lady Sabine to touch her but didn't. She leaned in even closer so only Sabine could hear her. "Advantage they'll take, of the weak and the proud, and all goodness they will destroy. Until the one girl, who answers to none, catches them in their ploy."

Cinder backed away and for the first time she saw true fear in Sabine's eyes.

Good. Let her be afraid.

Cinder pulled a parchment from the chest and faced the crowd. "This is my writ of lineage. Signed by my father, Lord Rondell." She set the parchment down and pulled out another. "And this is a letter from my father, explaining how he'd found out the truth about what Lady Sabine was and what she'd done."

"And what truth is that?" Lady Sabine asked.

Cinder rounded on Sabine. "That you're a fraud. And not even fae. You are a daemon."

Gasps sounded from all around the room. People moved back in terror and even Livy backed up a step. Only Cinder stood rooted in her spot unafraid.

Lady Sabine hissed, and her eyes grew red. Cinder dropped the silver box to the floor and swiped at Sabine with her open palm. Magick arched off her fingertips and a thick green rope bound Sabine like roots from a tree.

Sabine's nails grew long as talons, and she sliced through the rope like parchment.

"You have no idea who you're playing with girl. I

warned you not to cross me." Sabine's dress split and huge, leathery wings spread from her back as she lifted into the air. "Stupid fae. Ssssssso weak. Sssssssso naïve. Your time in this world is coming to an end. I'll come back with my brotherssssss and my mother, and then you'll see true power."

Sabine flew at Cinder, talons stretched out. Cinder fired her magick at Sabine hitting her in the chest and knocking her back.

A long slithering tail protruded from under Sabine's dress. The crowd screamed and ran for the corners of the room.

Sabine's tail shot out and caught Cinder by the ankle but Elise threw an arc of magic into the fray zapping Sabine's tail like lightning. Sabine screeched and shot higher into the room. She spit at Cinder who spun out of the way as a pool of acid landed when she'd just stood and burned into the stone floor.

Elise stepped next to Cinder as Cinder sent a bright yellow fireball careening for Sabine. Sabine ducked out of the way and flew toward the large picture window.

"We can't let her get away," Elise said.

Cinder pulled her magick in tight and threw it at Sabine in the same moment Elise did. Together their magick wound around Sabine like a million threads of spider silk. Sabine struggled and fought to cut the threads but for each one she got through ten more produced themselves. Round and round she turned like a pig on a spit, becoming more and more encased in a crystalline cocoon.

Sabine screamed, and cursed. Swearing her revenge on Cinder. Her revenge on Elise and her revenge on Rome.

Cinder and Elise continued to unleash their magick until the cocoon covered Every inch of Sabine's body, snaked over her mouth and finally the rest of her face, cutting off the last of her words.

Arms shaking, Cinder lowered her stepmother to the floor with a bump. She swayed as the room spun and Rome rushed to her side, wrapping his arm around her waist.

"I have you." He kissed her forehead.

She sucked in a deep breath, and focused her eyes on the glowing red stone necklace inside the cocoon. It pulsed once, twice, three times and then went dormant.

Cinder waited for the cocoon to explode. For Sabine to break from and fly out the window to the rest of her kind, but as minutes passed, nothing happened and she finally relaxed.

"Mother, are you all right?" The king walked to Elise who patted his cheek like a little boy and then brushed him off.

"I'm perfectly fine, son."

Olivia ran to Cinder and hugged her tight.

"It's all right," Cinder cooed.

"Are you sick?" Olivia asked.

Cinder threw on a warm smile. "I'm just tired. Guess I wasn't as healed as I thought." A niggling of fear trickled down her back. Would she ever be back to full strength?

Olivia stared up at Cinder, her eyes wide. "Was she really a daemon?"

"Most likely," said Rome.

Olivia blinked several times. "Does that mean... Am I–" She didn't finish the question.

Cinder pulled her little sister close. The truth was, she didn't know what that made Olivia.

The king stepped forward and beckoned the still cowering crowd to move closer. "Those parchments name Lady Cinder as Lord Rondell's heir. As such, she is given all rights of his properties, his holdings, and his name. And is thereby eligible to marry Prince Rome."

"You should kill the monster before it can escape," someone called.

"What if she gets out?" someone else yelled.

"What if others come looking for her?"

"Don't worry," replied Rome's grandmother. "We're going to put her somewhere no one can find her."

CHAPTER NINETEEN

R ome wrapped Cinder in his arms. "She'll be safe
down here. No one will get to her, and she won't
be able to get to anyone else."

Cinder stared at the horrid screaming face of Sabine.
She was sure Rome believed the words of comfort that he
spoke to her, but all she could think of was the red stone
necklace that Sabine still wore at her throat. Though it had
yet to make another sparkle since being encased, that didn't
mean it had lost its power.

Cinder had seen the sway those stones held and she
wasn't so quick to dismiss their abilities.

"Come," Stil said.

Rome ushered her from the iron-lined room and closed
the vault door behind them. Stil pressed his wand upon it
and nodded to Cinder. She laid her palm on the metal
searing her skin, and the heavy door sealed shut. Vines and
thick roots covered the door completely.

"Only the three of us, the king, and the queen-mother know about this," said Stil. "I've employed every magick I know to keep this location hidden. And between Cinder and I, the magick is powerful enough to withstand just about anything. If someone finds her, it will only be through one of us."

Rome took her hand, and together they climbed the steep steps that she'd carved in the heavy rock face of the mountain, to a door that when closed looked just like the wall next to it.

She looked over her shoulder as Stil joined them, just to make sure that everything looked as it had before they'd begun their excavation.

After several moments Rome tugged on her hand and they continued through the catacombs of their ancestors. Row upon row of tombs lay carved into the walls of the cavern. The scent of rich dirt and wet stone permeated the air but thankful no mold.

Bright lanterns floated around the ceiling, illuminating every surface. His grandfather's statue stood guard over the expansive mausoleum. His eyes ever fixed on the outer door.

"So this is all of them," she mused.

Rome nodded. "All the way back to Prince Verdagan." He snickered. "It still amuses me that, after all this time and everything you've been through, your blood is purer than mine."

Cinder sighed. "Is anyone's blood truly unpure? After all, we're all fae." Her thoughts turned to her sister. "Well... almost all of us."

"You don't worry about Olivia. We'll not let anything

happen to her."

Cinder was confident of that. Her little sister had suffered enough at the hands of her mother and she would be damned if she'd let anyone else abuse Livy.

"When she's feeling up to it, I'd like to speak with her," said Stil. "See if there is anything she might know about those who are attacking Fairelle."

"My sister knows nothing, I'm certain."

Stil nodded. "You're most likely right. But it would still be wise to make sure."

Over the last days, Cinder's protective instincts for her sister had grown considerably.

"I hope she's all right," said Cinder.

Rome squeezed her around the waist. "She is."

"I wish she would have stayed with us," said Cinder.

"She'll come back," said Stil. "She just needs some time to work through everything she's learned. About who her mother was. Who she is."

Cinder wasn't as confident. Their father had left Cinder the apothecary and the chest, which in and of itself was worth a fortune. To Olivia, he'd left the house and to Sabine, he'd left nothing. Young and without a job, Cinder wasn't sure how Olivia expected to keep herself. Cinder planned on paying for anything Olivia needed, but at some point, she'd have to stand on her own feet.

"So, I've been told there is to be a ball," said Stil.

They ascended the staircase toward the castle.

Cinder groaned. "I've had enough of balls and gowns and parties. They're tediously boring and half way through my feet ache."

They stepped into the hallway and Rome closed the door with a chuckle. "But I would have thought feet of your size would distribute weight better, and you'd be able to dance longer."

Stil laughed but backed away as Cinder rounded on Rome.

"Roman Geoffrey, are you saying I have large feet?" She flicked her fingers at him and a spark of magick hit his arm.

"Ouch." He stepped toward the staircase. "Not large per se. That is, if you compare them to, oh, I don't know, Stil what do you think? A dragon perhaps."

Stil held up his hands. "Oh no. You're on your own with this one my friend."

Cinder gasped. "A dragon?" She flicked magick at him again and he yelped.

A sly smile tipped Rome's lips. He ran for the stairs, and she chased after him. He hit the landing laughing and threw his hands in the air. "All right. Not a dragon. A troll maybe."

She advanced on him and flicked magick at his rear, making him jump. "A troll? My feet are smaller than a troll's."

"I'll just be going now," Stil called from below. "Check in with you later."

Rome paid no attention as he ran up the next flight of stairs with her on his heels. "Yes they are smaller. And they don't smell as bad."

She shook her head and chased him up to their room. "And just how do you know what a troll's feet smell like?" He flung the door open and raced to the middle of their room.

She magicked the door closed and locked it before flicking her magick at him again.

He was already removing his tunic. She ran her fingers down her spine, and the laces of her dress burst apart.

"Are you saying your feet do smell worse than a troll's?" he asked.

She stepped out of her dress and shoes. "I'm going to make you pay for that."

Rome looked her up and down, slipped off his shoes and dropped his breeches to the floor. She flicked her wrist and he fell back onto the bed.

His hands slid down her body making her quake. "You promise?"

She kissed him hard, then ran her tongue down the flat planes of his torso. He tangled his fingers in her hair and whispered her name. She traipsed her fingertips over his nipples and zapped him with magick making him buck beneath her.

She kissed over his hip-bones and down the inside of his leg.

"Cinder. You're going to be the death of me," he moaned.

She nipped his skin and ran her hands up between his thighs sending small waves of magick pulsing up over him.

She stopped kissing and looked up at him. "Oh no, husband," she said. "But I will bring you right to the edge."

THE END

BELLE AND THE BEAST

FAIRELLE BOOK SIX

By Rebekah R. Ganiere

CHAPTER ONE

SOUTHERN WESTFALL FOREST, FAIRELLE - NEW YEAR, 1213 A.D. (AFTER DAEMONS)

Belle's limbs shook, but she forced her face to remain impassive so as not to upset Chloe.

"Mama, my head hurts," her little girl moaned.

Belle grabbed a cloth and dipped it in a bowl of warm water before crossing to where Chloe sat at the kitchen table.

Chloe rubbed her forehead with her chubby little pink hand. The bracelet Klaus had bought her years prior hung from her wrist like a cheap buy-off. It took everything inside Belle not to rip it from her daughter's skin and fling it into the fire.

"Hey, Sugarpie." Belle shoved the corners of her mouth into a smile, cracking the split in her lip and making it ooze again. She ignored her own, and blotted the blood from Chloe's nose. "I know it hurts. Just let me get your nose cleaned up and then I'll get you some medicine."

The desire to kill Klaus had never run so deep. Over the

past year he'd become more abusive. Belle had been fighting to save up enough money to take Chloe and run, but it didn't matter anymore. She was ready to stomp down her pride and beg for help if needed.

Chloe raised her hand and cupped Belle's cheek. "Your eye is purple."

Belle swallowed down a sob. She'd tried to shield Chloe from Klaus' temper, but ever since he'd learned of Chloe's... *ability*, it had been harder to protect her from just about any facet of her father's personality.

Belle finished wiping the blood from Chloe's nose and then stripped her daughter's shirt off. "Let's get you into your sleeping gown and stockings."

Belle crossed to Chloe's small bedroom and pulled her nightclothes from the little trunk at the end of her wooden bed.

Klaus' use of Chloe's ability to enhance his criminal behavior was a new low, even for him.

She grabbed a bottle of extract from her medicine shelf and headed back to find Chloe staring into the fire.

"Here Sugarpie, let's get you into your night clothes."

Chloe continued to look into the fire; her eyes blank, bright blue and glassy. "Going on a trip into the woods. Somewhere new.""

"What?" Belle slid Chloe's gown over her head. "No sweetie. We're going to go stay with Uncle Jamen and Auntie Scarlet, Uncle Flint and Auntie Zelle for a while."

Chloe shook her head. "We're going to make a new friend. You'll like him. You'll like him a lot. He's going to like you, too."

A chill ran over Belle's shoulders as she stared at her daughter for a moment, then opened the vial of opia. "Sip this."

Chloe drank the medicine without a hitch, her eyes still on the dying fire. Since Klaus had been using Chloe's ability, her headaches had become more frequent. Belle needed to be careful with the opia. Using it too frequently would end badly; but couldn't stand seeing her little girl in pain.

Chloe yawned. Belle took off her daughter's breeches and pulled up her stockings. Then, Belle picked up her little girl and carried her to bed. She wrapped the already sleeping Chloe in a thick blanket and kissed her on the head.

Panic threatened to overtake her as Belle raced to her own room and closed the door before crumbling to the floor.

How many years had she tried to make it work? The lies, the infidelities, the robberies. She'd put up with it because her father had been the same type of man. But in the past year since Klaus' friend Craigen had died, things had gotten worse. She didn't know what had happened, he wouldn't say, but he'd become more and more paranoid. He'd moved them to a cabin far outside of Westfall and no longer allowed her to go into town. She'd tried to focus on a way to get out for months. But making gadgets and clocks and small things that moved and then hiding them from him so he couldn't see, had gotten harder and harder as the months had passed. When he'd brought home the two extra horses the week before she knew her time was close at hand.

But she couldn't wait any longer. Her black eye and split

lip were testament to that. Not to mention Chloe... Belle either left now, or she'd die in that cabin.

Belle sucked in a ragged breath and swiped at her tears, making her bruises ache. No matter how little she had in life, she still had her dignity and there was no way in hell she'd let Chloe grow up thinking it was all right for a man to shove her around.

Belle pushed to her feet, her mind made up. She needed to pack and get out before Klaus returned. She didn't have much time.

BELLE LIFTED THE GROGGY CHLOE ONTO THEIR HORSE, THEN pulled herself into the saddle. She shoved her blunderbuss into a strap on her bags and positioned her satchel of tools behind her. She didn't have tome to pack the gadgets she'd wanted to sell in Westfall, but it didn't matter anymore. All that mattered was getting herself and Chloe to safety.

She laid Chloe's cheek against her chest, then wrapped the leather straps she'd fashioned around Chloe's back and buckled them to her belt. Chloe snuggled closer before Belle covered them both with her cloak.

"Are we going to the forest now?" Chloe slurred.

Belle kissed her daughter's golden curls. "No sweetums, we're going to Uncle Jamen's, remember?"

Belle nudged the horse, and they trotted away from the small cabin, out of the woods. She fought the urge to turn back; to look, one last time, at the place she'd called home for nigh on a year and praise the gods that she would never have to look at it again, but she didn't. Instead, she kicked her horse again and headed for the road leading to Westfall.

THE MOON SHONE DOWN ON THE BARREN ROAD. IT WAS A good twenty miles to Gwyn Manor, yet the longer she rode on the open thoroughfare, the worse the pit in her stomach grew.

She glanced left and right but found nothing more than fields and trees for company. The night breeze pinched her cheeks and made her eyes water. The clunking sound of her belongings shifted with each quick step the horse took. A half hour passed, Chloe's breathing evened out, and a light snore resonated against Belle's breast.

Five years old. Still a babe, yet Chloe had seen, heard, and endured things no child should have. Hunger and cold. Fighting and drunkenness. All of them at Klaus' hand. None of them worse than using their daughter.

Chloe had been special from the moment she came into the world. She'd made not a peep when born. She'd simply looked up into Belle's face with those wide, blue eyes and stared. By the time Chloe had reached the age of one, she'd begun exhibiting strange behavior. She'd run to Belle's leg and hide her face moments before someone knocked on the door. One blustery night, she'd screamed out mere seconds before a tree limb came crashing through the window, landing where Belle had been sleeping.

And once she'd learned to talk, she said odd things. She knew things, things she should not know.

Belle had tried to hide the oddities from Klaus, but he'd

figured it out. And that's when the real nightmare had started.

He'd come home once again penniless and with a new scheme. Pulling Chloe into his lap by the fire, he'd told her a story. Within minutes, the story had turned to questions. And the questions had turned to demands. This time, Chloe's eyes rolled back into her head, and her nose began bleeding. That's when Belle had attacked.

Pulling Chloe from him, she and Klaus had fought. He'd caught her in the eye, but she'd brandished a knife and told him to leave. She'd thought, for a minute, that she might have to stab him. But finally, he'd grabbed his coat and shoved off.

She'd put up with the torment and terror herself. But she'd be damned if she'd let him ruin their daughter.

Hoofbeats pulled Belle from her memories. She reigned in her mount and listened. Several horses closed in at a fast clip. She glanced around, but there was nowhere to hide.

Her heartbeat kicked up and she urged her horse down the roadside embankment. It wouldn't hide them, but at least they'd be out of the way.

She waited as the horses drew closer. One horse. Two horses. Three. She pulled the hood of her cloak up and dropped her face from sight. She trotted forward and prayed the horsemen wouldn't notice her as they passed. Her hand rested on her blunderbuss.

Seconds clicked by, and her heart thumped louder with each pounding step as the hoofbeats drew closer. She could just make out their outlines growing larger. She kept moving forward, pulling Chloe in tighter against her.

Closer... Closer... They moved at a brisk pace, as if being chased. Less than twenty yards away now, they had to have seen her; but their horses didn't slow. She kept her head down and her fingers tight on the wooden hilt of her blunderbuss.

Keep moving. Just keep going.

They were less than ten yards... Her fingers twitched. *Five.* Her legs pressed into her horse's ribs, ready to spur him forward. *Two.* Her entire body tensed.

They passed by.

Relief washed over her. *Thank the gods.*

She waited a moment before looking over her shoulder. One of the men slowed and turned back.

"Belle!"

She kicked her horse. *Klaus.*

DAX STIRRED HIS GLUEY OATS, AND THEN SHOVELED SOME into his mouth without tasting a bite.

It'd been close to six months since Cinder had told him to stay in the abandoned castle and find his past. But he had yet to figure out what she meant for him to do there. Every waking moment had been spent tearing through the rooms. Looking through chests and drawers and cabinets. Reading books and parchments and maps — and still he was no closer to finding out who he was then he had been with the werewolves, the vampires, or even his time with Flint.

Evidence suggested that the castle had been deserted for months, maybe more than a year. The long-term food supply was plentiful, but a thick layer of dust covered every-thing. Much the same as when he'd gone with Sage to his hideout in the Wastelands. He feared that any answers he searched for had been taken with Morgana, when she'd fled.

Morgana.

Every day new memories built on the last, and he found, with each one he acquired of the place, the less he wished to know.

Morgana had kidnapped him. She had tortured him, and humiliated him. Everything short of raping him. It was inconceivable to him that she was Zelle's mother. Zelle was everything she wasn't; kind, loving, and the perfect match for Flint. But Morgana... All those horrible moments tied in her bed, the whippings and more, now plagued him. What he still could not remember though was who he'd been before that.

Dax dropped his spoon into the silver bowl and hung his head, clearing the panic that swept over him and dug its talons into his ribcage. He pushed his chair from the cold stone table and walked across the kitchen, rinsing his bowl in the washbasin and set it out to dry.

Out the open window, the moon hung above the trees in the clear sky. He took a deep breath. Being in the woods had left him lonely and even more desperate to find out who he was. But somehow, it also felt familiar.

Alabrax swooped down and peered in the window. It was a good thing they'd left Ville DeFee when they had, in the past months he'd tripled in size. There was no way Cinder would have been able to hide and feed Alabrax much longer. But out in the woods, Alabrax fended mostly for himself.

The dragon squawked, and Dax nodded. "I'm coming."

His nightly walks through the woods with the dragon did them both good. It offered Alabrax companionship and gave Dax an hour or so to clear a wasted day's search from his head.

He made for the back door of the kitchen. Though the castle appeared to be a ruin on the outside, and dust covered most everything inside, the castle itself was in good shape. The ruination was a façade meant to keep people out. The furniture was rich and all manner of finery adorned the walls as well as the shelves and tables. If a thief managed to get beyond the traps and spells, they'd become rich beyond imagining. But of the forty-seven traps he'd found outside, it was unlikely anyone without an intimate knowledge of the place would get within twenty feet of any door.

He walked outside and greeted Alabrax with a scratch to the chin. Alabrax purred like a kitten. Then, his head popped up and his ears flattened to his skull. His gaze whipped toward the front of the castle and he hissed.

Dax's gut clenched. Someone drew near.

Alabrax grumbled and Dax raced around the side of the castle, sidestepping the spell trap he'd fallen into the week before. Alabrax flew to an upper tier of one of the turrets, staring into the woods.

"What is it?" he called.

Alabrax hissed again, and Dax sniffed the air. The breeze swept several scents his way. Men, three of them, and two females. He hesitated. He could go back inside and wait them out, see if they made it to the castle, or if they headed a different direction. No one had come this close in a month.

A scream rang out and a chill raced up his arms. His inner bear growled. *Dammit.* Hiding wasn't in either of their natures.

He whistled for Alabrax and tore into the woods. His night vision allowed him to see clear as noonday. Following the scents of the newcomers, he prowled closer to the group. He stopped and listened, as another cry rang out. Smaller. Weaker. *A child.*

"Alabrax. Find them," Dax commanded.

To read more go to your nearest retailer!

Dear Reader,

Thank you for taking the time to read *Cinder the Fae*. This series is due to my love of fairytales and the fantasy genre. I have loved writing all of these characters in new adventures and new relationships. I hope that you will enjoy the rest of the series of our strong women and honorable men.

If you enjoyed the book, please take a moment to leave a review on your favorite retailer. Your reviews make all the difference to an author and the success of books.
If you'd like, email me and let me know what you liked about the book or who your favorite character is. I love hearing from readers. It makes writing so much more fun when I hear from my readers.
VampWereZombie@Gmail.com

To find out more about me and my Upcoming Releases, Join my Street Team for Swag and Freebies.

I also love connecting with readers! Stalk me everywhere! I look forward to hearing from you!
Rebekah R. Ganiere - BOOKS WITH A BITE

Award Winning–*USA Today* Bestselling Author

Rebekah R. Ganiere

Fairelle Series

Red the Were Hunter - Book One

Yanti's Choice - Fairelle Short Story

Snow the Vampire Slayer - Book Two

Jamen's Yuletide Bride - Book Three

Zelle and the Tower - Book Four

Cinder the Fae - Book Five

Belle and the Beast - Book Six

Gerall's Festivus Bride - Book Seven

Jak the Giant Healer - Book Eight

Wolf River

PROMISED at the Moon

CURSED by the Moon

RECLAIMED from the Moon

TAMED under the Moon

UNLEASHED with the Moon

FATED despite the Moon

NEWSLETTER

To claim your Two **FREE** Books and find out more about
Rebekah R. Ganiere and her other Upcoming Releases
You can Go Here:
www.RebekahGaniere.com/Newsletter